©2018
R. L. Migdal
Mythoprint Publishing

THIS
REALLY
SUCKS

WHO KILLED LUKE MANDRAKE?

Book I of

The Goddammerung

by

R. L. Migdal

Volume II:

Requiem for the Damned

A Just Punishment

Socrates condemned
His fellow citizens
By obedience.

                                        —RM

Luke opened his eyes, but it didn't matter. The blackness was complete, palpable. It was a gigantic cat lying on him, smothering him in his sleep. Or maybe it was a sphinx, heavy as stone, with the face and breasts of a woman. Anyway he was pinned in an enclosed space, and could barely move.

The tattered remains of the image of Kore still hung before his eyes, Kore peering around Hades's enormous arm, her long lashes wet with tears. Married, damn it. Married! Of course she was. All those ancient goddesses were married off young.

Had she just been playing with him? Had she done this before, taken a lover from among the dead a thousand times, and finally gotten caught this once?

Or did she love him, even now?

Not that there was anything he could do. But not being able to do anything, to move or even breathe, just made him worry even more. And Luke had plenty of complications to worry about. What would become of Charity now that he was truly dead? Lying in a coffin, deep underground, that's sure what it felt like, though he had no clue how he'd gotten here. He'd started to come to in the sun room, his eyes had opened for an instant, and then–

Nothing. Waking up in a box. It was the worst thing he could think of, to be stuck here like this, thinking about everything that he couldn't do anything about. Luke just wanted to go back to sleep now, forever. Fuck it.

But he couldn't sleep, no matter how hard he tried. He couldn't get his mind to shut up.

Luke was desolated, but he didn't feel like crying. He was still too angry. He knew that his current circumstances were Hades's doing. In fact, despite repeated assurances that he was living out some sort of personal destiny, he was positive that it was Hades who'd turned him into a zombie in the first place. It was so obvious.

Hades, that total dick of a pedophile who was hardly better than Zeus, the way he had ruthlessly seduced Persephone, an innocent young girl. If the god of the dead hadn't lured her from her mother's protection, Zeus would never have gotten his claws into her.

Poor Kore. She obviously still thought it was somehow her fault, that she had to make up for it by being stuck with a cold fish, a controlling, sadistic narcissist, for all time. Or maybe, maybe she was just so traumatized by the rape, that she couldn't really handle love at all. *Maybe she feels safer, somehow, with HIM.*

It was horrifying. Ugh. Ugh. Maybe Hades was fucking her right now. Luke was torturing himself with these thoughts. He couldn't stop himself.

Underneath his disgust lurked a deeper horror, one he did not like to think about: his own part in Kore's humiliation. Who was he in this story, he protested to himself, but a pawn of supernatural forces? Yet she was right, he had taken advantage, had behaved shamefully. She had wept on his shoulder, after all, called him "my lord." Why had she done that, unless she loved him? And yet he'd behaved as though she were the one behind all his troubles. What an asshole he'd been.

He could so easily picture Kore on her knees before him, her facile mouth– *No! Don't even let those thoughts into your mind!*

Better to direct his rage at the Lord of the Underworld than to dwell on Kore's fate very much. The chagrin was brutal. He had to think about something else.

Luke's dread began to mount when he considered that he might actually have all eternity to dwell upon . . . upon whatever uneasy thoughts toward which his mind was likely to stray. He was in no state to manage his wildly contradictory imaginings. He was worse off than Prometheus. Even without Buzz to torment him, he was doing a perfectly good job at eating his own brain, metaphorically anyhow. It frightened him to think he might lose his grip on sanity entirely.

Luke wondered, did Prometheus regret giving humanity fire? If he ever escaped his chains, would he still be a friend to man? Or would he be a vengeful demon?

How long could Luke remain a prisoner to his worst thoughts, before turning into a monster?

Maybe he really should be kept in here forever, maybe he was becoming a thing that ought never to be unloosed on the world again.

I'm a monster. I'm a monster, Luke started repeating to himself in a whisper. *Don't let me go, I'm a monster. Don't let me go, I'm a monster.* He began tapping with his foot against the side of the coffin, and singing.

> *I'm a monster. I'm a monster.*
> *Don't let me go, I'm a monster.*
>
> *You thought that you were rid of me,*
> *Monster, I'm a monster*
> *But I'm coming back to see*
> *Monster, I'm a monster*
>
> *Wanted you in charge of me*
> *Want you to be rid me*
> *Monster, I'm a monster, ow!*
> *Don't let me go, I'm a monster.*
>
> *Thought I could make it on my own*
> *Monster, I'm a monster*
> *I only want to be alone*
> *Monster, I'm a monster*

I'll never show my face to you
I'm standing right here behind you
Monster, I'm a monster, ow!
Don't let me go, I'm a monster.
Monster . . .

There was a sound coming from outside the coffin. Luke stopped singing and tapping his foot.

"Did you hear something?" a female voice said. A very familiar voice.

"It's just the steam pipes, Mrs. Mandrake. Nothing to be alarmed about."

"Oh, right, of course." *Charity! Charity's here?*

"Are you ready to make the identification, Mrs. Mandrake? Do you need a few minutes?"

"No, I'm fine. Please, go ahead Doctor." Her voice sounded husky.

Luke felt a lurch, and the noise of a heavy drawer sliding open accompanied a blast of light that blinded him. As his vision adjusted he found he was staring up into Charity's face. It wore an expression of shock and horror.

"Charity," he said weakly. "It's . . . it's only me!" Luke lifted his head, tried to sit up. When he moved his right arm, he heard the links of a chain clink.

Buzz was curled up on him with her head resting on his chest. Luke felt a rush of joy. *Kore!*

She was with him still, collared and bound to him by a fetter, the delicious goddess of his dreams.

But his heart sank again instantly. *If Kore is a vulture again, that means I'm still–*

But there was no time for Luke's realizations to sink in.

"Luke? What the fuck!" Charity's hand moved toward them.

Buzz skrawked and darted at her with a menacing hiss.

Luke's wife drew back with a shriek. She was staring at him with terrified incomprehension. She screamed again, "Oh my god! Oh my god!" and ran from the room, followed by a man in a white coat, who shot a panicked look back at Luke before slipping out.

Luke reposed in a body-sized drawer. He was in the morgue.

"Buzz, damn it! Did you have to do that?" he grumbled as he struggled to rise.

"Nice to see you, too, Bozo," Buzz remarked. Sobbing could be heard from beyond the double doors, one of which was still slowly shutting on its pneumatic hinges. "Let's get outta here."

"But Charity's–" Luke began.

"Charity does *not* need to see you like this," Buzz snapped. "Have a heart! The poor girl is in hysterics already."

"That's why I need to go to her. I have to let her know that everything's . . ." Luke looked at his greenish withered flesh with its rotting bits. There were bones showing through all over the place.

"Everything's all right? That's what you wanna tell 'er?" Buzz wondered sarcastically. "Sure, let's go. She'll be so relieved to see us."

Buzz was right, of course. The last thing Charity needed now was to see him again in this hideous form. He really was a living corpse, a monster. Maybe if he disappeared, she would think her eyes had deceived her.

"Time to get outta here," Buzz croaked. "Before the mortician decides to put us back in the locker."

Luke was sitting on the long drawer, his legs dangling over the side. "Uh, I seem to be naked," he pointed out. "I don't think we can promenade down the street like this in broad daylight. Anyway, there's only one door."

"What about that ventilation duct up there?" The vulture indicated a spot near the ceiling with a gesture of her beak.

"Ha ha, how do you propose we get to it?"

"Just climb aboard, Bozo," Buzz commanded. She launched herself into the air. Luke dropped lightly onto the condor's back, just as she pumped her wings. In moments they were high up near the ceiling, beside the cover to a ventilation duct. Buzz chopped a hole in the plastic with her beak and Luke got a grip on it, braced himself against the wall with one foot, and wrenched it off. The rectangle fell from his hands, and Luke looked down to see it strike the floor a few yards away from where the man in the white coat now stood, looking fearfully up at them.

"Go on, Luke!" Buzz hissed. Luke plunged into the duct feet first, and Buzz followed.

The racket inside the duct was beyond belief as the bony zombie and the enormous condor scrambled along in pitch darkness. Periodically, frigid air was suddenly forced through the tunnel, it hissed and blew. After a minute or so they came to what felt like a tee intersection in the duct, and Luke halted.

"Where the hell are we going?" he wondered aloud.

"We are going to look for a place to hide, and wait for nightfall to make our escape, okay Bozo?"

"How do we know if it's daytime or nighttime? Do we even know if we can get out of the building after dark?"

"Hmm, I see what you're driving at."

"Where the fuck are we? A hospital? The city morgue?" Luke's voice roughened and he felt the tingle of tears under his eyelids. Seeing Charity again, and especially her look of horror, had been an emotional trainwreck. *I've got to keep it together. I am not going to break down.*

"Still, we gotta try. Excelsior, right kiddo?"

"Okay," he said, "we're lost in the guts of an unfamiliar building, and we need a plan that allows us to escape, preferably one involving me getting some clothes. And it goes without saying that we gotta avoid being seen."

"Nobody can see us right now," Buzz pointed out.

"Oof," Luke shifted in the flimsy aluminum ventilation unit, causing it to snap and boom. "But we've been seen, and they can probably hear us moving around. Lord knows what kind of hell is about to break loose, but it's gonna if we don't vamoose."

"Well, whaddaya say, Bozo? We can go left, right or backward. You choose."

"No, you," Luke insisted. "I'm too emotionally fucked up right now to think straight."

"All right. But how about some light, at least?"

It seemed as though a firefly had somehow gotten into the duct, because at these words, a tiny light flickered on and off near Luke's armpit. It began to glow more brightly, steadily, not moving. He realized that it was the cowrie shell that contained the spirit of Charlotte.

His little Tinkerbell. Somehow, like Buzz, she had followed him into the solid world. Luke had to admit that was kinda nice. It would have been even nicer, though, if he had woken up in a non-zombie body. How did these things get decided?

"Lucky I gave you that shell, wasn't it?" Buzz croaked.

"Yeah, funny how it lights up," Luke said. He'd been meaning to ask Kore about Charlotte, but having reached the moment of truth, he decided not to bring the subject up. All he needed was to incite more jealousy.

"Hold it up," the vulture commanded, and Luke raised the shell on its chain. A narrow beam of light issued from between the pink and white lips, and he aimed it like a flashlight.

Buzz extended her neck forward and peered down the branches of the duct. "It looks like the tunnel narrows to the left."

"So let's go to the right."

And they set off to explore the windy network of rectangular extrusions. Luke recalled the duct he'd been sucked through on the Island of the Damned: so cozy, so abrasive, such powerful suction. It was there that he had found the intubated girl, the mysterious creature who now inhabited the cowrie shell.

Compared to that stone-built duct, this rickety vent was like a cheap movie set. In fact, the entire world of solids felt a bit tacky, badly put-together, especially compared to the rich sensory experiences he'd had in the afterlife. He'd always known that it was a whole lot of fakery, though. How had he managed to live this way for 27 years?

After five minutes of crawling, they came to a port set in the panel above them.

"This is promising," Buzz remarked. She mangled the cover with her mandibles until Luke was able to lift it off.

When they looked out, they had a view of the bottom of a wire shelf, upon which plastic tubs were stacked. Luke and Buzz emerged to find that they were in a refrigerated storeroom for organs. The door had a safety lock so that it could be opened from the inside. But the quiet chamber without was quite thoroughly locked. There were regular climate control vents in the outer chamber, but they were too small to be of any use.

Fortunately they hadn't let the door to the fridge shut behind them. Returning to their maze, the frail, depressed zombie and the agitated vulture continued squirming along until the refrigeration duct bent to the right, eventually joining up to a larger, circular tube that was vertical. This master duct proceeded downward another four yards, where it ended. Above, it soared into impenetrable darkness. Wire staples were attached to the walls of this freezing wind-tunnel as a ladder of sorts.

Luke climbed up these, and they found their way into another cold-locker, this one a storage room for plasma. But when they were about to exit, they heard footsteps in the room outside, and glimpsed the hats of security guards through the wire-reinforced window in the door.

"Shit," Luke muttered, dropping to the floor.

"Let's skedaddle," Buzz hissed. Luke crawled back over to the vent cover and slithered through feet first, pulling the condor in after him.

At the top, the main duct apparently connected with a gigantic refrigeration unit located on the roof level. Luke directed the cowrie shell beam upward, wondering if there was a way out in that direction. That's when Buzz noticed there were noises coming from up there.

"Somebody's opening up the machine," she rasped. "Go down!"

Luke hastily climbed back down the staples. At the bottom was an outlet to yet another cold room.

This duct was smaller than the others and Luke hesitated to try and enter. But there was a bang far above him and he heard voices. They were coming down to search the ducts. They'd been discovered.

He shoved Buzz into the hole, which was not much larger than a legal pad. She barely fit, and as for Luke, though skeletally thin, he squirmed into it anxiously.

"Good thing I'm not claustrophobic," he remarked as he wriggled along, pushing Buzz in front of him.

"Well I am," squawked Buzz.

"That was sarcasm," Luke gasped.

"I didn't used to be," Buzz replied. "But having these giant wings is enough to give me a horror of enclosed spaces."

"I'm with you on that," Luke agreed.

Eventually they reached a vent with an aluminum cover. The vulture would have made short work of this from the outside, snipping off the screws with her powerful beak, but from inside that was impossible. The cramped passageway made it awkward, but she gradually snipped away until she had made a hole through the center of the grid. Then Luke reached around and unscrewed the bolts from the outside.

At last Luke and his avian appendage found themselves standing in a storage facility for vaccines.

Luke peered through the reinforced glass panel, saw no-one, tested the door, then opened it, and bumped somebody. Apparently it was a couple of candy-stripers, making out on the floor.

There came a startled grunt as Luke shut the door and pressed himself against the wall beside it. He heard footsteps, the sound of somebody taking off down the hallway at a run. Moments later another set of footsteps faded away in the opposite direction.

"Okay, back into the hole," Luke barked.

"I don't wanna," Buzz complained.

"They could tell somebody. Go!"

Buzz dove reluctantly into the tiny channel, followed by Luke. They inched painfully along, with a good deal of gasping and choking and grumbling.

Suddenly Buzz halted. "Back up!" she screamed.

"Hush! What is it?"

Buzz didn't elaborate, she just hunkered down and refused to budge. Eventually Luke decided to squeeze past her, and as a result they got pretty badly stuck for a while.

When the two creatures emerged at last into the large vertical ventilator shaft, their pursuers were not in evidence.

"Let's go back toward the morgue," Luke suggested.

The duct they'd started out in felt almost roomy compared with that last one. When they reached the T-junction, Luke shed the beam of his cowrie on the unexplored option ahead. It was pretty obvious that the passage narrowed considerably within a few yards.

"I ain't going in there," Buzz rasped. "No way. I'd rather take my chances with your wife."

Luke took that as an admission of defeat, and turned left. He and the condor soon emerged exactly where they started, having left some feathers and a few bits of zombie behind here and there throughout the refrigeration system. The drawer had been shut, and the room was empty.

After dropping lightly to the cold locker-room floor, Luke said, "Probably she's gone." He looked at the double doors, with their high rectangular windows that provided a view of nothing more than the ceiling tiles in the adjoining chamber. "Anyway I'm going to find out."

Buzz raised no objection, perching on Luke's shoulder as he walked, gripping the bony jut of Luke's clavicle with her claws. There she swayed, effortlessly, while Luke hunched down and crept toward the door.

He would have put his eye close to the crack, but it was sealed with rubber flaps to keep the cold air in. He gently swung the door open just a few inches.

There was a shriek close by on the other side, and Luke let the door shut on its own. But it shut slowly, and for a second or two he looked straight into Charity's face. She had been about to come in.

Luke froze.

"I am not seeing this. I am SO not seeing this. So, so, so not–" Charity's voice must have been pretty loud, which it usually was, because he could hear every syllable. How like her to make the most terrifying episode of her life public. It was as if she were inviting whoever was in earshot to participate in her self-mocking denial of the impossible. "I definitely did not see that, people," she went on. There was a hint of panic in her voice.

Go home, Luke wished at her as hard as he could. *Go home and forget about it, forget me. Go hug the kids, but tell them nothing. Please, let your memories of me fade away as if I'd never been . . . !*

Luke was surprised at how vehemently he wished this. He'd thought all he wanted was for her to forget seeing him as a zombie. But now he remembered that the best thing for her, and for Cherry and Haddy, was to erase himself. That was as true now as it had been, when he made the decision to do so in the first place. Truer, in fact.

Reawakening in undead form among the living did not count as erasure.

Meanwhile there was silence on the other side of the door. Was she still out there? Luke held his breath, and waited.

"Luke?" Charity said in a tremulous voice. God, she was brave. He'd have been halfway to Eureka by now.

"Is anybody out there?" he asked.

"Just me," Charity said.

"Should I come out?" Luke asked.

"I–I don't know," Charity said carefully. "Is that horrible bird thing with you?"

"Gee, thanks, Missy!" Buzz squawked, "I won't hurt you if you don't hurt me."

"It can talk!" Charity said. "How the hell can it talk?"

"It's a long story," Luke said.

"Are you . . . dead?" Charity asked.

"Not entirely," Luke replied.

"Completely," Buzz said at the same time.

"I look horrible," Luke added. "You should just go."

"Luke? How can I–how can I just go?" Charity was definitely crying now. "What happened, Luke? What have you done?"

"I'll let you know when I figure it out, Boo," he said.

"No, I have to . . . I have to see you again, Luke. I have to know. I have to know what I saw, and what I didn't see."

"Are you sure? Charity, just go, let me get out of here, and you'll never have to see me again. You'll never even have to think about me. I promise."

"That's not true, Luke, and you know it. Whether I like it or not, I'm going to have to think about you every day, for the rest of my life."

"Then–then I want you to remember me the way I was."

Charity sniffed, and gave a sob that was half laugh. "Are you sure?"

"Okay, the way I used to look, anyway."

"Are you, like, a zombie?" she asked incredulously.

"Sort of," said Luke.

"Absolutely," Buzz interjected simultaneously.

"But–you don't eat brains."

"*He* doesn't," said Buzz.

"There's nothing to be afraid of," Luke said. "But, somebody could show up any minute and see me, and that would really be unfortunate. I need to go undercover until I figure out what to do. Go home, Charity. I can do this by myself."

"Luke, no. I'm your best friend. I have to know what's happened to you. I have to know the truth!"

And Charity opened the door.

Luke's heart was bursting with love for her. He closed his eyes for a few moments, so he wouldn't have to see her look of apprehension turn to horror and disgust.

"Ohh, Luke," she said. "Oh, Luke." He opened his eyes to see her tears. "You, you need a doctor," she cried. "My god, look at you!"

"No, no. There's not a doctor in the world who can cure me," he said. Maybe he had just coined his own epitaph. "No doctors!"

"But you're alive, you're somehow still alive!" She threw herself toward him as if to embrace him. He jumped back. "See?" she said, as if his reflexes proved something. "Luke, you're not dead."

Luke wanted to believe her, of course, or even to just go along with her, but the facts were the facts.

"Um . . . I'm pretty certain that I *am* dead."

"Pretty certain? Oh, pshaw."

"I'll prove it," said the vulture, she who had once been the Queen of the Dead. And with a swift pounce of her hideous head, she munched a portion of Luke's brain.

"Christ, leave Luke alone, you fucking vulture!" Charity yelled, grabbing Buzz's neck with both hands. She was fast.

"Help! I'm endangered!" Buzz skrawked.

"You sure are, you cannibal!"

"Let me go!" shrieked Buzz as she flopped into the air. "I'm warning you! I can snip those fingers right off."

"Stop it, both of you!" Luke cried. Charity let go.

"You have to get rid of that thing!" Charity folded her arms. "We are going straight to a locksmith."

"Nope, not going to a locksmith, not going to the doctor, not going anywhere except out of here. Out your life. Forever."

"*What?*" Charity's eyes began filling with tears.

"I'm sorry," Luke said firmly, proud of himself for the first time in ages, "that's just the way it has to be."

"But Luke, the kids!–Haddy and Cherry miss you so much! Aren't we even going to *tell* them?"

Luke pulled down on his face in exasperation, then popped a dislodged eye back in. Rubbing tended to work them loose. "You aren't making this easy, Boo!" he moaned. "Look, this is probably just temporary, it's a mix-up, a fluke. It's better that they never . . . ."

"Ohhh! Booo hooo hooo!" Charity surrendered to seismic sobs.

"Honey–honey! Whatever happens, I'll be watching over you, that's all you need to know. I can't be part of your lives, and I can't let anybody but you see me or recognize me. I just need to figure out how to finish what I started. Okay?"

Charity was pulling herself together now, but that was only because she was so angry. "So. I'm married to a zombie, and I can't even tell anybody?"

"That's right. Because if you do . . ." How could he get across to her how unpleasant it would be if everybody found out? Even if he got back to Famebeau one day, he'd never be able to erase the effects of so many minds, visualizing him as an actual zombie. He'd be stuck in this gruesome form.

"If you do, I'll never stop being one, ever. And you just can't condemn me to that, Charity! Please." Luke realized he was crying too. He had probably been crying for a while.

Charity stared at him fiercely. "Okay Luke, you win," was all she said. "I'm going to go right now and get a gurney, and wheel you out of here. Anybody tries to stop me, they get rammed in the hip."

"It's okay," Luke said. "Just bring me a sheet or something. I'll sneak out on my own. Less risky!"

"Dr. Lupercan was searching for you," she warned. "I told him it was probably a practical joke, or some sort of statement by a grief-stricken fan. Then he said he had to get some paperwork for me to sign. He'll be back."

"Haw, he's looking for schnapps in his office. He's probably off having a nervous breakdown," Luke opined.

Charity looked both ways down the hall outside, then raced off. She returned two minutes later with a thin blanket, some paper shoes and a hospital gown.

"Sorry, no pants to be had," she said.

Donning the gown was a puzzling exercise, since the sleeves were too small to fit over Buzz's chest.

Charity stood by holding the blanket. "Will that bird attack me?" she asked, eager to help, yet hesitant.

"You'll leave her alone, won't you Buzz?"

"Yeah, sure. Let bygones be bygones, I always say."

In the end, Luke had to tie the gown under his armpit.

"Buzz, you could be draped over my shoulders. I'll look like a hunched old codger."

Buzz arranged herself obligingly.

Charity pulled the blanket this way and that, looking at her handiwork critically.

"Looks too weird. You'd better carry the vulture in front. There you go," Charity said briskly as she helped Luke distribute the folds. Her hand brushed Luke's cold cheek and she shuddered. "Do you want my sweater?" she asked with a sniff.

"That's okay, thanks anyway." Luke pulled the blanket further down over his face.

"I'd better stay here in case the Doctor comes back," Charity offered. "To throw him off the scent."

"Great. You're a champ," Luke said. He shuffled toward the door like an aged man, something he'd once done mockingly onstage after rumors had circulated of his untimely demise. Now, he was afraid part of him might fall off.

"Well, see ya," he said. "I mean, 'bye. Don't try to find me, okay, Boo?"

He kept his head down. Luke heard Charity making suppressed sounds behind him, heartbroken sounds. He didn't look back.

Dennis Defoe groaned as soon as he realized he was awake. His head was throbbing to the rhythm of an irritating noise, and it felt as though a weight were pressing his eyes deep into his brain, pinning him in place as the repetitive sound bit down like a dentist's drill, stabbing a nerve in his parietal cortex.

He flung aside the pillow that covered his face. A lamp crashed to the floor. The merciless drilling went on.

The telephone. Goddammit. What time was it?

Defoe rolled himself angrily into a seated position, or at least he meant to. He had been closer to the edge of the bed than he realized, and he found empty air beneath him for a split second before his shin made contact with the corner of the fallen lamp.

Goddammit!

The phone continued to ring as he pulled himself upright and stumbled toward the bathroom. He dropped two tablets into a cup of water and downed the fizzing liquid, sucked air noisily in through his nose, and limped back toward the bed. He settled himself in with the bruised leg propped up on a pillow.

He lay there dazed, the agony in his head battling for his attention with the fiery pain in his leg. Eventually he reached a bearable equilibrium between the two, so that they almost canceled each other out to allow him to drift toward slumber.

That was when the telephone resumed its buzz-saw assault.

Defoe lunged for the receiver.

"What is it?" he snarled.

"Dennis?" Oh Jesus. It was his ex-wife. Of course it was.

"What the hell are you calling me for, at this hour?"

"It's one in the afternoon, Dennis. And you were supposed to be here at ten."

The contempt that woman could load onto her words was phenomenal. If the sentences were a train, each syllable was a car piled with lumps of coal, chugging down the bad-boy track and straight into his stocking. The stocking bulged to bursting, and Defoe exploded.

"Dolores, I'm on a freaking case!"

"Not any more you aren't. And I'm late for work, so please get over here as quickly as you can."

"I'm in Olympia, fercrissake."

Dolores sighed. And sighed again. "I'll have to get Ellen to come and watch Hilary until you get here, then."

"I can't take her this weekend. I told you, I'm on a case."

"Maybe you should turn the TV on, Dennis." The line went dead.

Defoe leaned back against the headboard and rubbed his face hard. What was Dolores talking about? Had he missed something? He reached for the remote, and clicked the television on.

It didn't take long to find the news. It was being reported on every channel except home shopping, and the station with *I Love Lucy* reruns.

Defoe stared at the clips that cycled in front of his eyes non-stop: the house in Portland he had visited two days earlier, the French doors to the sun room, the view within blocked by two police officers. The camera zoomed in toward the external window to the sun room, then cut to file footage of Luke Mandrake from a year ago, helping his wife strap the two children into their car seats in the back of a faded yellow Volvo wagon, then back to the reporter on the scene.

"Mandrake had been missing for six days when a telephone repairman doing routine maintenance spotted the body through an upstairs window of the couple's Portland mansion. The Coroner reports that Mandrake has been dead for three and a half days."

"Why that sonofa . . ." Defoe remarked softly. "He was in there the whole . . .”

Defoe stared at the TV screen while reality cracked his cranium like an egg, and scrambled his lobes with the wire whisk of revelation.

“They call that a mansion? These guys don’t know what the fuck they’re talking about.” Defoe felt inside the pocket of his overcoat for his travel flask. He shook the bottle, then poured the last few drops of whiskey onto his tongue.

“For one thing, that was no suicide,” he said severely, lecturing the empty bottle. “Charity sent me on a, a . . .” What was he trying to say? Honker? Gronker?

“A wild goose chase!” He was feeling very muzzy. It was time a drink. He rummaged in his suitcase and pulled out the half gallon jug of Badunoff vodka he’d purchased at the Savers Club a couple of days ago. It was nearly empty.

“It was that freaking leprechaun who did it, on her orders,” Defoe’s eyes glanced around the room, probably in search of a cup, “or I’ll be a fuckin’ unkie’s muncle.”

He hoisted the jug and poured some of the colorless liquid into his mouth. His throat was scorched and his eyes watered, but he gazed at the bottle affectionately before downing another swig.

As the pickled cells of his nervous system, fueled by ethanol, fired up, so did his ire against Charity Ball.

She had known all along that her husband was dead. She’d used Defoe as a patsy, made a fool of him.

A warm feeling rose up in his solar plexus, coursed down his legs and arms, and soon arrived at his cheeks, mottling the pallid skin with patches of red. And it wasn’t just the vodka. It was something more, something he hadn’t felt for a very long time.

It was a sense of purpose, propelled by implacable hatred.

I’m going to get that bitch if it’s the last thing I do.

April 4, 1994 – Brooklyn, NY

Rosetta decided to take a rest. Her throat hurt and she thought she might be coming down with something. The picture was nearly finished anyway. She cleaned her brushes, put a piece of plastic wrap over the wet blobs of paint on the palette, and put on the kettle for some tea.

She thought of continuing work on the sketches for the next painting, but her thoughts kept returning to the shock she'd had earlier in the day. It was terribly upsetting, not only that Luke Mandrake really was dead, but that the dreams she'd had every night during the days leading up to the discovery of the body seemed to predict it. *People who think it's romantic to have "psychic" experiences, probably haven't had too many of them,* Rosetta mused darkly.

The truth was, it was so disturbing even to think about the dreams, it made her dizzy and sick to her stomach. She even caught herself feeling guilty about them, as if she were somehow responsible for the tragedy. *But that's silly,* she told herself. *Just try and relax now, get some rest. There's no point in making yourself ill.*

The goal of relaxation gave her something easy and safe to focus on. Rosetta set up an exercise mat in the bedroom, really just several layers of blankets on the floor, and did some stretches. *I should try and do some sit-ups and leg lifts and Kegels,* she told herself. But she was feeling so tired. Maybe just the Kegels, then. She lay on her back and breathed deeply, while flexing the muscles of her lady parts the way her gynecologist had instructed her to do.

Squeeze . . . release. Squeeze . . . release. Squeeze . . . release.

Rosetta found herself as usual thinking of Aron and how distant he'd been recently. It was like they lived on two different planets.

She still hadn't told him about her period being so late. The last thing she wanted to do was bring up that subject, unless it became absolutely necessary, but she was starting to become unbearably anxious.

Tears gathered in her eyes and slipped down her cheeks. How silly she was being. She really was awfully tired. Maybe she should go to bed. But Aron would be home from work in a couple of hours, and she hadn't started cutting up the vegetables for dinner yet. She would go to bed early, and probably feel better in the morning.

She curled up with her sketchbook, and when the words of a poem started to form in her head, she wrote them down. Fifteen minutes later she read the lines over.

How I long to be adored!
But I soon retire, ignored
Or you trample my devotion
With a slight, disdainful motion.

Oh, I try to take it easy
Acting confident and breezy
While my bosom purveys plunder
And a heart, betrayed by thunder.

Deep within your limpid lover
Sunken treasure you'd uncover:
Nobler love I never gave
Gentle, generous and brave;
And of profanity's desire
I'm your lifetime soul supplier!

But the feast returns, a ration
From a poet without passion
One whose words are coldly measured
And whose wife I am: unpleasured.

Rosetta sighed. *Well, there you have it,* she thought. Should she even show this to Aron? Asking him to read it would probably only make matters worse. Anyway, he'd think it terribly arrogant of her to brag about the nobility of her love for him.

No, the poem wasn't much good, was it? But at least in writing it she'd gotten some comfort. It was better than crying her eyes out.

With another sigh, she got up and went to the kitchen, where their young roommate Bob was slathering peanut butter and jelly onto white wonder bread.

"How can you eat that?" she teased. "It's just plastic fluff and air."

Bob grinned. "Bread is merely a conveyance for the contents of the sandwich," he replied. He crammed an enormous bite into his face, picked up a glass of milk, and strolled off toward his room with the sandwich in one hand and the glass in the other.

Rosetta investigated the refrigerator. Luckily there was still some cheddar cheese, and a tomato, and a couple of English muffins left. She'd been planning on preparing a nut and mushroom paté, squash soup, and salad. The paté and soup would be a lot of work to make, more than she felt up to just now. But she concluded that she could sauté the shrooms with onions and garlic as a side dish, and serve them with the salad and a welsh rarebit made with tofu dogs.

Satisfied with her new plan, Rosetta thought there might be just enough time to stretch and prime another sheet of paper, before she started dinner. She wanted to get a head start on the bog mummy painting. Also, she needed to arrange for a female model–she needed to take photographs reproducing the positions of the bodies found in the bog. She could probably get Aron to pose for her over the week-end, for the male figures.

If only her throat didn't hurt so much. She wanted so badly to stay up late and keep working on the sketches.

*   *   *

22

Go to sleep, Jean-Baptiste moaned. *You're ill!*

It was two in the morning, and Rosetta was in her studio in front of a drawing board, smeared from head to toe with charcoal. She was obsessed with finishing those drawings of ancient corpses.

It made him anxious. It was dangerous for her to be working so late, in her condition, in this unheated room.

Jean-Baptiste had lost a mother and a sister as a child, had buried two young sons. He knew that he was probably over-solicitous in matters of health. This was after all a different age, the age of antibiotics. Still he couldn't help wishing that Rosetta would get some rest. It was merely common sense, for goodness sake.

Anyhow these bog mummy drawings, well, they were simply macabre. It had all the marks of an unhealthy fixation, to Jean-Baptiste, this fetish with the bodies of the dead.

If you must study death, don't let it be the death of you! the guardian angel muttered.

Back From the Dead

I warned you twice
I'm not too nice
Laugh this aside
It's good advice

From Planet Dumb
You look real smart
I wear this hole
You wear my heart

I see you, I can hear you speak
Callin' me back
Back from the dead
Callin' me back from the dead
Callin' me back from the dead

I think I'm zombie from outer space
On the night of the walking, talking dead
But that doesn't matter now
None of that matters now

I'll rocket home to your embrace
You'll wrap a grin around my head
You're super-human! You're the face
That summons me back from the dead
That raises me up from the dead

The Rubber Dahls, 1990

Charity pumped the knob of the vending machine, she thumped and clattered. Her body language was eloquent of distress, devastation. And most of all she was profoundly enraged.

"*All* I wanted were some Lorna *Doones,*" she informed her adversary in stentorian tones as she removed one of her bubblegum-pink Doc Martens. A knot of spectators were starting to accumulate around her in the family lounge.

"But you, you *infernal robot,*" and Charity raised the shoe, "won't put *out!*" She slammed the boot into the side panel of the tight-fisted device. She was aping her dad, she suddenly realized, and it had to be a little bit terrifying to watch. But she had embraced her demons long ago. When she summoned her Kali force, she carried all before her.

The Lorna Doones dropped into the dispensing tray. There was scattered applause.

Orderlies were running over here now from every which way. *That crazy bitch Charity is going nuts again, come and see!* Luke could slip out unnoticed in the chaos.

Yep, making scenes was her specialty, and she didn't even have to pretend this time.

There was a deprecating hand on her elbow. Dr. Lupercan had returned.

"Mrs. Mandrake-" he pleaded.

"It's Ball, Charity Ball," she snapped. "Always was, and always will be. Please make a note of it."

"Ms. Ball. Will you come into my offish please?"

"What is going on with this place?" she complained. "Yes, I'll gladly come to your office. I think you've got some splainin' to do, Dr. Lupercan."

The Medical Examiner sat down at his desk and leafed through the pile of documents that he had prepared, while Charity laced on the pink boot.

Dr. Lupercan opened a file drawer, removed another form, and proceeded to fill in the spaces. Charity tapped her boot steadily against the chair leg. The tempo would have come to about three hundred whacks a minute, but after fifty or so, the Medical Examiner spoke without looking up from the paper.

"I'm ashuming," he said, signing his name with a snockered flourish, "you'll be filing a poleesh report."

"Why is that?" Charity cooed.

The Doctor leaned toward her confidentially. His drunkenness only exaggerated the frigid intimacy of his manner, the manner of a man who chose performing autopsies as his profession, and Charity shivered.

"Mishez- Miz Ball, your husband's body has clearly been shtolen from this inshtitution."

"Dr. Lupercan. My husband had some . . . unusual friends." The Medical Examiner swallowed visibly as Charity went on. "Some very wealthy and influential friends."

The Doctor stiffened, spread his hands out on the desk, where they did spider push-ups. "Muh, muh-" he muttered.

"Has it occurred to you that one of them must be behind this prank?"

"You–you think thish is just a prank? Shome shelebrity hi-jinks! No, Ms. Ball, no." The man was beginning to appear somewhat demented. He stared at nothing. "I examined the body," he whispered. "He was dead, you know, had been for shome days. But not–not like *that* . . . And then tonight . . ." Dr. Lupercan shook out a white handkerchief and dabbed his temples. "The *eyes*," he squeaked, almost inaudibly, "*the eyes* . . ."

"Dr. Lupercan, please!" Charity said bracingly. "You are drunk!"

"A drink, what an exshellent idea! Would you care for a

schnappsh?" The Medical Examiner rummaged around at the back of the file drawer. *Luke as usual is so fucking psychic it's ridiculous,* Charity observed.

"Thank you. Doctor." She stood up and took possession of the pile of documents. "I came here tonight to identify my husband's body," she remarked as she examined the relevant form. "And that was certainly my husband."

The doctor, with a surprisingly steady hand, poured schnapps into two shot glasses, and silently handed one of them to Charity.

"We both know what we saw," she said softly. "Yet what could it possibly be but a prank? And before we bring the police into this, I'd like to do some asking around. Understand?"

Dr. Lupercan swallowed his schnapps, then stared at her helplessly.

Charity sipped hers, gazing limpidly into the Medical Examiner's eyes. "So . . . let's just sign these now, and you can release the body to me," she said. "The less said, the better. Don't you agree?"

"I . . ." the Doctor cleared his throat.

"Do you like Goldschlager, Dr. Lupercan?" Charity wondered, as she signed the release form. "I'm going to send you a whole case of it. Because you've been such a comfort, and so understanding of me in my moment of . . . distress." She really was an enchanting woman.

Charity reached over and squeezed his forearm. "Thank you, Doctor," she murmured. She leaned in close to him over the desk, and pushed the release toward him.

"He's out there," she whispered, holding his gaze with her enormous brown peepers. "And he's watching, and waiting. So . . ." She pressed a finger over her pursed lips. Then she turned abruptly away, and began to button her pea coat.

Dr. Lupercan picked up the release form. Underneath it was a small stack of hundred dollar bills. "Izh thish-" he began.

"Thank you *so* much Doctor, for your care and attention to my poor husband," she trilled, favoring him with a misty look. Lupercan signed the form, detached a carbon copy and slid it toward Charity. Moments later she was prancing down the hospital corridor, her heart beating fast.

Life with Luke had always been an out-of-the-ordinary adventure, Charity mused. His death was turning out to be an even bigger one.

*　　　　*　　　　*

"Lemme outta here!" Buzz grated.

"Not yet, Buzz." Luke whispered. He thought they were clear of the medical campus, but he could only see about a four-square-inch slice of street between the folds of the blue blanket he clutched at his throat. It was enough to catch glimpses of occasional pedestrians, who carefully ignored him as he hobbled along, disoriented, under a tangle of criss-crossing elevated highways and on-ramps.

He was making toward the tumble-down industrial district by the river. So long as there were people about, the appearance of an enormous and hideous vulture from beneath his wrappings would quickly put an end to the anonymity he currently enjoyed.

"I can't stand it, I tell ya!" Buzz complained in a muffled voice.

"Sh!"

Luke stumbled into a sheltered parking lot, and birthed the bird from under his hospital gown. Buzz sighed gustily as she flapped her wings and stretched her neck, wriggling it to get the kinks out.

"The things I have to put up with," she complained. She straightened her wing feathers with her beak. "I don't think I'll ever enter an enclosed space again."

"I hear you. Whaddaya say we fly somewhere less populated?"

"Sure, Bozo," Buzz agreed. Luke hopped aboard and she flapped her powerful pinions.

Buzz lurched into the air, lost altitude, climbed again, then started to sink. Something was wrong. Although as a zombie Luke couldn't have weighed more than 50 pounds, the condor weighed half that. Buzz was locked in a battle against physics. Apparently, physics was winning.

Buzz struggled on a bit, then dropped onto a rooftop, with a wheezing gasp.

"Look, a clothesline," Luke observed. There was an assortment of items hanging out to dry, including a couple of shirts, some floral pillow-cases and an enormous pair of corduroy jeans. Luke swiped the pants and a black hooded sweatshirt, which had an electrician's logo silkscreened on it in red. The brown cords were secured around his emaciated waist using the rolled-up hospital gown as a belt.

"You're gonna have to travel in one of these, I guess," Luke said as he held a pillow case open for Buzz to climb in.

"No fucking way, Bozo. I ride on your shoulder. No more claustrophobia for me."

"Buzz, if somebody sees you it'll excite attention. And it's actually illegal, I believe, to have a pet condor."

"I don't care. We can just wait till the wee hours, when nobody's around to see."

There was a bit more arguing, but eventually Luke gave up on trying to get Buzz into the sack. He shrugged and sat down. "I have no clue where to go anyway," he sighed.

"I have an idea," Buzz said suddenly. "I could play rubber chicken."

"What?"

"If anyone notices me, I'll pretend to be a fake," Buzz insisted. "Like this." And she struck a pose with her neck extended and her feet flattened against her body.

The vulture dropped to the tar rooftop and lay there, stiff and rubbery. Luke prodded her with a finger. Even her feathers felt like rubber. It was a pretty convincing act.

"How did you do that?" Luke asked. Buzz didn't answer. "Buzz?" He poked at her again. "Buzz!"

He lifted her up. She was light and flimsy, a hollow thing. He shook her and her rubber head waved and bounced on her rubber neck. "Buzz? What the fuck!"

Then the bird's body grew heavy in his hands. Moments later it was again like a living animal's, and he could feel feathers against his palms. Her head snaked around toward him and she blinked.

"Whaddaya think, Bozo?" she grated.

"I have no idea what just happened," Luke breathed, "but I bow to your infinite powers."

"Oh that's nothing," Buzz retorted. "I guess I could turn myself into licorice, or stone, or whatever material you want. But it's not a very useful talent, in most situations."

"I'm so confused," Luke lamented. "What's going on here? Are there even rules governing our existence? And if so, what are they? It would really help to know."

"It's kinda hard to explain," Buzz began. "You just gotta feel it . . ."

Luke certainly wanted to feel it. He wanted to feel a rush of power, transformation, insight–anything but the grinding misery that was, judging by his experience so far, to be his unending fate.

He closed his eyes and sought inside himself for clues. Beyond his momentary thoughts, the crowded sea of impressions from his immediate locale and the background chatter in his mind, all he could detect was the same looming enormity he had confronted every day of his conscious life. He called it the Wall.

He still had the same talent for hearing thoughts that had been his from an early age. In fact it absorbed an enormous amount of energy to shut out all those unwanted voices, and though he was used to it, his telepathy had always been an exhausting burden. It was bad enough in situations where he didn't much care. But the second he was emotionally involved with anyone, their conflicted thoughts began to slowly annihilate him, becoming at times a tormenting barrage of judging voices and confused murmurs. Knowing what people were thinking may have given him a strategic advantage, but it also ate away at his confidence, and made it difficult to focus.

As he listened, Luke could hear the thoughts of nearby people as clearly as words spoken quietly in his ear: *Get the hell out! . . . Macaroni and cheese . . . Why did you have to do that? Why? . . . seven more push-ups, six, five, four . . .*

Out beyond these voices he detected the babel of a city, with an underlying drone of the sick and dying, and on a global scale, the heavy, crashing waves of human misery. This was the true source of his physical pain, he knew, though he had never seen fit to reveal the fact to his doctors.

For 27 years Luke had striven to protect himself from the overwhelming stream of data that had eroded his sanity day by day. But the flimsy structures he erected in his mind were useless against the flood, while the drugs, sex and loud, thumping music had provided only temporary relief.

But the Wall was another matter. The Wall had always been out there, stopping him from seeing the big picture, occluding his understanding of his place in the universe. It was the Wall that he had tried again and again to scale, to overcome, to penetrate and destroy: driving his own body beyond endurance, pushing the envelope with illicit medicaments, screwing for hours on end. His desire to attain a blessed state of freedom from pain was also a quest for a state of greater awareness, one that was forever just beyond reach. Denied transcendence, he had bled and bled, had suffered inescapably, skating along a knife-edge of humanity's agony that cut deeper by the moment.

So much unwanted information rushing at him all the time, and the one thing he most needed to know . . .

"Penny for your thoughts," Buzz said. And now the obvious finally dawned on Luke: he couldn't read her mind. Yet he'd heard the thoughts of the goddess in the Hall of Ten Thousand Pillars clearly enough. The fact was, with the exception of the loudspeaker mental projections of the monstrous Bette Davis, he hadn't read a single thought during his entire stay in Famebeau.

But maybe she could read his.

I wanna fuck you, he silently shouted at Kore as an experiment, picturing her in his mind as he had last seen her, feeling her in his embrace, a voluptuous nude. The condor showed no sign of having heard, but then–

The Wall mocked him silently, pregnantly, withholding its secrets.

"I thought you wanted to get outta here," Buzz rasped.

Luke sighed and bent to pick up the condor. He buried his face in her feathers, imagining the skin of the goddess, its salty taste. He kissed her lips.

Luke opened his eyes in surprise. He still held the vulture in his arms, not the houri. And yet there had been a kiss, so momentary, so vivid and sweet.

"What just happened?" he murmured.

"I guess we all have our hidden talents, Bozo," Buzz croaked. "Come on. Let's try going down the fire escape." Luke knew she was gonna jump out of his arms in a second.

"Wait. Wait." Luke said gruffly, clutching the scavenger bird tightly. He was becoming increasingly frustrated at the way he was being kept in the dark. "Aren't you ever going to answer any of my questions?"

"I guess that depends, Bozo."

"On?"

"On what the question is, of course."

"I know there's something you're not telling me."

"And never will. Code of silence, orders from the highest level. Sorry, Luke."

"Damn it," Luke released the bird, sat down and folded his arms around his knees. "Why the hell are there so many questions you can't answer?"

"I can't tell you that."

"Okay then . . . can you just tell me what the fuck is really going on? Why are you still here? Did *you* want this? Did you want . . . to be with *me*?" Annoyingly, Luke's voice cracked a bit at the last few words.

Buzz sighed, and preened her ruff. A fine drizzle was falling, and the droplets glittered on her iridescent black feathers.

"I think . . ." she squawked at last, "I think that there are a lot of forces at work here. This is a deep game, Luke, and I don't know every move in it either. For example, that cowrie shell you have there. There's somebody inside, am I right?"

Luke should have known better than to try and hide anything from Kore. She obviously didn't miss much. Fortunately the condor didn't seem to expect an answer from him, beyond a shamefaced nod.

"Did I want to be here with you?" Buzz went on slowly. "I don't know if I ever had any choice, besides complete annihilation. Pluto surely thought that sending you back here to die would be the end of me, too. That . . . that hurt me badly. I never imagined he would be so vindictive toward me, although vengefulness is one of his primary traits . . ."

Luke picked up a fragment of crumbled cement, and threw it hard at the clothesline. It bounced off of a damp sheet and clunked down onto the tar-paper. "I just don't understand how you can still have feelings for the guy. He's such an asshole."

"Do you think I still feel the same about him after everything that's happened? I guess I'm not that big of an idiot." Buzz croaked indignantly.

"Well, I'm relieved to hear that. Good riddance to him." Luke stroked the vulture's back gently. "So what are our options now? Can you think of any way of getting us out of this mess?" *And if you did, would you even tell me?* he wondered.

"Wait and see. Something will happen, no doubt," she creaked serenely.

"Right." Luke remained miffed. "And what about the rules? I mean, our very existence here on earth breaks fundamental laws."

"Certainly."

"Yet the laws of physics are still something we have to deal with. We can't really fly. We can't just make shit up, and expect it to manifest itself in the world, like they do in Famebeau. Except . . . you just turned yourself into a rubber bird. I mean, what the fuck?"

"This is a completely unique situation, Luke." Buzz butted him with her head reproachfully. "I'm figuring things out as I go along, just like you. Okay?"

"Okay. But . . ." Tears started in Luke's eyes. "Why? Why won't you just tell me the whole truth, Kore? Don't you trust me?"

"It's not that Luke, believe me." The vulture inspected her foot, nibbled at her toe. "I'm already in deep doodoo right now, you know."

Luke sighed. "I know. There are other gods–Zeus, the total dick, or whoever–"

"No. Not Zeus. I don't give a flying burrito about what Daddy thinks." She looked over her shoulder and then stared Luke in the eyes and rasped, "I will tell you one thing, although I shouldn't, because–ack! ack!"

Luke felt excitement clench his gut. He was finally about to get a clue. He had to wait though, while Buzz coughed up something. It turned out to be a feather.

Then she put her beak right next to his ear. "I am pledged to help you," she rasped. "I was told to look for you, and give you aid."

"No shit!? Who told you to help me?" Luke demanded.

"Shh!" Buzz warned him. "We are being watched!"

"I don't get it," he whispered, "Why help *me?*"

Buzz put her beak to his ear once more, and spoke in the tiniest scratching whisper imaginable. "It's because of something you haven't done yet. And the more gods like Zeus and Hades try to prevent it, the more they're creating the perfect conditions for you to do it."

Luke opened his mouth, but before anything more than a bemused bleat came out Buzz snapped, "And I can't tell you any more, so don't ask."

It began to rain in large, hard drops. Luke didn't know what to make of Kore's information. It was going to take some ruminating.

"OK. Let's go." Luke stood up, and Buzz settled herself on his shoulder. He walked over to the door that led downstairs from the rooftop, and tried the knob. It opened, and he stepped through.

The girl on the landing below dropped her laundry with a shriek, baby clothes scattering as the basket bumped down a flight of stairs and landed face down.

Luke froze, scanning for information he could use to manage the crisis. She was filled with bitter thoughts, he had been feeling it for awhile, up there on the roof, without really noticing. She was distraught, in fact, over the death of Luke Mandrake. Her vivid thoughts of suicide, of throwing herself off the roof, projected wildly into his mind.

Luke pulled his hood further down and rushed past her, clutching the suddenly rubberized vulture.

"Hey!" she yelped. "Those clothes are my dad's!"

Luke should have fled, but instead for some reason he stopped one landing down and started scooping the baby clothes back into the basket. He couldn't help himself. Even though he was a slob about his own clothes, he was totally anal when it came to baby things. Seeing them on the dirty stairwell bugged him.

"Who are you?" the girl breathed. She was thinking of Luke

Mandrake. *He moves like Luke. Could it be?*

Forget about me! Luke shouted involuntarily with his mind. Could she hear him? Would she recognize him?

The undead Luke Mandrake walks the earth. That was not a rumor he could afford to start.

He paused in his task with a pair of onesies held to his chest. He was struggling to pick up the clothes while remaining concealed inside the tent-like hoodie, making fists and using them like a giant pair of tongs, but the flapping ends of his over-long sleeves were problematic, and the plastic vulture-on-a-chain even more so.

"You . . . you don't have to do that," she murmured. "It's okay."

Nakita, that was her name.

Don't do it, Nakita, he wanted to tell her. *Don't jump.* But if he spoke, she might recognize his voice. He tried to move like a hobbled old man, which was not that difficult since he felt like one already. But he exaggerated it, tried to be a different guy, a timid, odd but not a scary guy, head bowed, silently and painfully retrieving the diapers and booties and little sweaters, and placing them in the basket.

Nakita put her hand on her hips and shook her head at him. Somehow Luke had succeeded in letting her think he was just some shy, childlike old tramp who'd stolen her dad's work clothes. She even seemed grateful to him for dispelling her suspicions, and she didn't really mind the theft.

Nakita hated her dad. She was already making plans to take the baby to church after she woke up from her nap, to spend the whole evening there. Maybe even to spend the night at Paula's. That way, they wouldn't be home when Dad got mad. He always stayed mad for so long. He'd call his friends so they could egg him on while he yelled and cursed. They'd come over for the game, all of them drinking scotch and malt liquor, bossing her around, making comments about her weight. *It wasn't like this before Momma died.*

Nakita watched Luke from the top of the stairs until he hurried off. Somehow his act of kindness, loony though it was, had made her feel less desperate.

*   *   *

"That was a close call, back there," Buzz remarked as they tramped along under an overpass crammed with noisy rush-hour vehicles. It was still raining, and the passing trucks spewed muddy water up onto them as they stood at a crosswalk. Luke's paper slippers were falling to bits. Now one of them floated away and got sucked into a storm drain.

"Fuck. Fuck!" Luke replied.

"What?"

"Whaddaya mean, what? My feet hurt. I don't have any shoes. We're soaking wet. We don't have anywhere to go. And any second somebody could recognize me, and then I'm just . . . totally screwed!"

"How about we take a break, huh? Sit down in this thing over here, what is it?"

"It's a fucking MAX shelter. Where the train stops."

"Well, let's halt here for a minute," Buzz suggested. "I need to stretch my neck."

Luke slumped down onto the bench and put his head in his arms. "Buzz. Kore . . ." Luke had been trying not to weep, but his exhaustion took over now. "God! Why is this happening? How did I–I mean, how is this possible? How did we get here?"

Buzz rocked thoughtfully on the bench, from one foot to the other. Then she croaked, "I think it was a mistake. Hades doesn't ever permit undead things to inhabit the earthly sphere. He meant to annihilate us both, I suspect."

Luke sniffed. "Annihilate us? You mean, like, destroy our souls?"

"In a manner of speaking, yes. He doesn't know that it's impossible to dispense with you so easily."

37

Luke digested this. He wanted to ask Buzz what that meant, why he was so hard to get rid of. Was it simply because she was helping him? What was so special about him?

Now there was a commuter train approaching, and as much as he would have liked to get on that train and ride it to wherever it was going, he couldn't risk it.

"We'd better keep moving," Luke said tiredly, and tucking the vulture back under his sweatshirt, on he hobbled.

The gloom thickened and the rain let up. As they passed a seedy Motel 6, a car pulled up beside them. It was a beat-up Pontiac, and Luke could hear the driver rolling down the window manually.

"Hey, there, you okay? Need a lift somewhere?" a friendly voice called out.

Luke hunched further into his hood, shaking his head.

"I could take you to a place where you and your baby would be safe, have a hot meal and a warm bed for the night," the voice persisted.

Luke was afraid even to peer at the driver from the depths of his ill-fitting hoodie, but he picked up genuine thoughts of concern from the man. A glimpse in the side view mirror showed that he was wearing a clerical collar. Probably not a predator, but all the same, Luke had no desire for hospitality, he just wanted to get away from everyone and everything.

"No thanks, Reverend," he croaked. "We're almost home."

"All right, glad to hear it. God bless," the pastor said, rolled up the window squeakily, and drove off. Luke stumbled on, making his way down toward the river, the railroad tracks, the back alleys of nameless warehouses; limping toward anonymity.

His mind kept going back to the moment he woke up in the sun room, sure he was whole, sure he was alive. He had felt flooded with a sense of new purpose, of possibility. Moments later, it had somehow all been erased, and in the darkness of the grave, Luke had become once again a thing of decay, a walking husk of tormented flesh and brittle bone.

"Buzz, can you at least tell me one thing?"

"What's that, Bozo?"

"Hades's plan was to trick me into coming back here, right?"

"Obviously."

"Was what he said true, though? Was I still alive at that point?"

"I've been wondering that myself. He claimed that you could simply wake up, that you were in a coma. But it seems to me that I would have sensed that myself when you arrived," Buzz croaked thoughtfully. "Perhaps your connection to your body was closer to that of a spirit walker."

"You mean," Luke said, "like the spirit that dwells in a mummy?" He had read the Book of the Dead, and knew that Egyptian priests could travel at will in their astral forms, and even heal patients that way. After death, their preserved bodies served as home base for the material aspect of the soul, which they called the Ka. "So maybe I really was already dead."

"Maybe so. Hades was anxious to rid himself of you, either way."

"But what did he expect would happen? Did he know I would become an actual zombie?"

"I doubt it," Buzz replied. "He probably sent you back expecting that you'd be trapped in your body, or get lost."

Up ahead, a couple were walking toward them, holding hands. Buzz fell silent as they came closer. Their clothes were threadbare, their shoes were worn, and the woman's purse was old and cheap, but the two were lost in each others eyes, lost in conversation. The wet ragamuffin Luke appeared to be, barely registered in their thoughts, although the young man spared him a pitying look.

But then, lurking not far behind them, Luke picked up a much more sinister mind.

It was the kind of hopped-up addict who had descended almost to an animal state, a mind roiling with physical need, with violent thoughts and greedy urges. And that mind had fixed itself upon the couple as its target.

Get on by, little homeless fucker, the man was thinking, *get on by. There's a lonely stretch up ahead, and I'm fast with this knife, twenty bucks is all I need to get my fix, twenty bucks and a few quarters for a coke, they've got that much on them for sure, the smug bastards.*

"Buzz," Luke whispered, "This guy's a killer, what do we do?"

The ruffian was getting closer, he stared straight at Luke and then back at his quarry.

Fucking lovebirds, lost in the clouds. Easy score. I'll get him first, she won't be much trouble then, right to the neck with my blade, good and sharp, yeah . . .

Luke buried his head inside his hoodie and whispered, "He's gonna knife those people if we don't do something! I don't know if I can–"

"Unzip this thing, Bozo!" Buzz hissed. The man was right in front of them as Luke pulled down the zipper on the hoodie. Instantly Buzz's head darted out and snapped at the thug's crotch with her pincer-like beak.

"Fuck!" the man screamed, doubling over in agony. But even as he staggered, the long knife was out. Buzz rose up on her monstrous wings and bore down at the killer's upturned face with her claws. The blade flashed, but Luke intercepted the murderous stroke aimed at Buzz's chest, by neatly blocking it with his own.

As he felt the knife go in just under his left clavicle, a highly unpleasant sensation and painful as hell, Luke sincerely hoped that it wasn't going to be fatal. He seized the man's wrist with both hands and the murderous fiend let go of the weapon.

"Get off! Get off me!" The man was screaming horribly now as blood poured into his eyes from the lacerations Buzz had inflicted on his face and scalp. He fell to the ground, convulsed in a fetal position with his arms over his head.

Luke glanced up the street where he could just make out the couple standing on the sidewalk under the light of a street lamp, staring back toward them in shock and terror. Then the two young people turned, and ran.

"We'd better scoot," he said to Buzz, who appeared to be enjoying herself a bit too much as she ripped more holes in the would-be-murderer's hands and arms with that highly efficient butchery tool, her curved beak. The fellow cowered and screeched, scrambled wildly away, then loped off, stumbling and half blind, disappearing into the dark alleys of the waterfront district.

"Come on!" Luke took off at as fast a run as he could muster, with Buzz flapping alongside, until they achieved a lonely strip of weedy turf bordering a chain-link fence that surrounded a municipal power station near the banks of the Willamette. Here Luke dropped, panting, in the shadow of a shapeless boxwood, and took stock of the damage.

"You're bleeding," he said to Buzz.

"Maybe. Or just bloody," Buzz retorted. "But look at you, Bozo."

Luke looked down at his chest, where the knife still protruded just above the heart region. He gripped the evil-looking metal hilt, held his breath, and pulled the blade out.

No blood gushed forth, and he detected no sign in himself of impending unconsciousness or death. Just a smart sting at the opening of the wound, and an agonizing ache deeper inside.

"Ow, ow, ow," he complained. "That was weird!"

"Thanks for taking that blow for me, Kiddo," Buzz said. "You're a real pal."

"Don't mention it." Luke took a corner of the hospital blanket and gently wiped the gore off of Buzz's head, neck and feathers. "It looks like you've got a couple of bad scratches there," he remarked.

"You don't think that guy is dead, do you?" Buzz wondered.

"Naw, just cut up a bit."

"Too bad," Buzz sighed. "I was hoping to go back for a snack."

"I don't get it," Luke marveled. "I get stabbed through the body, and voilà, not a single drop of blood. But here you got scratched by some fingernails, and you're bleeding like a stuck pig. What gives?"

"It's not all *my* blood, you know."

"Still. Buzz? Isn't there something you wanna tell me?"

Buzz sighed. "All right. I'm not a zombie, okay? I look horrible enough to be one, but–here among mortals anyway, I'm just an ordinary bird."

"Ordinary? I don't think so."

"Well, ordinary in the sense that I can be hurt, possibly even killed."

"Oh. Shit, that's not good." Luke felt horrified, and horribly guilty. He would never have let Buzz attack that murderer, if he'd known. She could have ended up dead!

"And by the way, Luke," Buzz added, "I'm getting hungry."

"Oh man. All right, next dead thing we find, it's party time."

"Thanks, Bozo," she said bitterly.

"Well whaddaya want me to do? Offer myself up as your next meal?"

"Never mind," Buzz muttered.

It was getting late. A garbage truck rumbled by. The two of them huddled in the shadows, zombie and carrion bird. Unlikely buddies.

"So Buzz, remember what we were talking about, before?"

"Yep." Buzz was busy putting her feathers back in order.

"What did you mean by, *get lost*?"

"Let me explain about what occurs at the moment of death," Buzz said. "Brain activity goes on for thirty seconds after the heart stops. Thought-wise, that's enough time for plenty to happen, especially because this is when the physical mind begins to merge with a larger consciousness, the overmind."

"I remember that," Luke said. "It seemed like my awareness was opening up to endless possibilities . . . more than I could comprehend, really."

"Naturally. At the moment of death, some are able to view the entire hourglass of time: every event from the past that led up to that moment, and every potential outcome in the future that may result from any of their actions at that moment. At this intersection of consequences and possibilities, choices are made, and the path of the soul is determined."

"I don't recall choosing anything," Luke put in. "I just got pulled along."

"It often happens that the soul takes its chosen path without any conscious awareness of the reasons. But my point is that, depending on the circumstances, a lot can go wrong at this stage. The soul can lose its way."

"Lose its way? Like, become a ghost?"

"Exactly. If some force keeps the soul tied to its body, or if some traumatic event has never been resolved, the soul can fail or refuse to move on."

"That makes sense. So . . . there must be plenty of ghosts around," Luke observed.

A police car drove slowly down the road, and they shrank further into the shadows.

"Maybe we should keep moving," Luke whispered. As soon as the coast was clear, they set out. Luke insisted on carrying Buzz under the hoodie again.

"It's not that late, and there's still a chance of running into somebody," he said. For once, Buzz didn't argue.

They made their way past the silos and domes of the construction supply depots on River Street without encountering anyone, and emerged into a vast trackyard. There freight cars waited among the ribbons of metal that fanned out across the stony waste, and the smell of creosote mixed with the stink of river-wrack.

As he picked his way along the ties, searching for the track that led out of the yards and upriver, Luke was still thinking about ghosts.

"I've seen quite a few ghostly apparitions, but I never thought I'd actually BE one," he said.

"I would call you ghastly, not ghostly," Buzz retorted.

"I've been seeing ghosts for as long as I can remember."

"I'm not surprised," Buzz remarked. "Apparently you're an adept, skilled in the astral arts. Adepts often see spirits that others can't."

"Why do you say that I'm an adept?"

"You spent time in Famebeau while still linked to your body, that's proof enough for me."

"I read a scientific article that said, it's just a symptom of sleep paralysis," Luke mused. "That when your mind is awake but your body is asleep, you may imagine that you're flying around the house, or that you see a ghostly figure standing by the bed. It's supposed to be, like, a waking dream."

"Imagine," Buzz retorted, "if solids could actually see all the ghosts and spirits that surround them everywhere? They'd go mad."

"So you think people have built-in defenses against seeing ghosts?"

"Of course. Human brains screen out most information, and just report what's relevant for survival. But some individuals have heightened sensitivities, or to put it another way, their filters don't work as well."

Luke considered this. "I'm sure that's what happened to me," he said finally. "I always knew things other people didn't know, but it never benefited my survival much, I can tell you that. At first I tried to talk to people about what I'd seen and heard, but nobody believed me. I wasn't sure if I even believed it myself. Anyway I continued to look for answers, but I don't think science can explain the things I've experienced."

"Gimme an example."

"Ugh, my chest is killing me," Luke moaned. Buzz was getting heavier by the minute, and as he hobbled through the deserted train-yard, Luke decided he could risk letting the vulture out for a while. He unzipped the hoodie, and Buzz took flight with a grateful, raucous cry.

"Damn, I love it!" she squawked as she flew in a tight circle, then pulled him forward with powerful strokes of her pinions.

"Slow down!" he cried.

"It's fantastic, Luke!" she cawed, turning to beat backward and down, barely able to contain her energy, "having wings!"

"I know," Luke answered sadly. "I know."

And then, as Buzz flapped lazily along above his shoulder under the light of the rising moon, he told her a ghost story.

"When I was six, my Mom and Dad decided to go on a family camping trip to Crater Lake. Dad used to go there as a boy and he was real excited about it. Mom wasn't a big camper and us kids were pretty little, but when he told her it had actual flush toilets and even laundry, she finally agreed to go there for a week. And so early one Saturday morning in July we packed up all the camping gear into our big brown Oldsmobile and headed out.

"I remember when we drove away, about five minutes later I re-alized that I had left my favorite toy behind, and I started to cry, and wouldn't stop kicking up a fuss until we went back and got it."

"What was the toy?" Buzz wondered.

"Well, I told my folks it was the cowboy gun and belt set that I'd gotten for my birthday from Granddad, and that I needed it so I could play cowboys and Indians with the kids at the campground. But what I really wanted was a little tiny Tinkerbell figurine that came from inside a snow globe. I never showed her to anybody, I kept her in a hiding place inside my Batmobile. I called her Mia and I used to talk to her every night when I was going to sleep. When I realized I'd left her behind, I couldn't tell Dad, or he'd have made fun of me and called me a weenie-head. He didn't approve of me playing with dolls."

"Poor Luke," Buzz rasped. "And you were probably so good at it, too."

"Anyway, what with one thing and another we got a later start than Dad wanted to, and of course we had to stop a couple of times for bathroom breaks, and then Mom complained about the heat and made Dad get us all ice cream. When we got near Crater Lake National Park the cars were lined up on the two-lane road. Long story short, by the time we arrived at the campground it was full, and boy, my Dad just exploded, blaming every one of us for our various whims and needs, that had delayed us on the way.

"Pretty soon, though, he came up with a new plan. There was another campground a couple of hours away called Medicine Lake. It was also in a volcano crater and was supposed to have a spectacular view of Mount Shasta, and other interesting attractions, and you could even camp right on the lake. So Dad decided we should drive there. It was actually in California, but he didn't care, he was dead set on it, and back into the car we all went.

"When we finally made it to Medicine Lake we got the absolutely last camping spot, and of course, it was in a part of the campground off away from the rest, that didn't even have running water. Mom was fit to be tied, and even though it was already getting dark, she insisted on us all going out to Bob's Big Boy for dinner before we set up camp.

"We have to feed these kids, Jim," she said. I was really happy about that, since I always ordered French fries, my favorite food. But Dad was not pleased, since that meant he'd have to set the tent up in the dark.

"That took a long time, so while Mom helped him set up camp, Jody and I went to sleep in the back seat of the Olds."

Luke was by now tramping along a triple set of tracks that

issued from the yard between aged warehouses. Up ahead loomed
a windowed brick wall built to conform to the curve of the tracks,
painted with faded letters: *North Coast Seed*. Beyond that the tracks
bent past a cluster of container boxes on wheels, and on under an
elevated cement roadway.

Luke's feet were sore and he was continually treading on the
cuffs of his voluminous trousers, causing them to slip down. He
felt like a real hobo, and if a freight train had come along he would
probably have tried to jump up and hitch a ride. But all around was
stillness, except for a striped cat that jumped down from a pile of tires
and slunk away into the tall weeds that bordered the trackbed.

"I guess Mom and Dad decided that since we were already
asleep, they'd just let us kids stay in the car for the night and have
the tent to themselves. When I woke up and looked out the window,
they were nowhere to be seen. I spied their tent nearby, but what had
woken me up was the sound of an animal running: *cloppity cloppity*.
I could see it too, it was a deer or maybe an elk, galloping along just
past the trees that were at the edge of the campsite, toward the shore.
I don't know how I could hear the hooves so clearly from inside the
car, but I could. The buck paused a moment and looked back, and I
could see its big, branching horns in the moonlight.

"And then, a crowd of people came out from the trees and
moved down toward the lake. Some of them were riding horses,
but most were walking. There were women in long skirts, and their
hair was braided, and they wore woven hats that looked like little
patterned baskets. And the men had long hair, and tall stovepipe
hats festooned with feathers and jewelry, and they had long rifles,
and bows and arrows. Some of them passed so close to the car that
I could have touched 'em. There were children too, and little babies
wrapped up tightly in blankets. The horses dragged stretchers along
the ground, and there were bodies on the stretchers, all dressed up
and decorated with feathers. I thought that these were wounded or

dead guys, and that they were being taken down to the lake for some special reason, maybe to be healed. I mean, it was called Medicine Lake, right?

"All the time that I was watching the people walk or ride by, they never looked at me, but I knew that they were Indians. You could tell by the bent way they walked that they were very, very sad. And then at the end, the very last one, a short skinny guy, turned to look at me. He had a big L-shaped scar on his face that made one corner of his mouth turn up, but the other half of his mouth wasn't smiling. His tall turban was made of colorful woven cloth patterned with stars and flowers. This man looked me right in the eyes, and he pointed to his scar, and then he did smile: a slight, clever smile full of plans, an angry, I'll-get-you-yet, warning smile. It was when I saw his expression that I understood that tragedy had come to these people. Something monstrous had happened to them, I was sure, and the Whites had been the cause of it, and now they had nothing left in their hearts but grief, and a terrible lust for revenge. And I tell you, although I was only six years old, my innocence evaporated under that baleful grin. It scared me so much, I wet my pants.

"The next day we went sightseeing at the Lava Beds National Monument, and we stopped at the first attraction, and it was nothing but a thin white cross with some words written on it. Dad read the plaque to us and it said that the Modoc Indians had killed some Anglos right there, during a peace treaty talk. Further on we saw the caves and rock formations where the Modocs had hidden out after that incident. The sign told how, with only fifty-four warriors, they had held off the US Army for a year, and killed hundreds of soldiers before they finally got caught.

"When Mom read aloud that one of them was called Scarface Charley, I let out a yell. I screamed and cried and said that I didn't want to go back to the campground. That's when I finally told my folks about how I had seen the Indians come down through the campsite. I was sure they were coming back. Dad laughed at me and called me a wuss, and told me it was just a dream.

"You see, I thought that the man with the scar would be angry with me if I told on them. So I'd been walking around all day, scared shitless, but not saying a word. Also I thought that if I told, something bad would happen to the Indians, and even though I was frightened by what I'd seen, I also knew that what had been done to them was wrong. Medicine Lake was their place, not ours. So I just kept saying, *We shouldn't be there, Dad. We shouldn't be there!*

"And then Mom laughed and hugged me, and said she agreed with me. That day we packed up camp and drove back to Crater Lake, and as it happened, a camping spot had opened up. So we ended up spending the rest of our vacation the way Dad had planned."

"But were the people you saw actually spirits of the dead?" The condor said. "Or were you looking back into another time?"

"No idea," Luke answered, gazing up with awe at the mammoth array of concrete grain silos that rose between them and the river.

"I've got plenty more stories," he said to Buzz. "Here's one that you'll agree was definitely a ghost."

"Tell on, Bozo," the vulture cackled, "tell on!"

"Well, when I was growing up we had a neighbor a few doors down named Mrs. McMaster. Kids used to sneak into her yard and steal apples from her apple tree. Some of the kids would pick apples that weren't even ripe, and throw them at her house. Then she would come to the back door and yell at them through the screen door. Sometimes they would even break her windows when they threw the apples, and then she would put cardboard up in the windows. A few times I snuck over into her yard with my friend Bobby and we took one or two apples each, but we didn't do it that often. I was always scared she would come out and yell at me. I didn't like getting into trouble with her because I had too much of a guilty conscience.

"Mom said the kids should leave her alone because she had such a hard life. When her son Lester came home from the Korean war, he was never the same again, Mom said, and Mrs. McMaster devoted herself to taking care of him. Mr. McMaster had died or left, I don't know which. Mrs. McMaster cleaned people's houses for money. Mom or my Aunt Suze would always go over there on holidays with some cookies, a casserole or a pie. So growing up, I felt kind of like the McMasters were in some way our responsibility.

"On Thanksgiving when I was eleven Mom fixed up a bag of fresh rolls and a Tupperware platter of turkey and trimmings for the McMasters. The men were all watching the football game and the women were washing up in the kitchen, and I was just hanging around drawing cartoons, so I got nominated to take the food over to their house. At first I thought I would try to get out of going, but then my cousin (his name was Bernard but everybody called him Bangs) came in and started picking on me the way he usually did, wanting to wrestle me and play with my toys, which he enjoyed breaking. So I was happy to get out of the house.

"When I left, Bangs decided to follow me. He said he wanted to get some apples from the McMasters' yard, and I told him that it wasn't Christian to steal, which only made him start in on me, trying to trip me and throwing rocks. He finally took off when Mrs. McMaster opened the front door.

"She was a dumpy-looking lady maybe 60 years old with short gray hair and really thick glasses that magnified her eyes so they looked like a frog's eyes. She was wearing one of those aprons with a bib at the top, like overalls have, and she had on thick socks and ratty slippers. You could see part of the skin on her legs, and it was covered with varicose veins.

" 'Yes?' she said, blinking at me.

" 'Uh, my Mom told me to bring you this Thanksgiving turkey and stuff,' I said. There was a kind of funny smell coming from the house, a laundromat smell.

" 'Oh, you must be Luke. Come in,' she said. I wouldn't have gone inside for anything except that I knew that Bangs was out there waiting for me. So in I went, and she offered me a glass of lemonade.

" 'Now let me just wash this Tupperware out and then you can bring it back to your Mom,' she said. And while I was drinking my lemonade she started scraping out the turkey dinner onto plates.

"That's when I heard a strange sound, like this: 'Wuuuuhhhh! Wuuuuhhh! Wuh, wuh, wuh. Wuuuhhh! Pubata-pubata! pubata-pubata!'

" 'What's that?' I asked.

" 'Oh, that's Lester,' she said.

" 'What's he doing?'

" 'Military exercises,' she said. She took a dinner plate to the door of Lester's room and knocked. Then she went in and I could see that somebody was on the floor in there, on his hands and knees. She sort of shut the door behind her but it swung open again. He was real skinny and wearing pajamas and he had a long beard, and he was still making the same battle noises.

" 'Lester? Here's your Thanksgiving dinner,' Mrs. McMaster said. And Lester stood up and saluted.

" 'Sergeant, the enemy position has been shelled!' he said in a very distinct and military voice. 'I await further orders.'

" 'At ease, soldier,' Mrs. McMaster said. 'Retire to the mess tent.'

" 'Is there corn, sir?'

" 'No, but there's gravy,' she said.

" 'Very good sir,' said Lester, and sat down at a card table to eat. Mrs. McMaster came out and went to the sink to wash out the Tupperware.

" 'What's the matter with him? Does he think he's still in the army?' I asked.

" 'Sometimes,' she said.

" 'Why? Did he like it that much?'

" 'Luke,' she said as she dried the plastic lid, 'Lester saw some awful things in that war. Sometimes, people just can't let go of the past.'

"Lester started to make more noises from inside his room. 'Enemy approaching! Duhduhduhduhduhduh! Strafe the bridge!' And then there was a huge crash.

"Mrs. McMaster ran to the door and opened it. The card table was lying on its side and the food was splattered everywhere.

" 'Lester!' she cried. But he was thrashing his arms around like a windmill and yelling, 'No Gun Ree! Blood in the water! No Gun Ree!' I was scared he was going to hit Mrs. McMaster. But she went right up to him and grabbed him around the waist. And then he started to cry, huge dry sobs. 'Jake! Why didn't you stop 'em, Jake?'

" 'Lester, Lester,' she said, patting his cheeks. And he quieted down, and she came out and got a towel to clean the floor.

"She looked at me and said, 'Don't ever go to war, Luke. A nice, sensitive boy like you, you'd get eaten alive. They'll make you do things, horrible things you can't live with. It's still eating him up inside, poor thing.' She shook her head, and went back to clean up.

"I heard him still crying. 'There's blood in the water, Mama!' he said. 'Jake! Jake's down there!'

" 'You have to eat, pumpkin,' Mrs. McMaster said. 'To keep up your strength. Please put back the table, Lester.'

"But Lester just kept on crying for Jake, sitting on the floor. Mrs. McMaster had to pick everything up, and set things straight.

"I guess I could have just left, but I knew it would be bad manners to walk out so I stayed where I was, even though I was really uncomfortable. Finally Mrs. McMaster came out of Lester's room. Then she grabbed the other plate, the one that was supposed to be her dinner, and brought it into the room for Lester, left it there, and shut the door.

" 'That's a hard thing for a young boy to see. A grown man, crying and throwing his food on the floor,' she said.

" 'I'm sorry, Mrs. McMaster.'

" 'About what, Luke?'

" 'I'm sorry the kids break your windows, and steal your apples. They shouldn't do that.'

" 'You're a good boy, Luke,' she said, patting my cheek. 'Don't you ever go and break your mama's heart.'

" 'I can bring you some more turkey,' I offered. 'And mashed potatoes.'

" 'Don't you worry about me,' she said. 'Now tell me, how is your mama? She's a nice woman.'

" 'She's fine,' I said. But I began feeling guilty as soon as she brought up my Mom. I hadn't been a very dutiful son lately, not since the divorce. It wasn't so much Mom I was mad at, it was her boy-friend Tad I hated. But that's another story.

"Anyway I left with the Tupperware, and even though I liked Mrs. McMaster, I never went back there. It wasn't long before Mom got tired of my rebellious behavior and sent me to live with my Dad. Years later, when I came back to live with Mom for a while, I found out that Mrs. McMaster had died of cancer. Lester had been taken away to the veteran's hospital when she got too sick to take care of him."

"I hope you're not trying to make me feel sorry for the guy," Buzz put in. "It sounds like he was a war criminal with a guilty con-science, if you ask me."

"Well I felt sorry for him. Anyway, I'm just getting to the best part of the story, so listen up. One day, when I was seventeen and was living on the street again, I decided to break into Mrs. McMaster's house. It had been empty for years. There had been a For Sale sign on it, off and on, for a long time, but nobody ever seemed to move in. It was getting cold out at night, and I figured I could camp out there until I talked Mom into letting me move back into the house.

"Bobby had told me that the house was haunted, but I figured that was just idle rumor. Anyway Mrs. McMaster was a nice old lady. Why would I be scared of her ghost?

"So I pried open the loose boards on the back window and slithered in. It looked like other homeless folks had been camping out there, judging by the bottles and rubbish. The water was turned off, and the electricity too.

"I snooped around. A lot of the McMasters' stuff was still there, though probably anything of value had already been stolen. When I went into Lester's old room, I found a pamphlet lying on the bed. It was called *FM 10-63, Handling of Deceased Personnel in Theaters of Operations.* I sat down on the bed, and started to look through it.

"I don't know what I was expecting, probably pictures of bodies blown to bits, or at least lying under sheets or something. But it wasn't really very interesting. Mostly it was military-speak, using terms like Forward Collections Platoons, Mortuary Services and Personal Effects. There were a few diagrams and flow charts, in which the dead were represented by a cross inside a rectangle inside a circle, with the word *COLL* written underneath. Nothing too shocking.

"So I opened up my own little bundle of personal effects, mostly a couple of cans of beer and a few roaches–those are butts from marijuana cigarettes, in case you didn't know–and made myself at home. The bed had no blankets or sheets on it, but it wasn't too disgusting. I guess I could have slept in the old lady's room, but I admit I was a little bit creeped out by the idea, since she could have died in there.

"I snooped around more and gathered a few objects I thought I could sell, or trade for pot or a place to sleep. One of them was a brass sculpture of a lion, I think it may have been one half of a set of book-ends, but there wasn't another one around.

"Eventually I dug up a copy of Emerson's *Nature.* I spread my sleeping bag out on Lester's bed, crawled into it and started to read.

"I'd never experienced anything like it. We didn't have much in the way of books in our house when I was growing up. We got Life Magazine, Look, TV Guide. National Geographic was the height of intellectual curiosity for my folks. So Emerson was like . . . well, an undiscovered gold mine of ideas.

"*But if a man would be alone, let him look at the stars.* Here was someone who wanted nothing more than to experience the natural world, far away from all the taskmasters and the bullies, and the sanctimonious fools. I liked him, and I understood him. He was a rebel. How kind he was, I thought, how noble to have written a book, when he could have kept all of this wonder to himself and never shared it.

"If I'd been assigned to read a book of Emerson's at school, of course, I never would have gotten anything out of it. There would have been a list of questions: 'Compare Emerson's vision of Beauty with that of Thackeray in Vanity Fair,' or something along those lines. It would have killed it for me. As it was, I had discovered Emerson all on my own, and I devoured the book. When I had finished, it was getting dark.

"I was sitting there on the bed wondering whether I should go over to Mom's and try and get her to give me some dinner, or just stay there and go without. I had a few saltines and some scrapings of peanut butter to look forward to, that was it. I remembered old Mrs. McMaster and how she had given Lester her own Thanksgiving meal, after he'd thrown his plate on the floor. That to me was the ultimate maternal gesture, and I told myself that nobody had ever loved me that way, or ever would, and I started to cry. I wasn't making much noise, just letting tears of self-pity run down my face in the dark.

"That was when I saw him. At first I didn't realize what I was seeing, because the tears blurred my sight. But I thought that there was maybe somebody pulling into the driveway, that the headlights were shining in through the window. I felt that flash of panic that comes when you think you're about to get caught doing something you're not supposed to do, and dried my eyes, and I was about to get out of the sleeping bag when I realized that there was a glowing figure standing by the door. It was Lester.

"His back was to me, and he was looking out of the doorway, and up the hall toward where the old lady's room was. And I heard his voice.

"*Mama! Mama!* he called out in an anguished tone. *Mama! Are you there? Mama?*

"I was sitting there huddled in my sleeping bag, rigid with fear. He went on crying, *Mama! Mama? Are you there?*

"I would have run out of there, believe me, but the only way to get away from the apparition was through the door, and he was standing right in the doorway. I stayed frozen in my sleeping bag for fifteen, maybe twenty minutes while Lester's ghost called out for his mother. Finally, hesitantly, like he was venturing into a battlefield, the figure hunched down and stepped through the doorway, and turned right, toward Mrs. McMaster's bedroom, and vanished.

"As you can imagine, I got out of there fast, and I never went back. But I couldn't stop thinking about Lester McMaster, and the next time I was in the library I decided to try and find out what had happened to him. I went through all the newspapers they had on Microfiche, but I couldn't find anything about him, except a three-line obituary. It said he had gotten a bronze star for his military service.

"A year or so later when I was living in Portland, I met a nurse who had worked at the Veteran's Hospital, and I told her the story of Lester's ghost. She remembered Lester. Turns out that not long after his mother died, he strangled himself on a shower curtain."

Luke was now approaching the spot where the railroad tracks peeled off toward Steel Bridge, and he decided that the best thing to do was cross the Willamette and head upriver through the South Waterfront district. He had a place in mind, where they could probably hide out for a while.

Up above the light rail crossed the bridge. Since they had left the MAX shelter, Luke now realized, he had walked in a big circle, largely along trackbed for the freight lines that was covered in sharp stones and broken glass. If he hadn't been so worried about being spotted by a police car, he'd have walked along the MAX tracks, which were embedded in brick paving stones that would have been a mercy to his bare feet, and they'd be across the bridge by now.

On their current trajectory, they should cross the river on the lower level of Steel Bridge, out of sight of the commuter train, and the cars and bicyclists that crowded the upper level even at this late hour. However, pedestrian traffic below was likely to be pretty heavy.

"Can you get under the sweatshirt now, please?" Luke asked.

"Come on," Buzz grumbled, "can't we at least wait until we're down by the walkway?"

"Okay, but before we get on the bridge, you've gotta get out of sight."

"All right, all right."

"Hey, how 'bout we stop for a while first, and I'll rest my feet a bit."

"Suits me, Bozo."

So Luke scrambled down the embankment and made his way under the bridge, intent on huddling within the darkest shadow he could find. Luckily there wasn't anyone else huddled there. It was a form of safety with its own inherent risks, a stark and stony nook that smelled of pee and misery. As Buzz lightly landed on the bare, packed clay beside him, Luke tumbled to the ground with a groan.

"My poor dawgs!"

"Have you ever encountered a poltergeist?" Buzz wondered.

"Sure. Why do you ask?"

"I find it so interesting, after millenia of ruling the dead, to learn more about those spirits that never make it to my kingdom."

"I would have thought you and Hades were experts on that. He seemed to know what he was doing, when he sent me back here."

"Not really," she croaked.

"Not really?" Luke pursued. It was so hard to get her to come to the point. "Why do you say that?"

"Hades probably assumed that your body was already brain-dead. He hoped to confuse and dismay your soul once you re-entered it. As an adept, you would be tempted to interact with the world directly, and so would be all the more likely to remain trapped on the earthly plane, a lost spirit."

"As a poltergeist," Luke shivered. "But . . . lucky me . . ." he quavered in his gentle, nasal voice, "I get to keep this handy, zombie body."

"And I get to keep this one," Buzz creaked.

"There were so many bizarre encounters with spirits I haven't told anyone about. Aside from the fact that my parents never believed me when I tried to tell them about it, I ended up deciding that the best way to deal with ghosts was to do nothing, to not even acknowledge them. Like, when we were in the hospital I saw several ghosts, but I ignored them."

"Why?" said Buzz. "I wish you'd said something."

"Well, did you see that little kid in the hospital gown, who was running down the hall in front of us, jumping up and down and pointing?

"The one who kept shouting, *Zombie, Zombie*? That was a *ghost*?"

"Naturally."

"I have so much to learn about these things," Buzz sighed. "I can't even tell the difference! Next time you see one–"

"I'll pretend it's not there, thank you. Don't you know what a poltergeist is?"

"It's a spirit that makes noises, throws objects, moves or steals things, and so on."

"Right, but I'm talking about the psychology. It's an angry or

lonely spirit that wants to get your attention. That's why I never en-
courage 'em. Give 'em the slightest bit of what they're longing for, and
they'll never let you alone."

"I see what you mean." Buzz fluffed up her feathers. It was getting chilly.

"I read up on poltergeists and learned they're attracted to certain individuals, youngsters who presumably haven't learned how to
fend 'em off, yet." Luke rubbed his hands around in the dirt nearby,
looking for something. "A cigarette would be so perfect right now," he
remarked.

"So what's your story?" Buzz wondered. "About poltergeists, I
mean?"

"There are so many. But here's one of the most dramatic.

"When I was sixteen I spent a few months living with my Aunt
Suze and her husband. They had a ranch out along Highway 30, with
a berry-picking patch, a Christmas tree farm and a gift shop. I was
supposed to be helping 'em out around the farm and store for the
summer, in return for room and board and a little bit of spending
money. I was really pleased with the arrangement, since Suze was
always my favorite aunt, and Uncle Larry was a nice enough guy.
When I got there I thought, *if this works out, maybe I can stay here for
a while, get my GED, work and save up enough money to buy a car.*

"My room was in the converted attic of their Victorian, which
dated back to the 1880's. For the first five or six weeks I didn't see or
hear anything unusual around the place. I really pitched in, learned
to drive the big mower out in the tree farm, stuck labels on preserves.
Then one day in July, Suze asked me to help her with weeding and
planting, out in the herb and flower garden.

" 'There are some wild cucumbers growing like crazy near the
old willow tree in the corner of the garden,' Suze said, 'and your mis-
sion is to take 'em out.'

"I was especially interested in the plant, which grows all over the place around here, because the seeds are supposed to get you high, I'd heard. They call it manroot or old man-in-the-ground because of the huge taproot that sends out shoots every Spring. The spiny 'cucumbers' aren't edible, but when they dry up they turn into what looks like a torturer's loofah. Soak 'em, and you can take the spines off. They're naturally soapy as well, and Suze had tried selling 'em in the store, but nobody was buying.

"On the label she'd made for the sponges, it described how the Indians used to use the soapsuds from the manroot to catch fish in streams. They would throw in some of the pulp, the fish would get soap in their gills, pass out, and float to the surface. The label wasn't selling loofahs, but they added some local color to the gift shop.

"The taproot grows to an enormous size, so I had some serious digging to do, and it was tough going among the gnarled roots of the willow. I kept at it though, determined to prove to Suze and Larry that I wasn't the hopelessly lazy bastard of a kid that everyone said I was.

"I finally got down deep enough to get the shovel under the root, and I kept working the blade under it, levering the root up to free it from the soil. Eventually I got it loose enough to pull out. The root was about the size and shape of a toddler. Or, in this case, a very small midget with a very large hard-on, in the form of a smaller root that stuck out like a penis, just where the big taproot divided into two legs. I thought this was pretty funny, and when I showed it to Suze and Larry, we all had a laugh about the horny little man who'd been hiding under the ground.

" 'Did he scream when you pulled him out?' Larry joked. He was of course referring to the mandrake, a European plant with a root that divides in a way that looks like legs. Legend has it that the mandrake-man screams bloody murder when you pull him out, and unless you plug your ears, supposedly the sound will kill you. Of course this is just a ridiculous old tale, but still I always identified myself with the mandrake root, because of my name. So you can just imagine how fascinated I was by that man-shaped root.

"I took the manroot to the compost in a wheelbarrow, and dumped it. That's when I saw something sticking out from between the 'legs', on the butt side. I'd thought it was just a rock, but I observed now that it had an unusual shape, and a familiar color pattern.

"Looking more closely I realized that it was the head of a doll. An antique china lady doll with a dark bun, and simple, serious eyes painted in glaze on her porcelain head.

"When I saw that there was a china doll stuck in there, I became, ah–"

"Obsessed," Buzz supplied.

"I was going to say enamored. Anyway I went to work with a hatchet, and chopped off one of the leg roots. When Aunt Suze came to find me and lead me to the nasturtiums and lobelia that were going in where the manroot used to be, I was still carefully chipping away at the fibrous flesh of the root.

"Suze was almost as excited as I was about the treasure. But I didn't get around to the nasturtiums that day. It was dinnertime before the doll was finally released from her prison.

" 'Oh shit! Is she missing an arm?' said Suze.

"I raced back to the hole where I'd dug up the manroot. Sifting though the dirt, I found the missing arm, broken in one place and chipped, but fixable. I brought her to the kitchen.

" 'Oh, she's a beauty,' Suze said. 'Look at that silk dress.' The blue dress and linen petticoat were of course dirty and half rotted away, but what a pretty doll, maybe eight inches long, with brown eyes and a little round mouth. I coveted her with all my might, which Suze guessed immediately, and she told me I could keep her.

"I didn't even thank my Aunt, I was so busy exulting over the antique doll. She was made entirely of porcelain with joints at the arms and legs. Filled with triumph, I charged off to the workshop immediately to repair her.

" 'Luke!' Suze called after me, 'What about dinner?'

" 'I'll eat later,' I called back over my shoulder.

"First I washed Abigail's clothes and her body, scrubbing with a soft toothbrush. Yes, I named her Abigail. Then I glued the broken arm with super-glue. By the time I'd figured out how to string the arms and legs back on, and got the doll dressed and restored, it was late that night.

"Exhausted but ecstatic, I set Abigail up on the dresser in my room, where I could see her from the bed. I gazed at her lovingly before going to sleep. It was almost like having Mia, lost years ago in the madness of my hobo's life, back again.

"Have you ever had that feeling, when you were half asleep, that somebody's in the room with you? And they come over and stand by the bed, or even sit on the bed?

"Well as I drifted to sleep, I had that feeling. But waking up didn't make the thing disappear, this time. Instead, the small figure, a shadowy form seeming to be made of black gauze, slipped into the bed beside me.

"*Toby, it's me, Abby,* she whispered. I could feel her body against me, her arms going around me. Her small hands moving here and there on my body, searching me. Finding me!

"I was electrified of course, and found myself responding eagerly to her caresses, lost in a desirous stupor. To a sixteen-year-old virgin, this was simply a dream come true. But as I felt her fondling me, I realized that she was no woman, but a young girl of ten or eleven. I began at once to feel guilty and reluctant to proceed in the seduction. Yet when I tried to push her away, I was unable to. There was no solid form there to push. Suddenly terrified, I lay there paralyzed, feeling her touch me in a highly inappropriate way.

Oh god, oh god, little girl. Go away. I thought fervently. But she did not go away, she kept on assaulting me in a stimulating manner, and before long I came. Even then I could feel her arms and body covering me, her skin damp against mine as I lay there spent and trembling. I fell asleep and had dream after dream about Abigail, the doll, and the girl Abby, who had lived in this house seventy five years in the past. The girl who had brought her doll upstairs with her many a night when she went to the bed of her half-brother, Tobias, whom she adored. In my dreams I knew the two children had been playing a naughty game in secret since Abby was little, and now that Toby was a teenager, their play had become more physical, they were discovering things together, exciting and illicit things that they could never, ever tell anyone about.

"It had been Abby's idea from the start, but Abby had another secret that was even darker. Her stepfather was the one who had shown the game to her first. He had been coming into the nursery at night since she was six years old, and everything she learned from Papa Henry, she passed on to Toby. She couldn't tell Toby about Papa Henry because she knew what would happen if she did.

"If you ever tell anyone," she said to Toby, "I'll creep up on you when you're sleeping, and smother you with a pillow." It made Abby feel in control, to be the one who knew about the games, the one who could demand Toby's promise of silence.

"It was such a big secret, though, that Abby had become a taciturn, silent girl, anxious and furtive, often detached from reality. She was constantly being scolded by her mother for not paying attention to her chores.

"Abby began to worry that her doll, who had watched her and Toby in their play, might tell on them. One night she went out and buried Abigail at the roots of the willow tree, placing a stone marker over the spot.

"Then I woke up, and Abby was gone. *What a crazy dream*, I thought, *it seemed so real.* I felt exhausted and bemused after such a restless night, but I was immersed in a heady daze that had within it a creative impulse.

"One of the best things about Suze's place was that her band had its rehearsal studio in the basement. As soon as I had grabbed a donut and some milk, I ran down there and started screaming out a song about Abby.

"I worked it out on Aunt Suze's guitar. It was slow and spooky in the verse, with lots of bends and threatening minor chords, and in the chorus it got really loud and menacing. That got my blood up, which I needed because I was feeling kind of sick to my stomach, actually.

"All day I worked on the song, or took breaks from working on the song, smoking, staring at Abigail, posing her, dressing her in different ways. I was trying to figure her out. Christ, Aunt Suze must have been wondering about me, but I was too freaked out about what was happening to me, to care.

"Sing it!" Buzz commanded.

"Okay, errm, ahem." Luke cleared his throat and sang in a rasping, moaning voice, barely above a whisper:

> *She came from underground, between the manroot thighs*
> *She comes to me at night and scares me with her sighs*
> *Her china hands have soft electric rays that shoot*
> *Into the stem and swell the bud up from the root*
>
> *Abby, the dirty doll, Abby the dirty doll*
> *Abby, the dirty doll, Abby the dirty doll*
> *Get outta my bed girl, get outta my bed!*
> *Get outta my bed girl, get outta my bed!*

"There's more, but I can't remember it now," Luke said.

"Still, I have a feeling this story goes on," Buzz sighed.

"Boy, does it. Late afternoon, I was singing the chorus and then

I went into a really nasty guitar riff, when all of a sudden the plywood board that Larry was building his model train setup on, there in the basement, came crashing down from its sawhorse stand. A bunch of the little fake trees and houses got destroyed. Oh my god.

"Aunt Suze came running down the stairs at the sound of the train set smashing to the floor. Of course I said I hadn't done it, and of course she didn't believe me.

"What was I supposed to say in my defense? Let's see, how would the truth sound? *Well Aunt Suze, actually, it was the antique doll, that came to life–no actually it was the ghost of the child who buried her, a naughty little girl, an abuse victim, who got into my bed with me last night, and popped my cherry as it were, although I tried to stop her. And now she's mad at me for singing the song I wrote about her, and so, naturally, she knocked down the train set in revenge.*"

"I can see your dilemma," Buzz sympathized.

"One way ticket to the loony bin," Luke replied. "So I kept my lips zipped. But that darned little succubus kept molesting me, night after night, sometimes even during the day. I can't say I didn't enjoy it at times, but it left me a walking wreck, and wherever I went I had to be constantly on the lookout for things being destroyed. She would knock over vases, throw pans. Once she demolished an entire shelf of plants in the greenhouse, while I wasn't even in there.

"It was incredibly disturbing. I mean, she was abusing me, not the other way around, you know? And yet here I was being punished, harassed, and implicated all at once. So although I often walked around with an idiot grin on my face, I continued to have really bad stomach problems and could barely eat. Overall it was extremely unpleasant.

"I know what you're thinking. Why not just get rid of the doll? But I knew Suze would get upset if she found out I'd reburied Abigail out in the yard, or destroyed her. I tried moving the doll to the piano, the garden shed, the car. So many times I wanted to take her to the river and throw her in. But nothing I did made any difference, and I figured that getting rid of Abigail wouldn't help me now. The cat was out of the bag, you know? Abby was there in the house, she had her claws in me, and she was going to enact her weird traumatic memories on me, whether I liked it or not.

"The dreams were sometimes horrible. I dreamed her whole pathetic life. Abby and Toby continued their affair into adulthood, even after he married another girl. Isolated after the early deaths of the parents, Abby lived the depressed life of a borderline nut-case, eking out a living on the farm. She got pregnant, Toby of course being the father, and hid the pregnancy.

"This dream happened over and over. She'd hide in the house, living on tea and toast and whatever she grew in the garden, never answering the door. When the baby came, she'd smother it, and bury it in the yard. Ugh. I'd wake up and vomit. I don't know if this happened only once, or continued to happen repeatedly for years. Finally, though, Toby left her alone, and she killed herself. Her corpse wasn't found until weeks later, dangling from that old willow tree.

"As for me, my days at the ranch were numbered. I'd pretty much become useless around the farm. I was terrified of working in the garden for fear I'd find the skeleton of a baby, for one thing. And Larry never forgave me for my supposed destructive behavior. Although they were too nice to kick me out onto the street, as soon as the Fall came Aunt Suze and Uncle Larry sent me back to Astoria. From there it wasn't long before Mom threw me out of the house herself, for breaking her rule against smoking weed. Pot had become my first line of defense, helping with both my anxiety and the stomach aches it caused.

"Of course I left Abigail at Aunt Suze's house, and to my relief, Abby didn't follow me back into town." Luke shivered, and fell silent.

"Poor Luke and his troublesome ghosts," Buzz cackled. "Do you miss her now?"

"Come on, Buzz, it's not funny," Luke protested. "She really drove me nuts, you know. Ghosts like her have totally messed up my life!"

"I'm sorry, Luke, I didn't mean to laugh at your problems. I'm sure it was an awful experience."

"It's okay," Luke said. "I think if somebody had told me that story about themselves, I'd have thought it was kinda funny–in a horrible way." He fell silent again.

After a while Buzz spoke up once more. "So much sadness in human existence, eh kiddo?"

"And no hope in sight for most of 'em," Luke agreed.

"The gods aren't doing a very good job of it, are they?"

"Religion was never much help to me, that's for sure," Luke replied. "I always envied those who could take comfort in the church, but for me, it was just empty words."

"Maybe it just wasn't the right religion," Buzz pointed out.

"You wanna know what my faith is? I worship the three P's: Pussy, Punk and Poppies. The only things in life that ever gave me any real solace."

"Is that it?" Buzz retorted, a little miffed.

"Oh, well, I guess there's a fourth P, now," Luke said gallantly. "Persephone, Queen of the Dead: my Goddess forever."

"Thanks, Luke," Buzz said. "You're a Pal. With a capital P."

Luke thought back to his bitter feud with Lord Hades. "I was wondering," he said, "when Pluto sent me back, what was supposed to happen to you?"

"It was supposed to break the chain that bound us, sentencing me to destruction." The Condor puffed out her crop angrily.

"But come on, aren't you immortal?"

"There are ways to get rid of us. Like reincorporation, where other gods literally divide you into parts, cannibalize you, and take your powers into themselves."

"Christ!" Luke was slowly getting the picture. He was playing a part in something much, much bigger than he had supposed. He'd been caught up in a deadly game among beings who operated at a level beyond anything a mortal like himself could possibly comprehend. And of course, as usual, he had monumentally screwed things up. The realization came freighted with an all-too-familiar, killer dose of chagrin.

Luke caught himself with his hands pressed to his temples, and froze. Rubbing tended to rearrange his features in undesirable ways. He sighed.

"This is all my fault, isn't it?"

"Probably," the vulture admitted, tapping him lightly on the cheek with her beak. "But don't take it too hard, Luke. You were only being yourself."

Luke threw an arm around the bird, and buried his face in the feathers of her ruff. Buzz put her wing around his shoulder.

"I'm really sorry," he said.

"You don't know how hard I'm trying not to eat you right now," she croaked.

"I . . . I appreciate that," Luke said. He lay there in the dark, listening to the fading whistle of the train as it clattered past up above, and unconsciously stroking the condor's bulbous crop. "So, Hades wasn't expecting you to be here now? Does he know what happened?"

"I don't know what he knows. Powerful as he is, Pluton can be pretty dense. It's probably the coke. He gets manic and numb, and loses his grip on what's really going on–and of course, he always has to be right."

Luke scratched the back of his scalp, near the bottom, where there was still a patch of hair. "Why put on a show, though? Why the cat and mouse game? Hades could have just blasted me out of the underworld, right?"

"There are rules even Hades can't break. He had to trick you into waking up, he couldn't send you back here against your wishes. But he didn't anticipate what would happen."

Why was she being so cagey?

"So? What happened?" Luke demanded. "How did I end up like this?"

Buzz shook herself free of his embrace, and straightened her wing feathers. "Seems to me, Luke, that you must have returned to your body, you must have awoken with such strength of will, such power as to reanimate it, even after death. You took possession of your corpse like a hand going into a puppet." Buzz preened under her wing, then fixed her eyes on Luke.

"You must really love her," she squawked.

Luke was silent, except for a wistful sigh. Charity was not a subject he wanted to discuss with Buzz right now. It was time to move on.

"Ready to go?"

"Sure, Bozo."

He tucked the vulture into his sweatshirt, and scaled the embankment to the freight tracks. Stepping from tie to tie he followed them until they joined the pedestrian walk. It was past midnight now, and thankfully there were only a few walkers out. Soon they were above the river.

"Buzz, look at this."

Gazing out at the city lights spread winking and glittering all around, mile after mile, Luke caught a scent of pine forests on a breeze that stirred Buzz's ruff of slender feathers. *Maybe the real world isn't all bad.*

"Nice," Buzz said carelessly. "Looks hospitable." She was being very cool, Luke thought. Was she upset?

I must really love her, she said. Hoo boy. Actually, truth be told, he was in love with two women, and not for the first time. Not much chance of actually hooking up with either one, though. It was his shitty luck, and as usual, the better things seemed to be going in theory, the worse they were going in reality.

On the other hand, hope springs eternal, even in the breast of a zombie. And so does lust, Luke was discovering. His impulses were just as randy now as they had ever been. He remembered that kiss he'd stolen from Kore on the roof of the apartment building earlier in the evening. That, it seemed to him, proved that there had to be a switch he could hit, to reset both himself and the goddess to the forms they were meant to have.

Kore versus Charity . . . what a conundrum. If both of them were standing here in front of me, the real me–how would I choose one over the other?

And why should I have to choose? What if I could persuade them to agree to a three-way arrangement?

Back when she and Luke had first become lovers, Charity had announced to him that she considered herself to be a bisexual man, trapped in a woman's body. Luckily for Luke, she was a man whose tastes leaned toward sex with men.

"So another bi man is a perfect fit for me," she had laughed. Luke could still picture her rapscallion grin.

Luke had long been a secret cross-dresser, even as a young boy. There was a fluttery-sleeved floral print mini-dress in pale blue and pink, he recalled, that he had swiped from his mom's closet when he was thirteen, and stuffed with Nerf balls to achieve a buxom, renaissance wench look. Over the years he had naturally experimented sexually with other boys, probably to a bit more purpose than most, and he had once had an unrequited crush on a sweet-looking guy in his art class. But then, all his crushes had been unrequited back then.

There was however a practical side to teenaged Luke's interest in men, since he spent several of those years living on the street. His curiosity and avarice were equally aroused when one by one, the closeted gay elders of Astoria had formed a court of admirers. Luke had toyed more than once with the idea of finding a sugar daddy, or at least selling blow jobs for beer money. But in the end, he couldn't bring himself to go that route, knowing how people would talk. It would have been too humiliating.

His curiosity had remained piqued, however, and once he moved to the city, he'd engaged in various explorations of man-on-man lust. But he hadn't ever found a man who could fire his imagination the way certain women did. There was no denying that the almighty yoni remained the glowing flame at the center of his sexual universe. With women he felt an instinctive respect and adoration, and a powerful identification. That empathy invariably kicked in so strongly with victims of rape and abuse that the emotion was visceral and dizzying.

More than that, he felt a yearning for acceptance so devastating that it silenced him, paralyzed him, whenever he was near a woman of any age who had that certain something, a beauty and poise and authoritative presence that inspired him to awe and devotion.

They were nearly to the far side of the river now, and Luke decided to take the short cut down to Waterfront Park, which meant he had to jump the fence that separated the pedestrian walks from the tracks that ran down the middle of the bridge. Having crossed over, he took stock of the landscape that spread out along the South Portland Waterfront.

"That's where we're headed," Luke offered, pointing down toward the park. Buzz stuck her head out of his sweatshirt to take in the view. The greenway wound alongside the river, patterned with the pale fluffy balls of flowering trees, and crisscrossed by winding walkways. There were still one or two people loitering about.

As Luke wandered into the park, he was thinking about the times he'd strolled here with Charity, about that sexy, teasing walk of hers, swiveling and cocking her shoulders like a bantamweight boxer. This was the park you'd go to if you wanted to hook up with somebody in, let's say, an unconventional way. This was where they'd met

Marnie, that night after the concert at Satyricon.

When Luke had informed Charity that he was nine-tenths a lesbian, she was delighted. And so they had embarked on a union that expanded rather than limited their sexual personae. On several occasions before their marriage, a menage á trois had emerged when Charity hooked up with another woman.

Ah, those had been blissful encounters. Two confident, passionate gals who were ready to take charge, to take him in hand and make a pet of him, that was a menu ideally suited to the satisfaction of Luke's most insatiable appetites. But it wasn't easy to manage the complex relationships, especially the way girls were always competing for the role of alpha bitch. Nothing lasting had emerged from their experimentations.

But now that he was dead . . . well, it had to be good for something, didn't it? It was a new game, with new rules, and if he and Buzz could find their way back to their true forms, he would reinvent himself.

If only he could find a way, if he could retain *both* as his lovers. *Two hot wives . . . hoowee!* The idea of enjoying Charity, bossy and imaginative hellion that she was, together with the deliciously submissive Kore, was exquisitely stimulating. *This could be a breakthrough,* Luke thought excitedly as he drifted into a blissful daydream about the possibilities. That was when Buzz nudged him with her beak.

"Penny for your thoughts," she croaked.

Aw, hell. What was he thinking?

"Nothing. Nothing real," he said. Nothing at all real, considering that Mr. Woody was no longer what he used to be, these days.

Anyway, Luke needed to stay focused on what he *could* do. He had to keep an eye on Charity and the kids, at the very least. And now he was going to have to figure out, on top of everything else, how to deal with Buzz's jealousy.

Rosetta had not felt better in the morning. Her glands were swollen, her throat was worse than yesterday.

This is going to put a cramp on any lovemaking, she thought sadly. No kissing, for one thing, since she didn't want to communicate the bug to her husband. Plus, tempting Aron in the sack tended to involve deploying her facility with fellatio, and that was out of the question in her current state. She could forget about having any fun this week, contrary to her hopes. Rosetta reluctantly resigned herself to getting as much rest as she could.

She did permit herself to do a little bit more work on the fairyland painting. It was the finishing touches, a delightful stage in the process. She took a nap in the afternoon, and was awakened by the telephone ringing in the kitchen. She was too groggy to try and catch it, so it went to the machine.

Ah, Rosetta, it's Aron. We're just on our way to Phil's friend Marky's birthday party. It's at–What? Just a minute, I'm leaving a message. Anyway, we're going to Jekyll and Hyde's, if you want to meet us. Looks like fun. That's on Eighth Avenue, you know the place, it's the one with the scary dummies all over it. All right, ciao.

Well, at least she was off the hook for making dinner. Squash soup would have been great, but Rosetta couldn't face doing that now. Some tea, and more sleep, that was what she needed.

***Eternity,* Hades**

Hades bent down and lifted his wife's limp body in his arms. He stared impassively at her sweet childlike face, with its slack jaw and enormous, partly closed green eyes. Clutching her to his chest with one powerful arm, he reached with his other hand and passed it down her forehead and over her eyes, closing the lids. He then traced her cheek with his fingers. He held her chin and pressed his thumb down on her lower lip, released it. The flesh was still warm, soft and pliable.

Pluton's deep chest was heaving as his hand moved slowly down the goddess's neck and bosom. He could not detect a heartbeat. Suddenly his arms convulsed and he strained her body to him. Surprising himself with a demonstration of passion, he pressed his cold pink mouth to hers.

"Persephone," he uttered hoarsely, shaking her. Her head lolled back, and he caught his breath in excitement. "She's dead, dead . . ."

He couldn't remember the last time he had felt this attracted to a woman. She was so delicate, so helpless.

He was interrupted by a flapping of bat-like monkey wings.

"My lord," intoned Hanuman, bowing before him, "you summoned me?" The monkey god raised his curly head and gazed upon Proserpina. His tail drooped mournfully, his mouth opened in dismay as he looked fearfully up at Death. "My lord!"

"Help me onto my Gryphon," Hades spat.

"My Lord," Hanuman replied. The steed landed noisily beside them, and the Dark Lord mounted her. The monkey god handed the delicate burden of Persephone's corpse to Hades, and away he flapped.

Carrying Kore in his arms during the ride to the palace did nothing to disperse the animal urges that had begun to rise in Hades's

loins from the moment he kissed his dead wife's lips. No sooner had
he arrived at his palace, than the Lord of the Underworld made haste
to bring her to his own apartment, where he deposited her on the
deep couch where he was wont at times to recline.

Pluto had always taken an exquisite pleasure in caressing the
bodies of the beautiful dead. It was his right, and his duty, so he fervently believed, to honor them with his adoration at the moment they
fell beneath the scythe. But necrophilia was not a word he would have
used to describe the emotions that elated him when he consumed
their lives with an insatiable appetite. It was greed, yes, it was a kind
of acquisitive pride that he felt, the satisfaction of adding another
perfect specimen to his collection of caged beings. It wasn't exactly a
sexual feeling, though there was eroticism in it. To have engaged in a
carnal act with the dead at the point of departure would have offend-
ed his sensibilities. Death was a private affair, a lonely journey, and
he was, apart from his pivotal role as the harvester of souls, a witness
more than a participant. Not that he personally visited each mortal at
the moment of truth, those days were long gone. But, at least until his
recent period of disengagement, he had selected his particular prizes
with interest and care. As always, he had arrived punctually, holding
out a hand in welcome, embracing and kissing the beloved on the
lips with a grave and ceremonious courtliness. He would soon pass
the deceased to an aide who would direct the departed soul to the
proper agency, and assist him or her with the necessary paperwork as
required.

But this–this was his wife, his ultimate prize, stolen from him
by Zeus at the very moment of conquest. He had never trusted her
since, despite ample evidence that Kore detested her father. She had
been irrevocably defiled by the rape and he had forced himself to
overcome a certain distaste in order to love her again. Perhaps this
disgust even held a certain appeal. Certainly he had used her sexually
in ways that he might not have done, had he remained as enamored

of her innocence as once he had been.

He had begun by forbidding her to leave her chambers during her six months below ground. Sure that Zeus was bent on infiltrating the underworld with servants who might snatch her away if she were left unguarded, he'd posted ogre-like titans at every point of egress. When the time came to deliver her to her mother, he'd required Persephone to remain under guard year-round, on pain of his acute displeasure. But he had not stopped at jailing her, oh no. For when she returned to him each Autumn, she'd been in his eyes soiled by her absence from his protection. He'd begun to make a point of exerting absolute control, of intentionally humiliating her, he recalled with a flush of arousal. For a century or more, he had forced her to wear a collar–a queenly collar of gold and rubies, but a shackle all the same, with a chain of links forged in gold and cast about with powerful spells. This he had anchored to their marriage bed with a massive ring of iron. And when upon her return she had been thus secured, he had caused her to be stripped and washed before him by his body servants. These creatures, squid-like beings with bulbous black eyes on stalks, had cleansed her every pore, her every orifice, long and obsessively with their elastic tentacles, rubbing her with scented oils and unguents. Then and only then, when she had been thoroughly sterilized of any possible lingering whiff of the thunder god, when she lay spread open for his inspection like an oyster, with her limbs immobilized by the suckered arms of the cephalopods, only then would he come to her, biting her flesh with his sharp teeth until she cried out, before taking possession of her, his rightful bride, as a husband must.

But those salad days had faded long ago. She'd complained to her mother, he supposed, and he'd been bullied, tongue-lashed incessantly by Demeter until he agreed to omit the cleansing rites. Then both mother and daughter had gotten to work on him to allow Persephone to engage in unseemly interface with the denizens of the underworld. He'd eventually permitted her to sit beside him once more in the throne room, to attend the feasts of the dead. And at last, after eons of tormented jealousy and irritation, he had finally let go. Kore had become a creature he could no longer control, and he had ceded that to her. After a while, Hades realized now, he had even fallen reluctantly into a presumption of her loyalty to him.

But all that had changed when *whatsisname* came along. That popinjay, that centipede! He had defiled her now beyond redemption, for there was no question about it: she had wanted the boy, had *enjoyed* having sex with him. *The whore!*

Hades gazed down now with red eyes aglow at the body of his faithless wife, the delicious Persephone. He began to slowly undress her, running his hands over her, pressing his fingers deep into her flesh. He moved her limbs about, repositioning them this way and that. His breathing became hard and rasping.

I have to preserve her in just this state, he told himself fervidly. Death was not in the habit of making exceptions to his own rules for anyone, but hell, what was the point of being the boss? He bent down, opened Kore's mouth while pinching the nose, like a lifeguard resuscitating a drowned swimmer, and breathed the air of the Styx deeply into her lungs.

That should keep her from rotting for a thousand years or more. Enough time to have quite a bit of fun.

Hades felt like frisking about on goat feet, and so he allowed himself to take the form of a satyr before pulling the delectable corpse toward him. For the first time in a long time, he was going to screw his wife's brains out.

And she wasn't going to feel a thing.

April 6, 1994 –Portland, Oregon

Luke fluffed up the mound of fast food cups, leaves, branches and cigarette packets upon which he proposed to lay himself down for the day.

"You call that a nest?" Buzz complained.

"Yes, that's exactly what it is. It's a nest of litter."

"I call it unsanitary," Buzz sniffed.

"Well if you were a proper vulture, I'm sure you'd feel right at home in it." Luke distributed some wadded waste paper strategically among the detritus.

"I don't wanna feel at home in it. I gotta go out and fly free. I gotta find carrion."

"Look, we've been over this. We can't go out in the daytime at all, or risk being seen by anyone. You know you can't carry me around on your back for long, not anymore. We've got too much substance here."

Buzz steadfastly refused to see the sense of his arguments. She kept on accusing him of paranoia and avoidance behavior. "Hiding from the truth won't solve anything, Luke," she retorted now. "You've got to confront your trauma! You've got to get out there and face the music!"

What the condor really wanted him to do, astoundingly, was to attend his own funeral, to find out what was being said about him, how people felt and thought, even perhaps to take part in it somehow.

But Luke just wanted to go to bed. Did Luke need to go to bed? No, he did not. Did he even have a bed to go to?

No, he did not.

Still, the litter nest was softer than a pile of rocks, and it was potentially a pretty good place to hide, once he built up the height a bit more.

The nest was located under the Sellwood Bridge, in a long dirt cleft screened by weeds. Luke had already combed every foot of the River View Cemetery without finding a comfortable spot, where he was certain of being safe all day from inquisitive solids. Buzz had been keen to spend the night in a nice roomy crypt, but Luke felt ill at ease as an interloper among the dead. In the end, he'd wandered back down to the river, where he felt more at home.

He had of course chosen this urine-infested slope under the rattling roadway more out of nostalgia than a need for shelter from the elements. He'd spent enough time living on the street, that places like this held a certain primal appeal. It was a perverse urge, really, to look back fondly at one's worst moments in life, but that's what things had come to.

The nook had been cluttered with bottles and half-burnt rags, but it didn't look like anyone had been living there recently. Of necessity the hobos chose to either move south, or get themselves jailed for vagrancy just in time for Winter, and Spring was barely underway yet. Not exactly a place he would have picked to sneak off to for a grope, had there been anyone to fondle, or only as a last resort anyhow. But here, Luke decided, was where he would dig his foxhole.

Buzz had been carrying in her mouth a copy of The Oregonian that she'd found during their walk, and now she spread it out on the ground. "Lookit this, Luke," croaked the condor, pawing at the newspaper with her foot. "It's all about you."

"I'm too tired," Luke moaned, casting himself down on his bower, which welcomed him with a chorus of crunches. He lay with his eyes closed, longing for sleep the way a legionnaire longs for water. A phrase that had run through his mind a few minutes ago had stuck there, and he kept on repeating it to himself endlessly: *Now that I've joined the ranks of the living dead. The ranks of the living dead.*

Were there really vast numbers of the living dead? It seemed unlikely. He'd always thought of zombies as impossible monsters.

Luke supposed that he might be the only one. Was he a freak of supernatural nature?

Had Hades created other zombies, too? Not that Luke particularly wanted to hang out with other zombies. But in the movies they always came in gangs, searching for brains to eat. That was how they made more zombies, he recalled.

Buzz was by nature an eater of the dead, but Luke had no desire even to taste brains. He had briefly considered having some fries, just as an experiment, but he was reluctant to insert food into his Swiss-cheese body. He could picture the ketchup leaking out all over the place. No thanks. He had enough troubles.

Being a zombie really sucks.

Luke tried to imagine how it must feel to Kore to be trapped in the body of a vulture, and yet to be an ancient and powerful goddess. He had a hard time believing that she was unable to escape her fate somehow. Was Hades really that powerful? And yet it seemed that the Lord of the Underworld had successfully dominated Persephone from the time she was a child. It filled him with sadness and rage to dwell on her sufferings, yet he turned them over in his mind painfully. His obsessive thoughts of her, like hot potatoes, burned him because he had nowhere safe to put them, and he refused to just toss them away.

At least his mental torment distracted him from the agony of his brutalized feet.

Excruciatingly painful, that was how Luke described to himself their journey south along the Willamette River, in search of a hiding place. He had continued walking all night, first around the Zidell shipyards, an enormously long, squat building that extended to the water, then along the disused trolley tracks through the derelict industrial area.

He'd hobbled past the neglected lumber yards and the long-closed chemical plant, only to sustain a rude shock. The old furniture factory was being torn down, and the shabby Victorian homes that had once housed its workers stood condemned to be demolished.

This had been a thriving artists' community back when he lived there in the mid eighties, a seedy, tumbledown paradise where gays and hookers and junkies felt at home, where poets and painters worked, where the sound of punk bands rehearsing was part of the rowdy ambiance. But all that had been swept away during the past decade in a frenzy of gentrification. Luke now reverently explored haunted blocks where trolley rails bent and got lost under rubble, where the bombed-out walls bore the traces of illicitly wheat-pasted posters and graffiti art, paying silent homage to the neighborhood's bohemian history, when artists had turned crumbling factories into squats and communal galleries. High above, new-built condominium towers dominated the skyline. The way along the river was littered with crumbling tarmac and the bones of lost cats.

Luke hadn't encountered anyone until after he passed the old waterfront tavern, Tequila Willie's. It was still open at that late hour, and when he saw the lights and heard the laughter and music coming from within, he'd felt a wave of nostalgia. He hadn't really frequented the place much himself, being eternally too skint to afford such luxuries, but a friend of his had worked there as a singing waiter. Sometimes Luke had been invited to the parties, where he'd enjoyed sloppings of frozen margarita slush poured from an endless series of pitchers.

Now Luke trudged through the parking lot, keeping as far away from the restaurant as he could, fearful of running into somebody who might recognize him. He could see new high-rises under construction, their bare beams lit with red blinkers to warn away low-flying aircraft. When he picked up the greenway again, by the sign that commemorated the Heron Pointe Wetlands wildlife refuge, he'd noticed that somebody was walking along beside him.

It was a bent-over old guy in ragged, grease-splattered clothes, with a white beard and big round ears. His short, pug nose and prominent lips made him look simian.

"I remember how hard they fought to keep that park from being swallered up by developers," the old man croaked. It was like he was echoing Luke's own thoughts. Luke had shrunk up under his hood, not trusting himself to answer. At least Buzz was hidden safely under his sweatshirt, fast asleep.

There came the sound of something splashing, way out on the surface of the river.

"Ever watch the salmon run upstream to spawn?" the guy had continued. "Ever wonder why they swim up over rocks and jump up dams to get back to where they were born?" He didn't seem bothered by Luke's silence, he just answered himself. "They don't do it 'cuz it's easy, they do it 'cuz it's hard. If it was easy, then what would be the point? All the predators would be able to get to the eggs just as easy, too."

Who was this guy, and why was he lecturing Luke on the life cycle of salmon? The tramp turned toward him and his round yellow eyes reflected the moonlight. The hair on the back of Luke's neck prickled.

"No, my boy, the salmon go back there, to that remote hidden spot, because it was a safe place to be hatched. If it weren't, they'd never have survived bein' born there in the first place."

They kept on walking for a while. Luke was still thinking about the old man's freaky monkey eyes when he spoke again.

"Well, have a nice night, and take care o' that condor. That's one heck of a rare bird, ain't it?"

How the hell had he known about Buzz, hidden under Luke's sweatshirt? He must have seen them together earlier. Anyway, the strange tramp had walked alongside him for a little while longer, nodding and smiling in a friendly way, then vanished as quickly as he'd appeared, leaving Luke mystified.

Footsore and wary, he'd picked up the trolley tracks again at the sailing club, and followed them down past Willamette Park, where in the wee hours of the morning he'd finally let Buzz fly free. At dawn they had made their way to the Sellwood Bridge.

Now Luke was grateful to creep out of sight and lie down. Trying to ignore the pain in his bare feet, in his joints and guts and rotting musculature, trying to ignore the agony in his lacerated heart. Trying to sleep.

The commuter traffic was already lumbering heavily above, and Luke found the noise comforting. He needed an incessant racket to drown out his obsessive thoughts. But the funny thing about obsessive thoughts, is their buoyancy. No matter how many times you try and drown them, they always bob back up to the surface.

When Charity tried to take me into her arms, I didn't want her to touch me.

That was the obsessive thought that currently floated at the very top of the apple bucket. But push that one down, and what popped up? *Hades, that fucking bastard. Made me into a zombie!*

And then there were the twins. Luke was already scheming on ways of just, you know, *seeing* them. From a distance, or at night, or even on some sort of video intercom–wasn't there one at their new house? He had to figure out a way to keep an eye on them, that was all. If he had one purpose left in life, er, death . . . uh, undeath?

Whatever. If he had one purpose, it was to guard Cherry and Haddy, and of course Charity, from all harm. But how would he be able to do it, without being seen?

At night was no problem. He planned on spending his evenings lurking around the grounds of the house, keeping to the darkest shadows, listening and watching. There had to be real comfort in that.

But not all threats occur in the dark. The worst things that can happen, or at least the ones that usually do happen, occur in broad daylight. What could Luke do about crooked lawyers, snooping journalists, government agencies, corporate dicks?

He already knew the answer to that question: the best thing he could do now was to stay far away from his family. And that was probably going to be difficult.

Luke's sleepless reverie dissipated at the sound of footsteps crunching up the slope of talus and clods that formed an apron to their hidden perch. Luke burrowed deeper into the heap of refuse and sticks. Then the shrubs parted and a figure emerged, dressed in shapeless trousers and a red wool shirt.

"Fuckin' flamingo," the homeless woman was muttering. "I din't touch yer fuckin' *flamingo*," her voice rose to a shriek as a car clattered onto the bridge above their heads, "you fuckin' IM-buh-sill!" She was heavy around the middle and her trousers were filthy. She shuffled closer to where Luke and Buzz were concealed, and tossed her sack of paraphernalia down upon the pile of rubbish.

Luke was sure that Buzz would squawk when the heavy trash bag landed on them, but the condor kept still. The hobo woman moved a couple of yards off, squatted down and Luke heard the sound of splashing urine. Then she returned to her bag and started to rummage through it.

"Salami, I know there was some salami in here somewhere," she muttered, tossing aside a smashed packet of flaming orange crackers and peanut butter. It landed on Luke's thigh, but he kept quiet. The woman continued her search.

Okay, this was awkward. How long before they were discovered? It was a miracle that he and Buzz hadn't been noticed already.

The woman was clearly drunk. She removed several empty liquor bottles from her luggage and checked them for any drops of liquid that could be gleaned before tossing them into the weeds. Then she pulled out a plastic flamingo lawn ornament, and stared at it. She scratched her head, shook it a few times. She hoisted the flamingo over her shoulder and carried it away.

"Let's go, Bozo, before she gets back," Buzz suggested as soon as the hobo was out of whisper-range. Although Luke wasn't thrilled about abandoning their hard-won turf, he extricated himself from the refuse, and made a dash for it.

No sooner had he parted the weeds that gave the rustic retreat some degree of cover, than he spied a pair of vagrants ambling slowly along. They had just emerged from the underpass where the paved path that led from the riverbank to the cemetery passed below the access road. They were headed his way, one of them pushing a shopping cart mounded like a hay wain with stuffed plastic bags.

"Dammit!" Luke swore sotto voce as he scrambled up the slope, and dove into the thicket of shrubs that grew down along the embankment to either side of the bridge's foundation. From this vantage point he could see the hobo woman admiring the flamingo, which she'd set into the mud bank of the Willamette like a sentinel.

"Take a look," she bellowed. "A fuckin' flamingo!"

The two arrivals, both men, stared. "Get that thing outta here," the one with the oversized khaki army coat yelled. "You want the cops to pay us a visit?"

An argument ensued, which the man in khaki eventually won, and the plastic bird was removed from view. But Luke and Buzz had not yet seen an opportunity for escape. The three vagrants showed no interest in providing one. They kept wandering here and there, gathering rocks, taking dumps, and generally making themselves at home.

Two of them constantly shouted to each other in hoarse voices, of which only occasional words were intelligible to Luke under the rumble of the commuters, but their thoughts were clear enough. The black guy with the long green army coat was Shorty, and the woman was called Fay. The third hobo, Chester, never said anything, and nobody talked to him much. He was a pale man wearing a gray sweatshirt, a green knit cap and black trousers, and his clothing was relatively clean and respectable. All his thoughts were focused on his next fix. Luke wondered if he were homeless like the other two, or just hanging out for the perks. Chester busied himself with building a rock trivet upon which he set a can of Sterno.

Shorty had found the paper and was perusing it while Fay rolled him a cigarette. *Goddamn shame about that kid,* he was thinking. "You goin' over to Luke Mandrake's house today, Fay?" Shorty yelled.

"All the way up there?" Fay objected. "I dunno. Pretty slim pickins, them kids ain't got nothin.'"

"I just wanna go. Hear what Charity has to say."

Fay laughed unkindly. "She done it, I heard. For the money."

"Naw, that's just stupid. She didn't need to go and do that to get the money, man. She already *had* the money. Why would she kill the goose that laid the golden egg?"

"Well what I want to know," growled Chester, finally breaking his silence, "is what happened to Billy."

"Billy who?" Fay asked.

"Remember that skinny street kid with the green hair who came out here looking for smack last week? From Santa Cruz?"

"That boy? He was a nice kid. You ever get him hooked up?"

"He was a she," Chester said. "Billy and I go way back. Told me she hitchhiked all the way from Fresno with Luke Mandrake."

Luke bit his lips to keep from making a sound. He remembered that guy. Billy had regaled him, and the truck drivers who picked them up, with imaginative stories of his early sexual experiences with women. Luke had easily divined that Billy was born a woman. According to Billy, Donita from L7 used to babysit him, taught him everything he knew. Luke was able to detect immediately that this was bullshit. He had been fascinated by Billy, though: he was an entertaining, obliging and competent companion, and a daring and practiced liar. It had pleased Luke to grant him his wish. He was a he. Why not?

"She never came back around after that, Billy," Chester remarked.

The other two were apparently struck dumb by the implications of this revelation.

"She went back there with the smack, and she disappeared," the man said. "And that was the same night Weezy got a hotshot."

"Weezy's dead?" Fay asked.

"The stuff we copped for Luke was simon-pure, angel of death shit. Couple of greenhorns kicked the bucket over in Eugene, too. Ya gotta be careful, man." He lit the Sterno and began unpacking his kit with speedy efficiency. *Yup. Just his luck to fall in with a troupe of junkies.*

"So Luke Mandrake took a hot shot, and Billy probably high-tailed it when Luke kicked the bucket," Shorty said. "Made it look like suicide."

"Or, maybe Billy kicked it too."

As the three of them sat there silently, watching Chester cook something in a spoon, Luke thought back to how Billy had shown up in Famebeau right after him, carrying a pistol and wearing a Shambala jacket. The Shambala jacket, he remembered now, that he'd given Billy the night they arrived in Portland.

Billy had stolen that gun from his house. And now, obviously, he was dead.

"Imagine if they found out," said Fay. "Imagine if somebody went and fuckin' told them that Luke Mandrake's suicide was faked."

"We don't know that, Fay. And keep yer fucking mouth shut, fercrissake."

"I didn't say I was going to do it." Fay lit a cigarette. "I'm just saying that if they knew about this Billy, they'd know something they don't know now. And if they could find him–"

"Her," said Shorty.

"If they could find her they'd know something *we* don't even know."

"What's that?" Shorty demanded.

"The truth," Fay said.

"Well I ain't goin' over to Luke Mandrake's house," Chester said. "I'm gettin' outta Portland, and the sooner I can hit the road, the happier I'll be."

Fay became calm as the tiny dose Chester had injected into her arm took effect. He threw a plastic bag full of clothes at her.

"Get some clean pants on, Fay, you're on duty today."

"God Chester, you're such a fuckin' slave driver," Fay grumbled. She withdrew a pair of trousers from the bag and looked at them. "Size 32? I'm not that fuckin' fat."

"You will be," said Chester, "When those pants are full of bacon."

"Great idea," said Shorty.

"Why do I always hafta do it?" Fay complained.

"Tina's meeting us at Zupan's," Shorty replied. "You two can work together."

Luke had heard enough. It was high time to leave their hiding place, sneak down through the stand of bushes and away. But just as he was creeping along the edge of the slope of scree, Fay came crashing through the weeds toward him. She was going to her pee spot.

"Shit," Luke hissed, pulling his oversized hood down to shade his face.

Buzz stiffened and toppled from his shoulder. The bird he caught in his arms was as plastic and hollow as Fay's flamingo.

"The fuck!" said Fay. "Who're you?"

"Uh, I–I–I'm a friend of Charity Ball's?" Luke stuttered. Fay's face collapsed into a suspicious scowl, resembling a puffy glob of bread dough deflated by a fist. She looked at him silently from within deep folds. Luke realized for the first time how enormous she was.

"I–" Luke began again. "She's looking for some stuff. Do you–?"

"We ain't got nothin'," Fay barked. "So GIT!" Then, as Luke turned eagerly to obey, her eyes lighted on the plastic vulture. The dough stretched into the shape of a beatific smile.

"Oooh, you sellin' that?" she squealed. "I want it."

"No," Luke replied hastily, but Fay had already seized Buzz and was shaking the injection-molded condor energetically, like a child investigating a Christmas present.

"The fuck?" she repeated. "It's on a chain!"

Luke's head was bowed as he leaned in toward Fay and whispered, "Just so you know . . . Charity didn't do it!"

His hands emerged from the long sleeves and quickly seized Buzz from the surprised vagrant. Then he bolted, hoping that she hadn't noticed his green and rotting skin.

Luke thrust the condor under his sweatshirt and instinctively headed toward the old trolley tracks that followed the Willamette through the park and down past the fancy houses that clustered along the Riverwood shore. He soon regretted his decision. He hadn't expected to meet up with much of anyone on this route, hidden from the highway, but he immediately encountered a young couple who had crossed over from Sellwood on foot. Luke sped up to get away from them, but then another pedestrian, a lone plaid-shirted punk, emerged from a woodland path just ahead and joined the cavalcade. So Luke slowed to let the couple pass, plunging off the tracks over the ever-present broken bottles, as if he were taking a leak. He could hear them talking now.

"I got so fucking drunk last night."

"You worshiped the porcelain god."

"I know, I can't believe it. I thought about stealing my Mom's Valiums and taking all of them."

"Did you find any?"

"No," said the girl with spiky flame-red hair. She wore a dilapidated leather jacket over a vintage slip, torn fishnets, and heavy boots. "How 'bout you?"

"Nothing," Her girlfriend's tattered canvas coat was patterned with hand-sewn patches and marker graffiti, devoted to Luke Mandrake and Shambala. There were even lyrics from Charity's band, Void. "We're going to have to get through this cold turkey."

Luke watched them as they marched off hand in hand, stepping from tie to tie in their regulation-issue boots. He could hear their thoughts clearly, and it was creeping him out.

So depressing. Why the hell did he have to go and do that?

Luke fucking Mandrake, you shithead. We needed you!

Over the years he'd occasionally wondered if the voices in his head were the signs of madness, or if he could really hear people's thoughts. Now that he was undead, the ability was becoming more developed.

The interaction with Nakita, the girl with the laundry basket, had been a close call. He was not eager for more encounters like that one, but now it appeared to be inevitable.

A man with a green mohawk joined the two girls up ahead. They seemed to be coming out of the woodwork, his fans. And he really hadn't wanted to meet even one. Why had he set out in this direction? It was as though an irresistible lodestone drew him toward Charity, toward home.

The three punks ahead of him stopped to light cigarettes. There was nowhere for Luke to go but forward. Behind him was an angry girl with a shaved head and piercings. To the left, the river, and to the right the highway already lined with vehicles moving slowly, not toward the bridge as was usual, but on the southbound side, toward Riverwood. Beyond that bristled the thick woods of the wildlife refuge, a mat of branches and thorns that Luke feared would tear him to pieces if he tried to force his way through.

So he marched along the tracks, shuffling carefully from one plank to the next, his zombie feet hidden within the cuffed legs of the oversized corduroys that he dragged over the blackened stones.

"Hey kid," the girl with the denim jacket called to him as he approached, waving her cigarette. "Got a light?"

Luke shook his head. He really did not want to pass so close to these people, but he also didn't want to leave the train tracks again and take his chances on the rough, littered ground. As it was, his feet were never going to be the same after last night's sojourn, and this morning's panicked sprint had left his soles torn to ribbons.

"You okay?" the other girl asked. The three drew back and watched him limp past. The girls looked at each other. *The poor old guy.* The young man with the green hair coughed.

As Luke hobbled on, he pictured himself carrying their darkest thoughts away with him, like an old-time scrap peddler's burden of rags. *Tragic figures have that effect. I should know.*

"Found some matches," said Josie, the girl with the red hair

Luke thought that the dark cloud that hung over the group was thinning a bit. But maybe it was just his imagination.

"So we're going to the funeral," Buzz commented when they reached the end of the Marine Park. His house was still nearly two miles away, but there wasn't much of anywhere else they could go from here. Where the woods ended, the back fences of the houses began. No escape that way.

When they reached the first drive, a stream of kids who had parked their cars nearby converged on the tracks. Luke kept his head down, kept plodding, trying not to draw attention to himself. They were a solemn cortège walking south toward Riverwood singly, in groups of two or three or five. All of them were headed to Luke's memorial, and he was being carried along with them.

There was no getting out of it now. He was going back to the old homestead.

✳   ✳   ✳

"Mommy, wake up."

"Whad . . . huh?" Charity had been dreaming of crop circles, huge elaborate fractal signs, miles wide, that turned the expanse of deserts into hieroglyphs. Luke had branded them on the landscape, using fantastic powers which had been awarded him after death.

"Mommy!" Haddy poked her arm with a chubby finger.

"What is it sweetie? I'm trying to sleep," she moaned.

"Mommy, Tsehwy–" that was how Galahad pronounced his sister Cherry's name– "Tsehwy went down . . . downstairs."

Charity sat up and began to pull on her dressing gown.

The twins had slept one on either side of her. It wasn't her practice to bring the kids into bed with her, as a rule, but since Luke died, she'd been having a hard time sleeping. And after yesterday . . . seeing him like that! It was just too horrible. So she had needed their little warm bodies close to her, she had needed to smell them and feel their sweet skin. Otherwise, she might have gone and done something stupid.

"Let's go find her, okay Haddy?" Charity said, lifting the toddler in her arms. The twins were nearly three now and a real handful.

Ping pang bumpity, thump crash!

It sounded like somebody was practicing percussion somewhere, and at first Charity groggily imagined it was Luke, who had taken to playing drums a good bit lately. But of course that was impossible. Luke was . . . the image of her zombie husband rose again before Charity's eyes, and she felt uneasy. Luke was out there, somewhere. Had he decided to come home?

Pap! Papity papity ka-klang!

When she saw Cherry sitting on the floor in the kitchen surrounded by pots and bowls, Charity felt a burst of relief. The toddler had unearthed an old-fashioned mechanical eggbeater from the cupboard, and was using it to torture a steel mixing bowl, producing a bright staccato clangor.

"That is pretty awesome," Charity said, depositing Haddy on the linoleum so that he could join the fun. Before he could yank the eggbeater from Cherry's determined grip his mother hastily provided the boy with his own salad spoon and a fork.

"Be careful!" she warned. "Only hit pots, not people, all right?"

"Onwy hit pots, not peepoh!" the two tots repeated gleefully.

"Hit pots! Not people!" Charity shouted, using a pair of chopsticks to tap a smart tattoo on a bowl. They all joined in the chant together while bashing away at the improvised drum kit.

"Hit pots! Not people! Hit pots! Not people!"

"This song needs a good bass line," growled a voice from the door. It was Kaylen, her petite frame draped in a huge tee shirt with a devil hand-drawn on it in black marker. She was wearing long red-and white striped socks.

"I'm sorry, did we wake you up?" said Charity.

Kaylen grabbed a wooden spoon and a spatula and began whaling two-handed on a Tupperware flour canister.

"Hit pots! Not poodles!" she cried laughingly.

"Hit pots! Not puddles!" Cherry yelled.

Back and forth, the toddlers shouted their own silly versions of the rhyme.

"Hit pots! Not noodles!"

"Hit doodles! Not noodles!"

"Hit noodles! Not foodles!"

"Hit noodles! Not boodles!"

"You must be exhausted," Kaylen said to Charity over the storm of giggles. "Go back to sleep."

"No chance of that," Charity smiled. "Let's make breakfast." There were too many disturbing thoughts clamoring in her head, and she had to shut them out, focus on something, well, normal. Kaylen bounced over and gave her a hug.

Charity had known Kaylen for a few years as the bass player for

Workingman's Fiend. They had shared the green room on a couple of tours, but they had not been especially close. Six months after joining Void, Kaylen was proving to be the friend Charity could depend upon in her darkest hour.

"I'm glad you're here," Charity said. Both women blinked back tears.

Kaylen grinned. "Where's the freaking coffee?"

There wasn't much food in the house, but they found eggs, milk and some stale French bread. A brick of frozen strawberries was warmed with sugar. Before long a pile of fluffy French toast was on the table.

After the berry-licious breakfast, Kaylen packed the kids up and took them to the grocery store. Charity was left alone with her ghastly memories. She found herself in the study, taking the Medical Examiner's report out of the desk drawer.

She simply couldn't figure out why the cause of death would be listed as "self-inflicted shotgun wound." What the fuck? She'd noticed it the night before, but she hadn't questioned Dr. Lupercan about it. She'd been focusing on other priorities.

She wandered into the family room and turned on the television. Nearly every channel was still running bulletins and updates about Luke. She hadn't been able to, couldn't bear to look at the tube or even the papers since yesterday morning when the accidental discovery of his body had become international news. Now, the reports brought her up short.

Suicide, by shotgun! Why hadn't anyone told her?

Where was Liam? He sure had been making himself scarce. She'd dropped the kids and Kaylen off yesterday upon her arrival, and had driven straight to the morgue. When she returned to the house, Liam was nowhere to be found. There was a note saying he'd gone to his Dad's place out in Scappoose. Something about a pregnant goat.

She badly needed to talk to him, but it didn't seem like she was going to be able to leave the house today without being tracked by reporters. There was a hullabaloo outside already and the day had barely begun. She could hear voices shouting, a heated discussion over parking. There was not a single parking space on the street, and someone was trying to park in the driveway. She'd had to bribe a guy who'd arrived by motorcycle to keep it clear.

And there were scores of kids huddled here and there on the lawn, occasionally staring furtively at the house like it was the fucking spaceship in Close Encounters of the Third Kind.

As Charity gazed out the kitchen window, watching photographers trample the pachysandra, she spied Liam making his way toward the back door. Thank goodness. She could hear him enter the house and, with his unmistakable, uneven footsteps, go into the ground floor bathroom, shutting the door. She ran down and knocked.

"Liam?"

"Yeah?"

"When you're done, could you please come to my study?"

"Sure," he replied in a cautious voice.

When she showed him the report, his reaction puzzled her. He gave a huge sigh of relief.

"Well, so far, so good," he remarked. "Did you tell Doug?"

"Why would I tell Doug? Let him read about it in the papers."

"You did talk to him though. Right?"

"He came to my place yesterday and told me about the letter, yes. The fucking scumbag couldn't wait till Luke was laid to rest before sticking the knife in. God damn . . ." She trailed off. Liam was looking at her very strangely.

"What is it? Liam?" She walked over to her old friend and put her hand on his arm. "Please tell me, Liam. Why does this paper list the cause of death as suicide?" she asked. "What the hell happened yesterday?"

Liam's face was white and beads of sweat dotted his upper lip. "Charity . . . didn't Doug tell you about the plan? He–he was on the phone with you. He said you okayed it."

Charity stood very still as a thundercloud gathered over her high forehead. She closed her eyes and said, slowly and carefully, "Okayed what, Liam?"

Liam didn't answer. She raised her eyelids to see him huddled in the leather armchair, both hands pressed over his lips.

"Okayed *what?*" Charity repeated, the hair prickling on the back of her neck.

"Doug said . . . Doug thought that it was the only way to turn the ship around . . ." Liam whispered. "He said that sales had been dropping since Paris. You know as well as I do what the word on the street has been, about Luke going onstage like a zombie, leaving his fans dissatisfied. Doug told me that the public had no patience with Luke's drug habit, that they were turning against him."

"And?" Charity thought she knew what was coming. But she didn't want to believe it.

"That if–if we could transform the narrative . . . if it were ruled a suicide, if there were a note–"

The note. There had been a copy of it in the envelope of documents she'd been given by the police. She pulled it out and scanned it again.

I have a goddess of a wife who is the hardest-working woman in music.

"It's the last page of the letter he sent Doug," Liam offered.

Charity understood now what Luke had been trying to accomplish with the letter. He was saying goodbye to his fans, of course, and at the same time, he was passing her the fucking baton of fucking stardom.

Luke had long blamed the pressures of the music business for propelling him into ever-deeper dependence on drugs. Her recent threat to divorce him if he didn't clean up, had decided the matter for him. He'd already been desperate to retire, it was something he'd been talking about with longing for over a year.

When he sent that letter to Clinquant, he'd been trying to save their marriage. And he'd been trying to save his own life. Charity's eyes filled with tears. Poor Luke. It had already been too late for him. They'd all known it, even while they were staging that fucking stupid intervention. They'd all known it was coming, Luke most of all. He'd been flirting heedlessly with death for as long as she'd known him.

Fuck, fuck, fuck. What had they done?

"So tell me," she murmured, wiping her eyes with the sleeve of her dressing gown, "how was some idiotic hoax supposed to make things any better, Liam?"

"Doug . . . was positive that staging Luke's suicide was the only way to get the numbers we need. The only way you and the kids were gonna be able to keep the house."

Charity's wet cheeks burned and her eyes blazed.

"Jesus! I'm not that broke!" she shrieked. Both of them looked out the window and she lowered her voice. "You should have fucking called me, Liam! I had no idea you were planning to–to . . ."

"Jesus Charity . . . you know Doug. He just . . . takes over."

Charity thought back to Luke's appearance the previous evening. He'd been greenish, dilapidated, emaciated. And, the top of his skull had been missing. She rounded on Liam, who shrank into the leather armchair, his eyes swimming. She knelt down next to the chair, drew up close to him, and hissed out the words that only he could hear.

"So you guys decided to blow the fucking brains out of poor Luke's corpse for dramatic effect. That's brilliant, just brilliant. You are *so* fucking lucky nobody caught on." Her knees were trembling, and she had to sit down.

"I . . . I was doing it for you, Charity," he said simply. She finally looked at him then, actually looked at him. Oh god. He loved her. Oh god. She was so sorry. Not for what she'd said, but for not remembering that, for speaking so angrily.

But what could she do? Did she need another junkie lover right now? *Hell, no.*

People were singing outside. She turned in her seat, twitched the curtains and peered out. They were gathering in little throngs. She was going to have to go out there and talk to them, eventually. But first, she needed to talk to Haddy and Cherry. They had to be told, by their mother, before they learned the details of their father's death from a stranger.

She could see the old Volvo creeping up the driveway now.

Charity sighed, stood up, and turned to Liam. "Just tell me one thing," she said gently. "Who did it? Who pulled the trigger? Was it you, Liam?"

Liam shook his head spastically. "No! I couldn't–I could never do that!"

Charity stared at him searchingly. "We're in this together, Liam. Just you and me, and that vulture . . ." she stopped for a moment and closed her eyes. "Nobody at Ded Leper can be trusted. Not Clinquant, not anyone. They are not our friends, Liam. Try to remember that."

"I'm sorry Charity. I really fucked up. Now," Liam swallowed, "now you'll never trust me again."

"I still trust you, Liam. I understand what happened, and why. Don't blame yourself." Charity sighed. "I'm going to tell you something I wouldn't entrust to anyone else. It's the hugest secret in the world."

Liam gazed at her in awe. The color was budding again in his hollow cheeks.

"Luke's body," she said quietly, "has been . . . stolen."

"What!?" Liam gasped. "By who?"

"Nobody knows who did it, but I'm looking into it . . . and so far I've been able to keep it under wraps. Let's hope it stays that way, because the last thing I want is to get the cops interested in us, any more than they already are. And . . . I think, Liam, that you'd better go on vacation really soon." Charity gave Liam a pointed look. "Like, maybe tonight."

"Okay," said Liam morosely.

"A really long vacation," she called over her shoulder as she stalked out.

*   *   *

Liam leaned back in the armchair. He let out a strangled sob.

There was something he would never tell Charity, or anyone, a secret that he was going to have to keep locked in the deepest recesses of his mind for as long as he lived.

He had seen Luke's body, had gone into the room and looked at the scene after Clinquant had completed his grisly task. He'd seen something that horrified him beyond telling.

When Liam had found Luke dead on Saturday in that freezing cold sun room, the musician had appeared to be peacefully asleep, slumped in a chair by the window, clutching the Remington, his rifled wallet on the floor. Billy, who was surely the last person to have seen Luke alive, had been nowhere to be found.

Doug had gone over all the details of the plan with Liam, had proposed using the note, and they had agreed on everything together. Doug had offered to do the deed, acting like a heroic soldier going into battle. Afterward, Doug reported that Luke had fallen backward in that chair from the recoil of the shotgun. He had decided to leave the corpse on the floor. It was more realistic that way, he'd said.

But there were two things about Doug's carefully-staged tableau that could not be explained.

First, the body was flat on its back, in a totally different pose

99

from the one in which Liam had found it. Yet surely rigor mortis would have begun well before the record executive arrived. How had Clinquant been able to reposition Luke so easily? How could Luke have retained that kind of elasticity?

And how–and why the hell–had Luke's eyes been *open*?

*   *   *

"They were the best band that ever lived," a girl with pink tufts of hair and faceted metallic plastic studs on her faux leather gear complained, and smacked her gum. "Then Charity showed up, and ruined everything."

The attenuated boy beside her with tear-streaked mascara sucked hungrily on a cigarette and then croaked, "Yeah."

Luke was watching and listening from behind the cypress hedge. It was a great spot to hide, as he had figured out not long after they moved in, because you couldn't tell that there was so much space back here, unless you squeezed through to explore it. The hedge was dense and imposing, but the soft flaps of fragrant foliage were pliable and admitted his skeletal body silently, allowing him to slip out of sight in moments. He had avoided several potentially uncomfortable encounters this way.

The lawn was crowded with fans, and Luke could detect their thoughts and conversations at will. Though most of the attendees were local kids, there were voices in a host of languages and accents, from Portuguese to Scottish brogue, Dutch to Swahili. Above the sub-dued hubbub of mumbles and sobs, the clank and clatter of buckles and bling on boots and jackets penetrated the haze of marijuana and tobacco, imparting a paradoxically military tone to the gathering.

And the mourners kept coming. On motorcycle and on foot, by bus and by boat, there was a mob converging on his house, and Luke's alarm mounted. His family's refuge was aswarm with histrionic

100

punks, roughnecks, dope dealers and narcs.

Charity had sent someone out for water and there was a large cooler set up on the picnic table, and a stack of cups. People had brought booze and some were picnicking on the lawn. Luke relaxed a bit when he realized that the constant bitchy refrain about Charity was mostly nothing more than catty chitchat. It enraged him, of course. But at least this was no angry mob.

However, many of the unspoken voices were violently despondent, and self-destructive thoughts hung like a dark nimbus over the group, every bit as detectable as smoke to Luke's agile perceptions. The more he listened in, the more his concern shifted from worries about his wife's safety to fear that someone would commit suicide publicly, or overdose on the scene. There were vast quantities of drugs concealed on these people.

A thick, silent knot of mourners gathered at the makeshift altar that was being assembled within the derelict koi pond, a grubby sky-blue cement basin near the overlook. More than one desperate mental cry of anguish could be detected from that quarter. Luke's dismay grew into a sense of impending doom.

He was splashing in puddles of woe. He wrested himself away from one depressive vortex, only to be sucked into the next.

What's the point of living? a mind noiselessly wailed. *Put my head in the oven, that's what I'll do!* The youth's brain was a buzzing hornet's nest of unpleasant thoughts, but Luke tuned in automatically. He found himself inside a ratty laundry room lit by a fluorescent bulb. Clothes and blobs of lint were everywhere, and a girl was crying. She turned and screamed at him, *you don't own me, asshole!*

Sinking deeper, Luke plunged into a reservoir brimful of self-loathing, milked from a lifetime of judgmental pronouncements by the boy's sick and hateful mother. Floating in this toxic soup was the woman's face, one side slack and the other twisted with anger, a dribble of spit on her chin. Luke heard the skitter and crash as she stumbled drunkenly through a room full of rubbish, and her voice, guttural and spewing hurtful words. *Coward! You're no son of mine! Get out! Get out of here, before I call the cops!*

Luke was drawn yet further into the dark thoughts, swirling down a rabbit hole as the lad's unstable mental state imprinted itself on his trembling heart. At the bottom of the well, a baby cried and cried, hour after hour, alone in his crib in a shit-filled diaper. No word of comfort, no embrace, no response to urgent need, only the moaning and mumbling of a croaking voice that occasionally yelled, *shut up!*

Luke struggled to escape, swimming upward with frantic strokes, until he broke into the air, waking with a grunt after what was probably a total of thirty seconds of hell.

"God, what a way to get some sleep," he whispered.

"What?" croaked Buzz.

"I was just picking up the inner thoughts of one of those poor fuckers out there, and I fell into a waking nightmare."

"Don't listen," Buzz warned. "You'll get lost if you're not careful."

"I can't help it!" Luke shook his head from side to side. "Isn't there a way to shut them out?"

"You tell me, Luke," she rasped, looking at him strangely.

At that moment the fleshy green fans of the cypress bushes parted, and someone pushed through. Luke shrank down into the shadows as a voice whispered,

"It's me!"

It was Charity. She stopped short and eyed the vulture warily. There was a pair of jeans draped over her arm.

"I brought you some clothes."

Buzz puffed out her crop a bit but otherwise remained calm. "I hope nobody saw you come in here," she cackled.

"Kaylen is making an announcement at the altar right now, so most everybody went over there." Charity was staring at Luke. In his ill-fitting ensemble he would have made the most pathetic hobo appear dapper.

"I'm glad you came," she said, with a catch in her voice.

It was such a relief to see her crouching there, just outside of the reach of Buzz's darting beak, that Luke had to force himself not to throw his arms around her.

"H–how did you know I was here?"

"I saw you through the window."

Luke had forgotten that the back of the hedge was fully visible from the dining room. "Did the kids see me?"

"Almost," she said.

Christ, he had to be more careful. Luke fought back tears as he said, "How are they doing, okay?"

"Okay. They miss their Daddy."

Charity handed him her offerings: Levis, his Mudhoney tee shirt, a thickly lined plaid wool shirt, a pair of flannel pajamas, a hunting cap with side flaps, tube socks, and a pair of black converse sneakers.

"Awesome," he said, "nobody will ever recognize me, wearing these."

"Oh. Do you want something else?"

"Hmmmm. How about that lovely gown you wore at the Grammies?"

"Luke!"

"Naw, you're right, too revealing. Seriously, though, your hooded bathrobe would be great. With the enormous sleeves."

"The purple velour one?"

"Yeah, that's it."

"And some raw meat would be nice!"Buzz put in.

"You got it." Charity turned to go and then paused. "Oh yeah, I brought some scissors," she said and tossed a pair of sewing shears toward Luke. Then she slipped out between the cypress, and was gone.

Luke stripped off the stolen garments and gratefully donned all his familiar clothes, starting with the pajama pants. The extra layers would, he hoped, make him look less like a walking skeleton. The shoes were especially welcome, a godsend to his poor feet.

It wasn't easy to get the tee shirt on over Buzz's bony form, and the long sleeves of the other shirts had to be slashed. He put the oversized black hoodie on last, having first removed the right sleeve completely.

When Charity finally returned with the robe, he was trying to convince Buzz to wear the sleeve of the sweatshirt over her long neck and chest.

"It'll hide your crop," he said. "The pink really stands out, you know."

"You don't get it," the condor objected. "My neck is totally retractable, see? If I wear that thing, I'll have to stretch it out in order to see, and that'll get old fast."

"But if you can pull your head inside, so much the better," Luke argued, trying to slip the sleeve on over Buzz's monstrous head.

"No! Look, it's just gonna irritate me in so many ways. It'll crush my ruff. It'll hamper me."

"I'm going to have to address the crowd soon," Charity announced, depositing a plastic-wrapped package of ground beef on the moss. "So if there's anything else you two need . . ."

"How 'bout some fresh brains for this Bozo?" Buzz rasped. "He seems to think that he can dress me up like a pet cockadoodle." She hopped over to the Styrofoam tray of meat, sliced through the packaging and began gulping it down.

"What can I say?" Charity shot back. "Maybe he's just trying to fit in. After all, his fashion sense was dictated by the taunts and blows of schoolyard bullies."

"Conformity," Buzz remarked between swallows. "The curse of all tailors." Charity let out a grudging chuckle.

Luke felt gratified to note that the two were sharing a joke at his expense. Maybe there was hope for his lascivious scheme, after all.

Braving the beak of the now-sated vulture, Charity helped Luke and the bird into the wrapper, which had wide bell sleeves and an enormous cowl beneath which Buzz was somewhat effectively concealed. Charity completed the look by draping a bright fuchsia feather boa around Luke's shoulders.

"Isn't that going to attract too much attention?" Luke worried.

"No, it's perfect," Charity insisted. "You're gonna be hiding in plain sight."

Luke caught a glimpse of his reflection in the window. There were pink butterflies embroidered on the robe. He looked like a cross-dressing sorcerer, but his face and body were well hidden.

"Are you gonna stay for the memorial?" Charity asked.

"I . . ."

"How can you pass up the chance to attend your own funeral?" Buzz croaked.

"I don't know," Luke said. "I should go, I think. I don't want to hear people saying sappy things about me."

"Oh, don't you," Charity said bitterly. That was when Luke realized how pissed off she actually was.

"Okay," he said cautiously, "then maybe I should stay."

"God, look at these poor people," Charity fumed. "They're all just so . . . heartbroken!"

Here it comes.

Tears began to slip down her cheeks as she went on. "Some of them aren't going to make it, do you know that? And it's all because you had to be so selfish, so idiotic–!"

"I'm sorry, Charity. Okay? What I did was totally stupid."

"Why? Why did you just run off like that? Why didn't you just talk to me, Luke? I thought we were best friends," Charity sobbed.

"I thought . . . you didn't want me any more. Why would you?

You told me . . . that I had dropped . . . dropped Cherry. On her head! And I don't even remember doing it."

Luke coughed for a while, hoping his eyes weren't going to explode. Salt water spattered, but the eyeballs stayed intact. *Better not try wiping the tears away. Too risky.*

"I'd become a shadow, a waste product, you know that, Charity. What you needed . . . was something I couldn't give you. You needed somebody better, somebody who wasn't . . . me."

"Oh, Luke," Charity said. "I needed *you*. I needed *you*."

Luke longed to wrap his arms around her then, to feel her against him. But that wasn't going to happen, he had to wait, to try and get his true form back somehow. Then he would return, then he would tell her how much he still loved her. Then he would find a way to satisfy her every wish. He swore this silently to himself, huddled in his robe, putrid, hugging himself with his own emaciated arms.

"They blame me, you know," Charity went on, her eyes flashing. "They've decided it's all my fault you died."

"*Your* fault? How the hell is it *your* fault?"

"Well I do feel guilty, of course I do. There were so many things . . ." Charity trailed off, shook herself. "And I don't know if they're ever going to leave, until–" Charity looked at him, and for the first time, he saw a glint of fear in her eyes.

"Okay, look. It was *my* fault. You–you have to tell them, it was my fault, it was my own stupid decision. Taking drugs is the dumbest thing that they can ever do. Tell them that."

Charity heaved a deep and quivering sigh. "I'd better get ready." She stared at him searchingly for a few moments. "Please don't go away, Luke."

Luke hesitated. What could he say? When he finally managed to speak in a cracking voice, he said "I'll be back one day."

But by then, she was gone.

"Great job keeping out of sight," Buzz remarked.

"We'll need to find another place to hide."

"What for? This spot is as good as any."

"I can't just keep opening up old wounds with Charity," he whispered.

"Then why not get outta here?"

"I've gotta make sure she's okay before I . . ." Before he what? Set out on his quest to regain his true form? He had no idea how to go about it, or where it would lead him. But the longer he continued to inhabit this body, the more unusual abilities he discovered in himself. If he could learn to master his powers, there was no telling what kind of secrets he might not discover. If he couldn't . . . well, then he would probably end up as a gibbering lunatic.

"Testing, one two," Liam's voice rose upon a screech of feedback. He was setting up the microphone for Charity's speech. Luke picked out thoughts and emotions from the swelling crowd. A profound craving for answers, for meaning, drove them to gather round the makeshift altar where the mic stand was. He practiced decoding the thoughts without getting drawn into the subjectivity of the individuals. It was much harder when the emotions were powerful. Fortunately, these folks were easy to spot since their minds were also the "loudest." It was like listening to the crowd in a concert recording, and trying to ignore the screams and yells, and pick out the words in nearby conversations.

The most powerful mental projections sounded like this:

"NEED DOPE! NEED SOME DOPE!"

"GET A GUN AND BLOW MY HEAD OFF–"

"LUKE! WHY? JUST TELL ME WHY?"

"HATE CHARITY, I HATE HER!"

The quieter thoughts came through this way:

" . . . Should I invite Pamela to come over after the–"

"Where's Rufus? Been waiting for an hour . . ."

" . . . Crotch itches, oh god, is it crabs? Maybe Josh . . ."

And then there was a soft hubbub of spoken voices:

" . . . Motorcycle looks like the one that . . ."

"Do you remember the night Shambala played the Cathouse Bar?"

" . . . Made that card, the one with the rainbow ribbon glued . . ."

There was a soft rushing sound that grew to a low roar as Charity stepped up to the mic.

"Hey, guys," she said. Luke couldn't see her himself, but the image of her standing there, hunched over a bit with a tissue clutched in her hand, was vivid in the minds of anyone who could. He could see every detail of her from all sides, from the chipped nail polish on the fingers that rested on the microphone, to the bits of grass plastered on her patent-leather mary janes.

"Charity!" a voice called out.

"What the fuck happened?!" yelled another.

But Charity ignored them, and plunged ahead.

"Thank you all for coming here to share this sad day with me, with our family. I want you to know that you guys are all a part of our family, every one of you."

Man, she was good. The crowd was now quiet except for a few coughs and sniffles, expectant.

"I hope we can turn this day into a celebration of Luke's life, and of his great, great music. I know that's what he would have wanted. So the first thing I want all of you guys to do is to close your eyes, and think about your favorite Shambala song. It'll be like a prayer for Luke, wherever he is."

In the silence that followed Luke could hear the songs. His records were playing in the minds of everyone there, and not just the big hits. There were obscure songs from his early recordings, and to his surprise one that rose above the others was the refrain of *Burgeon*:

They know not what they do, they know not what they do . . .

Tears streamed down Charity's face and she wiped her eyes.

"Luke, you goddamn asshole!" she suddenly shouted. "You were a fucking light in this world. We needed you! Why did you leave us?"

Most of the people in the crowd were weeping openly now. What she was doing was cathartic. Luke had always admired his wife's ability to speak to the heart of things. Right now, she held this mob of outcasts in the palm of her hand.

"He left a note, a bullshit, self-involved rockstar note. I'm going to read it to you. It's all we've got to help us understand, so here goes."

Luke sat up at that. A note? What the heck was she talking about?

"Speaking as a wasted, whining, low-life bloodsucker living off the entrails of a corrupt system, I have to say that I just haven't gotten any pleasure from playing music in too many years."

It was from the letter he'd written to Clinquant. It was his good-bye note to his fans.

"It's not you guys, those of you who understood my music, whether you were on the scene from the start, or just discovered this music, and I mean by that not Shambala but all the bands I've been influenced by and learned from, the way I discovered punk rock years ago. You are the greatest friends anybody ever was blessed to have, and I feel incredibly guilty not to appreciate it more than I do.

"But the business of music is a long way from the experience that I used to share with my true fans, the feeling of being one, as it were, with a group of misfits like myself. Now it's all about the money, and it's all about me, and I'm not a strong enough person or even an important enough person to have that much attention from an uncaring swarm of plankton focused on me every minute of every day."

Charity took a swig of water before continuing.

"They say I was always meant to live fast and die young, oh you fucking asshole!" Charity editorialized, *"so I guess this is sayonara. I'm going to disappear, find another plane where the weight of all the pain and all the pressure are finally lifted from me."* Charity's voice broke

here, and she paused, unable to go on. Liam put his arm around her shoulders as she wept. He took the paper from her, and kept reading.

"*I have a goddess of a wife who is the hardest-working woman in music, who makes sacrifices for my sake every single day. I have two small humans who are at the center of my universe, who look to me to understand what it means to be a person. What kind of an example am I giving them, with the way I live my life? And yet what choice have I had? I'm just a morose little sacrificial lamb, trying to dull the pain of the poison I've swallowed by taking more poison, and it's all too much. I'm not fooling anybody, not even myself.*

"*The thrill is gone, and so, I'm outta here.*

"*I'm sorry, I really am.*

"*Galahad, Cherry and Charity, I'll be watching over you.*"

"I did not fucking write that part," Luke whispered savagely to Buzz.

"*Goodbye, cruel world.*

"*Luke Mandrake.*"

Luke was in shock. What the hell?

"I don't get it," Luke whispered to Buzz. "Where did they get that?" He had mailed the only copy to Clinquant at Ded Leper. It was certainly not meant to be a suicide note. At least, not consciously.

"That's what I've been trying to tell you, Bozo," Buzz rasped. "But you refuse to listen to me, or read the newspapers."

"I'm listening now, okay?"

"According to the papers, you shot yourself."

"No way. I OD'd. The last thing I remember was watching Billy squeeze the syringe, then pop! I was . . ." Luke stopped, the events of the past few days whizzing through his mind. Recalling how he'd woken up in the sun room for just a few seconds before everything went black. "No way," he said again, feeling a sickness growing in the pit of his stomach.

"Okay, so you overdosed, I'll buy that. But when you came

back . . ."

Luke's eyes widened in dawning horror. "It sure as hell wasn't me who pulled the trigger," he said. "Somebody set me up!"

"I tried to stop you, Luke," Buzz said. "I knew no good would come of it, if you–"

"Buzz, look!" Luke interrupted. He was holding up his left hand.

"What?"

"My fingers! They're . . . changing!" Last he'd checked, the finger with the wedding ring on it had been the only one that wasn't rotted down to the bone in several places. Now the index finger was whole again, and the other fingers all seemed to exhibit less decomposition than before. He knew this was so, because frankly he was kind of obsessed with constantly checking on his level of decomposition.

"Goodbye Luke," Charity was sobbing. "I love you. Everybody here loves you. We will always remember you, the way you were. We will never forget the music you made. I promise you that."

As she spoke an image of Luke rose up, shot out on a hundred projector-beams, and glowed against the clouds: Luke as a clear-eyed youth, sweet-faced and smiling his faint, wry smile. At least, that's what Luke saw. Not one member of the crowd looked up, but the picture could be read in each of their minds.

As Luke gazed up at his perfect self, another lesion in his rotting flesh closed its lips, and was erased. And another.

The healing had begun.

Dearest Robin,

I have been pacing the cell-like chamber where I spend the off-duty hours of my incarceration, and thinking wistfully of you. What are you doing now? Perhaps you are hosting a soirée for contortionists, or providing therapeutic comfort for the ghost of a frustrated Amish sodomite; or maybe you have been laboring to devise a lavish entertainment for Aphrodite and Humberto (I do hope young Humberto is still in her favor!) featuring a selection of fine absinthes long unavailable to mortal connoisseurs. Whatever you are up to, I sometimes wonder, who will wash the sheets? Certainly not the god of love, ha ha.

The thought of the mess I am sure to come home to when I finally return to your side ought to irritate me, but it is so comforting to picture reuniting with you, my beloved, that I almost look forward to the mountains of laundry, empty champagne bottles, and melon rinds with which you and your guests are surely filling the palace on the upper slopes of Olympos, where you and I have shared so many delicious hours.

Alas, I am beginning to doubt that the day of reunion will ever come.

Why must my punishment be so protracted? It hardly seems fair to be separated from you for an indefinite period in this heartless fashion, all for the insignificant infraction of conducting souls directly to your abode. Good gracious, the Council knows that the great Eros doesn't have time to visit the underworld to personally interview every single one of his deceased worshipers. You are already so dreadfully overworked!

By rights, it ought merely to be a rubber-stamp process when it comes to managing the disposition of your stream of spirit-devotees.

Pluton's arbitrary, reduplicative policies are no more than a way of contesting your primacy as the eldest of the gods.

And so of course the Council upholds Death's lawsuit. Violating the Olympian Code, indeed! But their authority is founded, it seems, on the precedent of punishing others for the same crimes that Zeus himself commits daily with impunity.

It's bad enough that I must take the form of Hanuman, the monkey god, and do the bidding of Hades in all matters going forward, unless summoned by one of the Olympians for special duty as messenger of the gods. But to make you, the Lord of Love, the one exception–no longer allowed to employ me in any capacity at all–it's cruel, it's utterly despicable for the Council to do this to us.

Don't they care that they're breaking my heart?

Yes, I readily admit that the plan we hatched was an encroachment on Hades's authority. But if the Lord of the Dead had been fulfilling his duties, had he been keeping up with the times to any reasonable degree, we wouldn't have been driven to it.

I will always maintain that it was a noble effort to assist you in rescuing your worshipers from eternal torment. Bypassing Hades's nightmarish maze en route to your therapeutic spa and rehab center, simply enabled you to provide whatever healing services the devotees of Love might require before moving on–as mandated by the very Code I was convicted of transgressing!

I cannot allow myself to indulge in regret. In my moments of self-doubt, I need only recall any one of the affecting stories from the battles you and I have fought on the front lines in this war for justice. And the abuses continue–even as I write, victims of rape and incest are routinely condemned to eternal torment.

Everyone else on Olympos, or at least every deity with any common decency, agrees with us on this point. The harsh sentences Pluton inscribes for what are at worst missteps–for one can hardly consider adultery, fornication or sodomy to be the direst of crimes–

are inhumane. And yet Zeus refuses to intervene, or call his brother to task.

And I don't have to tell you that abiding by the regulations imposed by Hades, that bureaucracy-obsessed sadist, has become not merely a cause for incessant vigilance, but a nearly impossible task, requiring absurd amounts of paperwork.

There was just today yet another example of the damnation of a teen call-boy who'd been murdered by a mob of vigilantes–a casualty of society if ever there was one. And yet the redemption of such a one still involves producing an endless stream of affidavits and motions on your part, my Lord of All Hearts, and witnesses and testimonials to follow. It's absurd, in this day and age, to have to expend such massive resources to save every one of the flood of unjustly-damned souls that accounts, on a yearly basis, for fully sixty percent of the deceased. But you know that, my beloved, far better than I.

What angers me most is that the Council behaves as if these draconian laws were an inviolable tradition. Yet the judicial system hasn't always been excessively punitive. My sweet mother Maia often described to me the golden age when Themis, the ancient Titan who could scry the future, ruled as divine judge. Eternal punishments were rare then. The dead were treated kindly: given rest, reunion and healing before returning at last to Gaia, great Mother Earth, to be reborn.

Perhaps one day you will explain to me how Themis the Just, Mother of the Fates, was forced by Zeus to cede her place as judge of souls to Pluto, while Apollo seized her Delphic Oracle. For I am told that not one of the Olympians came to her defense.

Hades certainly doesn't seem to remember the good old days very fondly, if at all. "Rules are rules," he rumbles, and then numbs himself by snorting another five lines of highly potent cocaine. He's never been a jolly fellow, but I recall that back before he was "born again," Death was at least capable of a merciful form of justice. I blame his recent conver-

sion for inspiring him to enact ever stricter laws, moralistic and absolute, mandating cruel punishments out of all proportion to the crime.

It's hard to imagine how Hades could possibly embrace monotheism, a patently illogical and nihilistic stance for a god. But lately I realized that the Lord of Hell identifies with the Devil. Apparently this faddish new religion makes him feel powerful and important. If only it could be uprooted, but for some reason it has become so popular among mortals that the Council is obliged to tolerate it.

Naturally Hades leaves all the busy-work to the paper-pushers: he has an army of functionaries, and they are readily bribed, I might add. It's a practice that Ares, with his endless supply of ill-gotten treasure, has perfected to an art form, ensuring that his worshipers escape accountability for their numerous crimes. Thus it is the victims of violence and exploitation who suffer disproportionately under the new laws, in particular women, children and that recently concocted, so-called minority, "the gays."

I would suggest that you resort to extending gratuities yourself, my lord, but we both know that the Council enforces its laws selectively, and would quickly condemn you, if you made any attempt at graft. The good are always held to higher standards than those who kill.

All in all, from what I've seen here, little compassion is meted out to the dead anymore. Knowing that makes the job of guiding spirits to Hades an excruciating exercise.

Proserpina had been making an effort lately to correct some of the more egregious miscarriages of justice and common sense. But I'm afraid I have distressing news to relate regarding the Queen of the Dead. In response to her dalliance with a certain mortal spirit, I have been pressed into duties on behalf of her husband that I find violently distasteful–I am forced to spy on her. Pluton has taken the singular step of transforming her into a gruesome vulture and setting her to feed upon her lover, who is doomed to walk in an undead body.

An unfortunate affair, that, and rather shocking, considering that

Hermes put down his pen, read the letter over, folded it and
held it up before him. He gave a soft whistle. Instantly a dove appeared in a flash of light, and seizing the parchment in its beak, vanished again. The familar of Eros, the messenger dove had the ability
to slip past every obstacle unseen.

The god rose and strode across the room in two steps, then
back again. He was a tall, graceful fellow with curly dark hair, full lips,
dimpled cheeks and large, black eyes. His skin was deep in tone, his
coloring warm and ruddy, his arms thick and his thighs powerful.
Though his winged hat and boots hung from pegs inside the door,
when he walked he rose up and floated slightly between steps, so that
his progress resembled that of an astronaut on a moonwalk.

Hermes stopped to open a shabby cupboard and gaze at the several bottles on the top shelf. He removed a pinot noir and a stemmed
glass, uncorked the bottle, sniffed its contents, and poured himself a
large portion of the wine.

"To poor, dear Persephone," he said, lifting the glass with a grimace before taking a draught.

What Mercury knew, but had not dared to reveal to Cupid, was
that Proserpina had not only been murdered by her husband, but was
unexpectedly incarnated, still chained to the zombie boy, as a vulture.

I must find a way to help her.

Demeter must be informed of Persephone's predicament. But Hermes could not risk sending her a written note. He would deliver it himself. It would be risky, but if anyone could manage it, he could.

If he got caught, no telling how dire his own punishment would be. But to hell with the danger to himself. Persephone was his favorite sister, and she was in deadly peril. If she were killed while incarnated in mortal form, it would be the end of her.

April 6, 1994 –Brooklyn, NY

Rosetta woke up with a terrible headache. Her throat felt like it was on fire. She got up, careful to avoid waking Aron who slept on the outside, and took some painkillers and an antihistamine. It was not going to be easy to sleep again until they took effect.

When Aron got up to go to work, Rosetta was dozing on the couch. She roused herself.

"Honey, I don't see how I'll be able to do the rehearsal tonight. I'm just too sick to sing."

Aron looked at her unhappily. "That's a drag," he said.

"Can you call everybody and reschedule, please?" his wife croaked. Aron didn't respond except to heave a long-suffering sigh.

"And can you please pick up some canned soup on the way home?"

"Soup?" Aron replied incredulously, visibly put out. "Like, chicken soup?"

Rosetta got up, dragging a blanket after her, and walked into the kitchen area to get a drink of water. "Any kind of soup. Chicken or lentil or whatever you want. Maybe–maybe get a couple."

"Right," said Aron, backing toward the stairs. "Well, I've got to go."

"Thanks, honey," Rosetta rasped.

After the Spring Equinox, 1994 – The Caverns at Eleusis, Greece

Demeter perched on the tiny round stool, her enormous spheroid buttocks bulging around the green velvet upholstery like a mushroom cloud. She bent her head over an expansive, gilded Italianate escritoire with an inlaid marble top. Her elaborate coiffure resembled a beehive or an inverted basket, comprised of hair of every possible natural hue, interwoven with living flowers and leaves. As she worked her head nodded gently, and the foliage brushed the desk's tiny drawers, with agate pulls carved in the shape of ripe heads of grain. There were drawers in such multitude that they rose to an improbable height from the desktop toward the light-streaked roof of the cavern.

Small balls of phosphorescence bobbed around Demeter's head, shedding their glow upon the desk to light her in her work. The goddess was writing a letter to her daughter.

Dearest Persephone, the letter began, *I know how busy you must be, reigning over the spirits of the dead, especially since Hades has taken to indulging in those vices of which we have spoken in the past. So I do not reproach you for neglecting to reply to my last*–Demeter paused for a moment and tickled the end of her dainty nose with the feather quill as she reckoned up the number–*thirty-seven letters. However, I do have some additional items to which I would like to call your attention, as I prepare for the joyous occasion of your return to my bosom.*

Here the monumental bosom of Ceres heaved a deep and melancholy sigh, a movement that was immediately manifested in the depths of the Banda Sea south of Maluku, Indonesia, where a vast, circular submarine canyon expanded and contracted slightly, resulting in a small tremor felt by villagers on the island of Pulau Kasiul, and a few hours later, local tidal flooding.

There are as you may imagine a growing number of flowers in great danger of extinction. Here is a list of but a few of these that must

be archived immediately: Purple Spurge, Gibraltar Campion, Summer Lady's Tresses, Jade Vine, Darling Wine Cup, Lake Darlot Hemigenia, Parrot's Beak, and the Utah Beardtongues.

And remember how we were thinking of reintroducing that lovely orange pendant passionflower that you designed for me, Passiflora Parritae? Well, its habitat is gone, I'm afraid, completely destroyed by those greedy verminous apes. Perhaps we can find a suitable spot somewhere in Ecuador, but darling Kore, I worry about pursuing this course, as micro-climates are so fragile. I sorely need your advice on this matter. However I think you will agree that the sweet little yellow phlox called Linanthus croceus can safely be reintroduced along the Pacific Coast, now that the logging and cattle-farming craze has truly passed.

Do reply, dearest Kore, and let me know how your own itinerary is shaping up, as I would like to organize a visit with Hecate, to discuss plans regarding our ongoing search for poor Artemis. And you know Hecate's schedule is terribly crowded at this time of year.

Your loving mother,

Demeter

With delicate brown fingers the goddess dusted the wet ink with fine golden sand, which she shook off onto a small rosewood tray. She folded the crackling hempen sheet in half and slid it into a wallet of moss green, along with three brightly-hued feathers. She then removed a ring from her little finger and sealed the thick envelope by stamping her monogram upon it: an exquisite honeybee, imprinted on a wafer of warm yellow beeswax that the goddess had softened by holding it under her tongue.

Demeter rose from her seat and, attended by her glowing firefly lights, moved majestically up a crystalline spiral staircase that shimmered, nearly invisibly, against the luminescent walls of the cave. Her smooth skin was the color of coffee, her eyes were enormous and black, her lips resembled the opening bud of a pink camellia.

Her bulk was considerable, and yet she moved with a lightness and grace that was indicative of the great vitality of her being. To say that she was fat would be to belie the awe-inspiring beauty that her form embodied. If a pomegranate be fat when it swells and bursts with gemlike fruits, if an ocean wave be fat when it rises to fifteen feet in height before it bends and tumbles as an iridescent rainbowed tube, if a mountain be fat as it reigns in grandeur over the flower-starred plain, then yes, Demeter was fat. Her fecund belly was swollen and hard. Her breasts bulged like melons, the large erect nipples, pointing upward, the color of coral. Ropes of pearls held her gauzy white gown aflutter against her polished skin as she skipped up the stairs lightly, on small brown feet ankleted with a thousand bells, her glorious body rippling and dancing up and down to the rhythm of her movements.

At the top of the stairway perched six splendid peacocks, their jeweled feet gripping large rings of silver that hung from the arched roof of a niche carved into the wall of stone. Demeter hesitated before them. Perhaps she should deliver the letter in person. Then she could learn for herself why Proserpina delayed her return. Persephone might resent the intrusion, she knew, but what if something had befallen her precious girl? As she held the letter pressed to her heart, a thunderclap startled the kingly plumaged birds and they stirred, their silver chains tinkling.

The goddess turned with a frown as, in a flash of brilliance, a muscular form materialized in the air, mounted on an outsized eagle. Turning her back at once to this apparition, she quickly handed her missive to one of the peacocks and unlocked his fetter with a small key, which she wore on a chain around her neck. She watched the bird flap upward with the wallet in his beak.

Before Demeter could turn again to greet her guest, a brawny arm had circled her body, just below her sumptuous bosom, and pulled her from her feet. The gigantic eagle pumped its wings under the added weight as the voluptuous goddess kicked and struggled in the grip of the titanic bearded fellow. Though her fingers ripped tufts of reddish fur from his chest, the man only laughed heartily.

"Sister!" he boomed. "What a welcome! And why art thou sore this time?" He deposited her on a soft bed of moss beside an underground stream, and seizing her jugs in his massive hands, began to nip and nuzzle at them like a hungry baby.

"Damn you Zeus!" she snarled, elbowing him aside. "Why wouldn't I be sore? You show up unannounced, and never once has your errand been to ask me how I fare, much less to assist me with my many vital tasks," Ceres complained. "Get thee hence, I don't have the leisure to entertain you. You expect me to open my legs to you at your command? Next time, make an appointment!"

"*This* is my appointment," Zeus rumbled, lifting his chiton to reveal an erection of inhuman proportions. "Now, can you imagine any other being, beast or human, mortal or immortal, upon whom I would dare to inflict this monstrosity? Whom must I murder, in order to spare you this pleasure, darling Ceres?"

The goddess narrowed her eyes. "That is a pile of horseshit, brother. Let thy gonads be ever so blue, let them be the hue of the sky, yet will I declare, it is no duty of mine to submit to this indignity!"

"No duty, dearest Demeter, but an honor and a great distinction!" Zeus implored, his blue eyes dancing as he stroked the goddess's magnificent flanks.

"Pah!" the goddess spat. "You indiscriminate beast! Take your importunities elsewhere, and begone!" And she withdrew from him, and rising to her feet, turned to depart.

Zeus gazed with ecstasy at her monumental derrière, and cried out in anguished tones, "Ask what you will of me, divine Demeter, and it shall be thine!"

The goddess looked back at him over her shoulder, and shifted her weight, causing a seismic wobble in the gravity-defying buttocks. Jupiter moaned.

"Anything?" she wondered scornfully.

"Anything! I'll bring thee pearls by the bushel, jeweled elephants, jaguars! I'll even put aside Hera, and make thee mine own wife!" he swore.

Demeter laughed. "What, you offer me slavery, to comfort me in my state of neglect? Tempting, but no." She brushed some his chest hair off of the shoulder of her gown, and looked at him sideways through her long black lashes. "But . . . there is *one* thing," she said slowly.

"Name it!" Zeus barked in a strangled voice.

"Persephone . . . has not returned to me at the appointed time. I fear that Hades has given her grief, and this she will not confide to me, because once she defied me, to marry him."

Zeus appeared relieved. "I'll gladly bring the girl home to thee, Demeter. Only ope thy blessed crevasse to my spelunking!" he declared.

"You must swear, on your divine phallus, that you'll not deceive me!

"I swear it!" Jupiter cried, his hand on the sacred object.

"And you must swear that you'll not molest Kore, nor touch her, nor even speak to her, lest she never forgive me for sending you, her hated sire, on such an errand."

Jupiter moaned and cursed. "Damn thy tongue, woman! I swear it!" he finally blurted.

"And," the goddess purred, "you must ensure, whatever may come, that my precious girl be returned to me unharmed within three days!"

"Done!" shouted Zeus, and leaping forward, he seized his promised reward. Taking possession of the stately bottom he kissed and caressed it with savage glee, then lifting her in his powerful arms, he probed her with his mighty tongue until the juice ran down in rivulets of fragrant balsam. The goddess, not one bit unwilling now that she had exacted the god's obedience, wrapped her plump legs around his muscled waist. For a night and a day, the caverns echoed with cries of ecstasy, and the earth itself trembled to the rhythm of the rutting of the divine siblings.

Waiting for the World Serpent

I've been in this house before
Old photographs on the walls
I've been up these secret stairs
Memory . . .

A room where no room could be
Upstairs, everyone is there
Go to the window, see the sky
Starry night

But in your arms I'm warm
In your arms I'm warm
But in your arms I'm warm
In your arms I'm warm

The water down below is deep
Let's go to the other side
Walk round to the far shore
Let's go in . . .

Have you heard the legend of
A golden egg beneath the waves?
One man chosen to dive down
Water blue

What brought us together?
Jugglers and minstrels
Lawyers and ladies,
On the roof dancing

Everyone waiting
Knowing the diver
Has gone to the bottom
Won't be returning

Waiting for the World Serpent
Touched by the first flakes of snow
I look up, I see stars . . .

Stars, I see falling stars, I see falling
Stars, I see falling stars, I see falling
But in your arms I'm warm
In your arms I'm warm
But in your arms I'm warm
In your arms I'm warm
Ahhh

Clockwork Robin, 1994

April 6, 1994 – Portland, OR

Luke lay sprawled on the mossy loam behind the cypress hedge, watching Buzz eviscerate the remains of the Styrofoam meat tray, and feeling absolutely devastated. Finally it was really coming home to him, how monumentally he had screwed things up.

He'd felt elated not so long ago, when he realized that Charity's unconventional memorial speech, or the public response to it, seemed to have in some small way reversed the decomposition process that ravaged his zombie corpse. He'd begun to detect a ray of hope for himself. For the first time since he'd come back, in fact for the first time in much longer than that, he'd felt the soggy blanket of despair lift from his heart.

But the problem with those damn hope rays was, sooner or later they always exposed a flaw, a deal-breaker, a canker in the rose. More disappointments were sure to follow.

The first flaw was that the physical change in him was so slight. Here it was, his fucking memorial, and so far just a tiny shift in his appearance had occurred. Events like this were a one-time affair. How would it ever be possible to change enough people's minds about him, to get him back his angel body?

The second and more serious flaw was that the error was built into the process. From the start Luke had eagerly given the world what it wanted. And what the world wanted to see wasn't just a sarcastic adolescent who can't do his chores without saying something petulant. They'd wanted to see the underbelly of their own guilt, made flesh in a form that could be ruthlessly exterminated.

Luke had known all along that the mass culture was the voice of the enemy. A reflexively paranoid druggie and avid bum whose fondest dream had been to seduce and corrupt his listeners, fellow devotees of the Church of Punk, into sharing his ritualized cathartic mayhem, he had carefully flaunted his agenda inside incomprehensible lyrics and incoherent tirades. Even at the time, Luke had understood that his self-mocking, nihilistic stance, destructive tantrums, even his occasional moments of earnestness, would all be co-opted the moment that his work entered the media stream and passed through its marketing mechanisms. But he had believed that he'd somehow be able to transcend all that through his art.

And now he knew that he was wrong. In fact, he'd done exactly the opposite of what he'd intended. He thought that by continually one-upping the system with his genius for irony, he could infect society with a kind of subversive skepticism that would serve to reveal the tissue of lies that was popular culture. Instead, Luke had become the instrument of everything he despised.

Inspired by the need to anesthetize his own suffering, he'd forged a sound that, though discordant and screaming, was somehow dance-able, addictive. Whether loosening the sinews with its rapid-fire frequencies, or grinding along slow and relaxing as a vibrating recliner, it was a music that galvanized the dissatisfaction and disillusionment of the MTV generation, of the destitute and discounted, in a way that was both liberating and comforting.

Into the post-punk corporate rock wonderland of the Reagan era, a world where rebellion was best defined as a hairstyle, Luke had indeed by this miracle succeeded in injecting his virus of unkempt rage and hormone-infused dysphoria. It metastasized, and as Shambala's music spread out across the globe, the band's corporate overlords had rubbed their hands gleefully and smiled. Luke had founded a monster brand of canned catharsis, all unsuspecting that he had merely provided the establishment with an effective new inoculation against the revolution.

The final, fatal flaw was that what was done was done. And what Luke had done, he could see now, was fail to defend himself from the violation of the crowd while he was alive, and there was no way to go back and change that now. He had been hustled up the slaughter-house ramp like a calf, and had willingly bared his neck for the blade, all the while taunting the butcher and daring him to strike. What a rube he'd been. And what had it all accomplished? Nothing but misery, for himself and his family.

As Luke lay there swimming in a bottomless reservoir of self-reproach, he became aware that Charity's voice was once again echoing from the PA system.

"Hey guys, Brandi Whip from Muckleberry is here, and she wanted to share a few thoughts about Luke," she said in a voice that sounded raspy from crying.

"Thank you, Charity. I just wanted to say . . . I came up with Luke from the days when we were playing no-money gigs with shitty equipment, and getting bottles thrown at us from the audience. We were brothers and sisters then, everyone hyped each other's bands, everyone had each other's back, and though we didn't have much, we were a tribe. And Luke remained a brother, even after he made it to the big time. If it wasn't for Luke and Shambala, Muckleberry would still be playing no-money gigs with shitty equipment and getting bottles thrown at us from the audience."

"Shut the fuck up!" shouted an audience member, hurling a plastic water bottle at Brandi. She dodged the missile with a smile.

"Like so many of the bands that Shambala generously brought into the public spotlight, if it wasn't for Luke, we'd still be scraping along, unable to afford a home to go to, a family life, or any of the rewards that we'd dreamed of during those grueling years on the road. So thank you Luke, for being a true friend. We'll miss you, brother."

Then another voice spoke up. It was Chevy Celica, Luke's best friend since high school: towering over Luke by a foot, with the long legs of a heron, the master of the drubbing bassline had remained a loyal sideman all through the years.

"Luke was the kindest, most caring friend anyone could have,"

Chevy said softly. "And he never stopped believing in the punk way. Nobody was more of a somebody than anybody else was, that was Luke's credo. All he ever wanted was to be part of something real, to give it his all. Luke Mandrake, as long as your music lives, you'll live on. Anarchy forever!"

Luke was not really enjoying the speeches. He couldn't stop thinking about how he had dis-invited Chevy and his wife Kirsty from their lives. How he'd permitted his lawyers to renegotiate the music royalty contract to get a larger share for himself.

Their friendship had been strained over the last two years, and listening to Chevy eulogize him now was little short of excruciating. As for Brandi Whip–why, he hadn't seen Brandi in years.

Luke had distanced himself from most of his old friends–anyone who wouldn't let him get away with using to the point of nodding out, without giving him some serious shit about it. He'd become so self-conscious about his drug use, that he had intentionally isolated himself.

Someone else had taken up the mic and launched into another tribute. It went on for over an hour, this relentless orgy of gratitude and sorrow and undeserved deification. Luke found it agonizingly embarrassing.

But, he also did not fail to notice that the more people extolled him as a saintly figure, the more his rotting bits firmed up, grew back or scarred over.

"By the end of this, I might actually be able to jerk off," he mused. At least there was the possibility of some compensation for the discomfort he was enduring.

Luke's mind strayed and he began to idly pick up on the thoughts of those nearby. The vicinity was crowded with people, thousands of them. There were several reporters lurking about, pontificating on camera, interviewing stragglers, ringing the doorbell in hopes of getting a few moments of conversation with Charity, or anyone else who would talk to them.

I'll make you pay! The mental projection hit Luke's mind from close at hand.

Jules!

Jules was thinking about Charity when he sent that curse out into the universe. Luke zeroed in on the thoughts of the bearded, thirty-something biker dude, who was lounging a few feet away on the other side of the hedge, with his helmet under his arm, wearing a fringed red leather jacket and leather leggings over, incongruously, padded cyclist tights. He liked to protect his balls, did Jules. He especially liked getting his balls cared for and groomed by professionals, did Jules. A cock-of-the-walk he was, and the enormous saddlebags on his motorbike were full of dope and firearms. This guy was the cheerfully dangerous dealer who had visited Luke in his hotel room, just a few days before the fatal overdose.

If she rats me out, Jules was thinking, *there will be hell to pay for that bitch. And Liam too.* Jules smiled innocently at a couple of girls who went by, raising his beer jovially. But inwardly, his mind seethed with schemes related to the circumstances of Luke's demise. He really shouldn't even have come, but the temptation to return to the scene of the crime was too great. Not out of guilt, but out of the desire to display a sort of barbaric brutality in his willingness to hawk heroin at Mandrake's funeral. Jules felt that this was the correct move in the psychological game he was playing with Charity. What he didn't realize, Luke divined, was that Charity knew nothing about the deal.

But there was more to be gleaned from the manic stream of Jules's consciousness. A private investigator working for Charity had been snooping around, asking all kinds of stupid questions. People were freaking out. But the guy was a moron, he'd believe anything, people said. A lot of 'em had been amusing themselves by telling outrageous tales. And many of Luke's old friends had a grudge against Charity, blaming her for the way Luke had changed.

Those jealous, spiteful jerks, Luke thought bitterly. *Why wasn't I allowed to fall in love and be happy, retire from the public eye, to immerse myself in the pleasures of family life?*

Jules was pleased that Charity had proved so unpopular with the locals. It would be easy to turn public sentiment against her. All they needed was a good story, and somebody dumb enough to "squeal."

Luke was going to have to keep an eye on this dude, and on that private investigator, wherever he was. Luke scanned the neighborhood, wondering if the fellow was around. He picked up a conversation inside the house that interested him.

"What was their relationship like? Did they fight?"

"No more than any couple might, I guess. Charity is very straightforward and . . . Luke could be sensitive to that sometimes." That was Liam, Luke knew.

"What about the property? Did Luke have a will?" Who was this guy? The gumshoe?

He suspects Charity. Thinks she murdered me for my money. Christ, what a moron.

"I wouldn't know anything about that," Liam said. "I'm more of a family friend than, like, a lawyer or something."

And Liam, Liam has something he's hiding.

He assisted in the cover-up of Luke's overdose. Assisted . . . Doug Clinquant from Ded Leper!

It was all starting to make sense now. Luke's heroin death was too much of a 70's rock cliché, of course. They had to make it look more dramatic, in order to protect the consistency of the brand. In order to sell more records.

Those money-grubbing fuckers!

Luke turned his vigilance back upon Jules. That guy was going to be a serious problem. How could he get rid of him? If only he could get into the gun safe . . . but even if his thumb-print was still intact, which Luke doubted, and even if the lock were still functional, which it was not–Well, picture that! Zombie Luke bursting out of hiding in a blaze of gunfire at his own funeral?–not the ideal solution to Charity's problems, or his own.

He needed a plan.

Touching on Jules's mind, he detected an uneasy urge to depart. A cop car had already parked up the road a piece with its lights flashing, and another was pulling into the cul de sac now. It was getting a bit too warm.

I've made my point, Jules was thinking. *Time to hit the trail.* Luke extracted the coordinates of the dealer's hideaway, and filed the information away in his mind. He might just have to pay a visit to Jules. One day soon, when he was better armed.

Eternity, **Hades**

Pluton sank both hands deep into the chest full of sparkling cut gems, fingering them, feeling them slide against his skin. The coldness, the hardness excited him. His eye caught for a moment on the ring on his left hand, the one Persephone had presented to him as a wedding gift. The rubies, amethysts and emeralds, cunningly fashioned in the shape of an orchid, winked at him. For his part, he had prepared not a ring, but a collar of diamonds, dripping with pendants and clusters that fell, sinuous and heavy, over her breast and limbs. It had suited her perfectly.

The splendor of his wedding gift was eternal, the purity of the diamonds flawless . . . unlike his wife's fidelity.

Hades had disported himself with Proserpina's corpse for some days without rest. Now, having possessed her body in every way that he desired, he felt nothing but disgust for the cadaver. It was decided.

"Let her eat diamonds, drink diamonds, forever more!" Hades murmured.

He would fill a vug with gems, and there he would entomb his late bride in a nest of ice and fire, within a chamber of reflections and sharp angles. Here he would keep her, forever perfect, forever preserved.

Hades snapped his jewel-encrusted fingers, and ten thousand sleek black rats emerged from the shadows and corners of the vast treasure-room. He snapped again, and ten thousand moles crept from crevices and holes. A third time he clicked his middle finger and thumb together, and ten thousand enormous army ants swarmed out from the cracks and chinks in the floor and furniture. He turned to Hanuman, who stood nearby respectfully, and gave his orders. The monkey god bowed.

Soon the rats began their task of gathering all the diamonds in

Pluto's storerooms into a single gigantic pile. The moles hastened to the work of polishing and planing the refracting surfaces in the tomb, which was to be within the subterranean vacuity of a celestine geode twenty feet across, its inner surface bristling with sword-like, pale blue crystals.

"Let her at last be slowly pierced from all sides as these crystals grow, until, bones shattered and calcified, riven flesh reduced to its chemical essence, she is one with the stone," Hades whispered to himself with ineffable satisfaction, as he watched the marching line of ants carry their burdens, gems beyond price, into the opening and deposit them on the floor of the spike-walled chamber.

"My Lord," Hanuman said at his elbow, "when shall I bring her to you?"

"She must be cleansed, and attired in silk and pearls," Pluton rumbled. "Then let her be brought here to me."

The monkey god, with a question-mark curl of his snow-white tail, bowed low before Hades and departed to execute his commands.

The Dark Lord continued to watch the caravan of insects for a long while, as they filed in and out of the sarcophagus of living stone. Now that in his mind Persephone had been utterly disembodied, a curious notion took shape: in digesting a goddess, what powers might not this massive geode, this crystalline gut, gain? Would this space not take on an oracular status? He was intrigued by the possibilities, and it irritated him that the natural process must occur in a geological time-frame. Could he not speed it up? For he missed her, his oracle of divine beauty, his orchid of night, and he had not yet even buried her. He needed to erase her, and yet simultaneously to preserve her essence in some way, as quickly as possible.

Hades at length began to wonder how the preparations for the burial were proceeding. Whom had the monkey god selected to wash and anoint the body? What jewels would be chosen? Would Kore be dressed in a rich gown, or bound, nude but for her fetter-like gems, in winding-sheets of pale silk?

He would not be satisfied, he concluded, unless he attended to these details himself.

∗   ∗   ∗

Hermes, still in the form of a winged ape, flitted in haste through the caverns of Hell, toward Hades's glistening palace of obsidian. His heart was leaden, and his mind raced with schemes for defeating the Dark Lord's vile purpose. It seemed possible Hades did not yet know that Persephone lived on in the body of the vulture.

He would have to bring the bird back here, alive, to resuscitate the Queen, and he could not light upon a plan to do so that did not involve disobeying Death. This he could not risk, for not only was his own future at stake, but if he defied his master in attempting to restore Kore to life, the outcome would be unpredictable. Hermes had enemies among the gods, who were Hades's allies. They might even persuade Zeus to ratify Proserpina's death sentence.

No, what he needed to do was get a message to Demeter. But how could he, if she did not summon him? It was distressing, this loss of freedom and agency.

Robin would never use me so.

He had to win his way back to his beloved Eros. But how?

Hermes entered the apartment where Persephone's body lay. He had sent for her handmaidens, and the women had already gathered there. Childlike Madame Du Barry was tearfully and tenderly brushing her mistress's hair, while hook-nosed Cleopatra found fault with the burial raiment that Dido was embroidering. Voluptuous, cow-eyed Dido erupted melodramatically with portentous declarations of the punishment she believed would befall Hades for the murder of his wife. Meanwhile Mata Hari, graceful and remote, prepared the unguents and spices for embalming.

136

Quickly Hanuman informed the women of Hades's wishes regarding the preparation of the corpse. He was interrupted by an unmistakable clap of thunder. Zeus was paying Pluton a visit.

To avoid any suspicion falling upon myself, I must arrange for Death to be caught red-handed with the Maiden.

Wince felt his heart lighten as he sprang out to the portico to welcome the Ruler of Heaven. Zeus was helping Demeter out of the dragon chariot.

"Welcome, your Majesties," Hanuman said with a bow.

"Hermes, damn you! Where is my daughter?" Zeus thundered without preamble.

"My King, for which daughter are you searching?"

"Proserpina, you banana-eating numbskull!" roared Jupiter.

"She's not in her chambers, nor are her maidens. Where is she?" Demeter demanded, wringing her plump hands. "Where is my darling girl!?"

"The Queen is missing?" The simian deity replied, opening his eyes wide. "Oh my, oh my. I will inquire into this issue immediately, and when she is found, I'll bring her the most urgent message that you desire her to attend upon you without delay." He bowed profoundly, with a graceful flourish of his tail.

"But surely your Majesties will require refreshment during your wait. Please, seat yourselves," the monkey god gestured toward the grand couch and armchair that furnished the underground patio, "And I will procure delicacies for your amusement."

"Skip the refreshments, and bring me Kore," Zeus bellowed, but Hanuman had already produced, in the twinkling of an eye, a golden tray laden with goblets of wine and small tarts filled with fig paste, which he set down on a low table carved from purple chalcedony.

*　　　*　　　*

137

The King of Hell had long been used, when he did not wish to be observed, to making his way through the halls of his vast domain in the form of a large and powerful bat. It was thus that he spied upon his subjects, taking pleasure in their punishments, and surveyed the counting of his riches. If especially concerned about secrecy, he wore the cap of invisibility, but that was rarely necessary within his own borders. Now Pluton fluttered and whizzed through a labyrinth of chambers and flues, until he arrived at his private apartments. And there, upon the portico that opened from the antechamber to his own retreat, he spied Zeus and Demeter, the latter sitting stiffly on the cushions adorning an ebony settee in the Egyptian taste.

Hades backed in the air and settled on a crystal crag to listen in with his bat ears.

"Surely Kore has been troubled of late," The Earth goddess turned from the king of gods to Hanuman as her complaints echoed in the vaults of the cavern. "For she has not answered a single one of my letters in many a day."

"Has Hades grieved her somehow, that she would neglect her mother so?" Jove demanded.

"Only the Lord of Night can answer that question," the monkey god replied, "and my lord is not within."

"Well if thy lord returns not before I lose my temper . . ." Zeus's thunderous voice died out threateningly.

"I shall go at once and seek him, but first I must search for an item from his chambers, which he has sent me to retrieve." Hanuman bowed profoundly, then vanished through the curtain that hung in the entrance, emblazoned with the image of Cerberus.

As the rich, thick brocade of the curtain fell closed, the eyes of the three-headed demon-dog glittered. The heads seemed to shift when the curtain moved, staring at the two deities.

"I've never been in there," Zeus admitted cautiously.

"Well I'm going to enter, and Pluto's spies be damned!" Demeter said, rising from the divan. Zeus folded his arms and watched her as the goddess put her hand up to the drapery. Instantly the woven heads began to bark and snap, but she ignored them, and resolutely drew the curtain aside.

"Demeter," Hades purred, landing lightly on the portico while transforming from bat to man, "are you perchance looking for me?"

Zeus shouldered in front of the corn goddess as she turned to face their elder brother. "Where is my daughter, Hades?" he thundered, "and be quick about answering, for I'm mightily annoyed!"

"Why Zeus, Persephone is but now taking her diamond bath, a pleasure she's recently adopted. It leaves the skin smooth and translucent–you must try it some time, dear sister," he nodded to Ceres.

"Lovely. I'll gladly join her immediately," Demeter pressed.

"It would be best if you waited for her here," Death replied.

"Fine. I'll wait," said Demeter abruptly, dropping back onto the settee with such determined force that it screeched backward, its gilded paws shuddering across the marble pavement. Then she glared at Pluton impatiently.

Zeus anxiously regarded the matching chair, which looked particularly uncomfortable with its golden rosettes along the backrest, and Anubis figurines carved one on each side, inlaid with carnelian and lapis lazuli. "I will come with thee, Hades. I would see this diamond bath," he rumbled.

"No you shan't!" Ceres said firmly.

"Sit, sit, brother," Hades murmured softly, "I will bring her to thee." And he entered the bedchamber hastily, pulling the curtain shut behind him, and then quietly closing the iron-studded door.

Hanuman was nowhere to be seen, and the massive couch was unoccupied. *Good. He has taken the Queen's body out through the secret door.*

"Well, don't just stand there weeping," Hades snarled at the women. "Follow them!" And with a wave of his arms he transformed

the four into birds: Du Barry a chubby dove, Cleopatra a pied fal-
con, Dido a white cockatiel and Mata Hari an osprey. The creatures
whirled above his head, skreeking.

"Hush! Quiet!" he hissed. "Come along!" and he led them into
an alcove where he pressed a certain button of onyx hidden among
the inlays on the ebony paneling. The panel slid aside, and chous-
ing the birds along in front of him, Hades transformed himself once
more into a bat, and made his escape.

*   *   *

Demeter selected a fig tart, and popped it into her mouth. But
before she bit down, she had opened her lips again in surprise, for
out from between them flew an iridescent hummingbird. The tiny
creature zipped around her head and then lighted on the goddess's
thumb. In less than a second, a slip of paper no larger than a basil leaf
had unfurled from its tiny beak. Ceres seized this note and examined
it closely.

"What does it say?" Zeus demanded.

"You are invited to attend the Gala Entombment of Queen
Persephone," the goddess read out. "Follow me!"

The tiny bird rose into the air and hovered, awaiting them.

"To the chariot!" Zeus hollered.

*   *   *

Hades, the handmaidens and Hanuman converged at the vug,
whither the monkey god had carried Proserpina. The diamonds were
spilling out of the opening now like a waterfall. Sparkling pebbles
rolling down into the still pool below. Atop the mound of gemstones

140

Hanuman knelt, laying Kore down in all her glowing beauty. There were ropes of pearls, twisted together with diamond-studded chains, wound around her neck and waist, across her bosom. Her wrists and ankles were heavy with chains of pearls and white gemstones. A cocoon of silk caught to her body under her breasts and about the knees by jeweled bonds concealed nothing of her form, and her thick black curls were crowned with fresh lilies braided into straps of crystal bead work. Hades drew in his breath sharply when he saw her.

He was beginning to regret having killed his wife, and to cast about in his mind for what could be done to remedy the situation. It was of course highly irregular, but he might have to try and bring her back. This would solve both his problems: that of deflecting Zeus's anger, and that of avoiding telling the Ruler of Olympos the humiliating story of Persephone's faithlessness. But there was only one problem with recalling her spirit: it would require petitioning the three Fates. He would have to think of some way to ensure their silence.

The four serving women were clustered around Kore's body. Hades parted them and lifted his wife's corpse in his arms. As he turned around, there was a blinding flash and a peal of thunder, and a chariot appeared, drawn by winged serpents, and with Zeus and Demeter its riders.

"My baby!" Demeter shrieked, vaulting out of the chariot toward Hades. She came on like a charging rhinoceros, with Zeus close behind, and threw herself on the bosom of her daughter.

"Persephone," she cried, "speak to me, my love!" But though the distraught mother shook her and kissed her and chafed her wrists, the youthful goddess did not respond.

"What is this, Hades?" Zeus thundered. "What have you done to her?"

The Lord of the Underworld opened his mouth to speak, but nothing came out.

"My darling Kore breathes not! She is gone!" wailed Ceres.

"Calm thyself, sister," Zeus said soothingly. "I will soon set things to rights." He took his daughter tenderly from her husband's arms, handed her limp form to the monkey god, then turned and, as fast as lightning, caught his brother such a blow to the temple that Hades's head whipped around backwards and he flew up into the air, legs flailing, before crashing down onto the pile of diamonds.

"Explain yourself, Pluton!" he bellowed. Hades groaned.

"Not dead, I believe, but merely sent to Earth in another form!" Hanuman interrupted, looking down at Persephone. "Show him, my Lord," he said, nodding to Hades encouragingly.

The Lord of the Underworld lifted himself with a whimper from the tinkling hoard. What was the simian servant saying? Persephone not dead? How could that be?

There was one sure way to find out.

Hades raised his left hand, emitting a greenish glow from the palm, that glinted on the facets of the precious stones. In that light it could now be seen that all around them, the cavern was crowded with the luminescent forms of the whispering, unseen dead.

"Look!" cried the monkey god. A thin sallow thread of marsh-light trickled from Kore's nostril, ran along the ground a short distance, then angled up and away through the stone roof above, up toward the land of the living.

Demeter rounded on Hades with blasting fury in her eyes. "How did you dare?! You –you sent her to be incarnated among the– the filth, the wretches, the *living*?"

"Call her back this instant!" Zeus commanded, menacing his brother with a monstrous fist.

"I would gladly do so," Hades flinched, "if I only knew where she is, or what she has become."

"What!?" roared Zeus, over her mother's despairing wail, "Is this how you care for my daughter, you rogue?!"

"Gracious King, allow me!" Hanuman handed Kore to her

parents reverently. He then made obeisance before them, flirting his tail as he declared, "I think I know whither she has gone." The other three deities gazed at him expectantly. "My King, and thou, goddess of all that is good," he went on, bowing again, "I promise that your daughter will be restored to you on the morrow. But I must advise Hades of my thoughts, and seek his advice in return. We must plan and labor together to regain her. Will you give us leave to depart on this errand?"

"I still don't understand what she's doing among mortals in the first place," Demeter scowled. "My brother Pluto has offered no explanation!"

"The Lord of the Dead did not wish to reveal to the mother the secrets which must come only from a daughter's lips," the monkey god said delicately, glancing at Hades, who merely rolled his eyes away and tapped his toe in irritation.

"She has a paramour, is that what you're suggesting?" Zeus surmised. "Ah ha ha! She's her father's daughter, after all!" he crowed. Then he favored Hades with a look of such insufferable smugness that the cuckolded husband's face turned gray and he began to tremble with fury.

"Hades," Demeter hissed, "you have twenty-four hours. If you fail to restore my Persephone to life by then, I'm bringing you up before the Olympic Court on charges of murder!"

"Dearest sister," the Lord of Night protested coldly, "you forget yourself. I am the injured party here, and Proserpina's punishment was decreed by Themis and Hecate!"

"Oh, was it?" Ceres snapped. "I shall consult them myself, brother, and you may depend upon it, I will learn the whole truth."

"As you wish, Demeter." Hades could not suppress the sarcasm in his voice. "But now, au revoir, for I must hasten if I am to comply with your demands!" With that he leaped onto the gryphon that stood by, and the beast clapped its wings.

The monkey god rose up on his blue pinions and followed his lord, calling down to the pair of gods below, "Twenty-four hours, on my honor!"

"Do you believe them?" Jove wondered.

"Well, Hanuman is up to something, and poor Hades appears to have no more clue what it is than we do," Ceres replied. "But Hermes will find her, if anyone can."

"Leave it to Mercury, I always say," Zeus responded. "The guise of monkey god makes him ridiculous, but he's far cleverer than Hades will ever be."

"Poor Pluton. His blindness is a malady none can cure, I fear," Demeter sighed.

"You pity him?"

"I pity my daughter, to have married such a living statue of a man," the goddess replied tartly.

The divine pair seated themselves in the serpent-drawn chariot, Holding on their laps the body of their precious child, they vanished in a clap of thunder.

*   *   *

The Lord of the Damned hastened toward his chambers, and Hanuman followed in a feverish state of apprehension. He felt sure that Hades was going to accuse him of betrayal, and he considered attempting to arrive before him in order to dispose of the evidence. However, this struck him as damningly suspicious, so he decided to feign innocence for as long as he could.

Fortunately Pluto strode right past the tray of message tarts on the patio without giving them a second glance, and Wince was able to slip them into his leather wallet before going inside.

Hades had of course made straight for the blow, and was already feverishly cutting lines with a razor blade on the polished obsidian surface of his desk. He ignored Hanuman and sucked up a deadly quantity of the stuff before leaning back in his batwing chair. Then he turned to the monkey god.

"Damn it, there are no mirrors here, I suppose?

"My lord, I can supply you with a mirror," the blue-and-white ape replied. He opened a drawer in the sideboard, and extracted a powder compact, which he handed to the King of Hell with a bow.

"Will this do, my lord?"

Hades took the tiny case in his enormous white hand, and flipped it open. He held it up so that he could get a good look at the discolored bruise that had risen on the side of his temple, probing it delicately with a finger, and wincing. Then he dabbed some of the pale powder on it, hissing with pain. As he did so he muttered.

"That's it! Infernal thug, interfering clod! Great Zeus, ohh, right! I'll boil your churlish buttocks in oil, I'll–" he halted, remembering the presence of Hanuman, and rounded on him.

"Can you find her?" Death demanded.

"Your lordship, I believe I can . . . I can but try."

"TRY?!" The god of the dead slammed his fist down on the stone surface so violently that Wince was sure he must have fractured some bones, but the crazed deity was apparently too benumbed by coca to feel it. He merely snorted another huge pile of the drug, and commenced muttering again. "It's that cursed zombie, he's still out there, he's alive somehow. I must destroy him! But–but not until I've restored her to . . . " Hades scrunched his face into a grimace, eyes squeezed shut. "Damn it all, Hermes, what must I do?"

"My lord Hades, if I may suggest?"

"What? What is it, Monkey-man?" Pluto's mouth hung open and he breathed through it harshly. "Speak!"

"Give me the key, my Lord; allow me to unlock the chain, and set the bird free. If this is done in the presence of Kore's divine body, her spirit will return to its rightful home."

Hades narrowed his eyes, "Why should I give it you? It is I alone who must turn the key." The Lord of Night inverted the stone jar that held his stash, shook it, and a few last yellowish chunks bounced out onto the desktop. He eyed them greedily.

"Assuredly my lord, and yet . . . if it be you who turns the key, there is a chance that the bird will die at the touch of your hand. And if the bird dies, might not Kore then die, and be lost to you?"

Hades sighed, and sat slumped and still for a while as the gears turned in his battered brain. At last he lifted his fevered, bloodshot eyes to Hanuman's face.

"You speak truly, Mercury. But see here," Death rose up to his full height and fixed Hermes with a manic gaze, "you must not fail to deliver the undead creature, the zombie boy, to me for vengeance, or . . . or his fate will be visited upon you in his stead!"

A shadow swept over Hades's face, and yet his bleary eyes glistened as he pointed toward the door with a long claw.

"Go, monkey god, and return as soon as you may, to report to me what you have found. Then, perhaps, I will give the key into your keeping. Now go!"

April 7, 1994 –Brooklyn, NY

"What exactly is wrong with you?" said the emergency room doctor. She was young and pretty, with a dark pony-tail, and a sharpness to her voice that brought water to Rosetta's eyes. Rosetta wasn't usually this over-wrought, but then she'd nearly fainted on her way into the exam room.

This was not the way her body usually responded to a simple cold. Rosetta was almost never sick, but just now her throat was so painful she could barely swallow. She had been resting and taking care of herself, hoping to throw the malady off, but it wasn't working. Her glands were painfully swollen, she had a fever, she ached all over, and she felt confused and dizzy.

"I have a really bad sore throat," she whispered, "and I went to the clinic, and they said I needed a pregnancy test, and they told me to come here."

"Are you pregnant?" the doctor demanded, looking at Rosetta suspiciously.

"I don't know . . . I haven't had a normal period for a couple of months. They . . . they said at the clinic that they couldn't give me a prescription unless I got a pregnancy test."

"Don't they do that at the clinic?"

"Not until Monday," Rosetta replied. She felt so tired. Tears trickled down her cheeks.

"All right," the doctor said grudgingly. "I'll take a throat culture, and arrange for your test."

She had walked a mile to the clinic in a daze, and nearly collapsed in the waiting area, hardly able to keep her head up. Luckily Methodist Hospital was only a few blocks further.

She waited in the hospital emergency room for hours before they called her again. This time a different physician sat down with her.

"The pregnancy test was negative," he said. "We won't have the results of your throat culture until tomorrow."

Walking home, the wind cut through Rosetta's coat as it drove tiny flakes of snow up against the windshields of the cars that inched along Seventh Avenue. She pulled her scarf tighter around her neck and ears, and worried about the cherry blossoms and the daffodils at the park. Would they survive a freeze?

Her throat felt dry and raspy. She stepped into a small newsstand shop, and selected a packet of cough drops from the candy display.

As she stood in line at the register, Rosetta stared at the newspapers and magazines on the racks. The face of Luke Mandrake, wearing a tormented expression, was plastered on the covers of half the periodicals. The headlines saddened and upset her: *Death of a Rock-and-Roll Legend. Luke Mandrake, Voice of a Generation. Luke Mandrake's Final Hours.* Even though she had never met Luke, Rosetta felt the tragedy personally, and not only because of the oddly prescient visions that had come all unbidden to her in sleep. There was also a natural identification with Luke and Charity, parents who struggled to raise a child while pursuing careers in music. What happened to that poor couple was so sad! Tears stung in her eyes again. Boy, she was an emotional wreck.

Arriving home in the afternoon, Rosetta took some Tylenol and fell into bed. She had woken up burning, but now she was shivering, her whole body ached, and she had a stiff neck.

Right before falling asleep, Luke's anguished visage rose before her mind's eye once again. What did he want from her? Why was he haunting her this way?

I hope you find rest, and peace, Rosetta prayed. *Let your soul fly transcendent toward the light.*

Still he gazed at her disconsolately, as if to say, *For me there can be no redemption, no escape from the prison of guilt.*

Her heart overflowed with pity, and moved by an impulse she didn't fully understand, Rosetta cried out to Luke with her mind: *You are forgiven! Not that it's my place to forgive, not that it comes from me. I just want you to know that the forgiveness is there, that a profound and limitless grace surrounds you. Only hold out your hands, your heart; only close your eyes, and you'll feel the kiss of mercy on your eyelids. Only believe!*

Cherishing this thought in her heart, Rosetta slipped into the deepest of slumbers.

April 7, 1994 – Portland, OR

Hermes sank slowly through a thick, chilly layer of cloud. He had shed the guise of Hanuman, the monkey god, and his hat was dripping with condensation. In his hands he held a deospectrometer, among the most useful of his many inventions. It looked a bit like a small movie camera, with its rubber eyepiece.

It had been surprisingly easy to locate Luke and Persephone using the device, which displayed a brightly colored image of whatever it was pointed at, in which certain energies were visually enhanced. This one had a setting for detecting mortal ghosts and spirits, another that revealed the presence of advanced supernatural beings, and one that picked up artificial intelligences and mechanical beings. There was also an infrared setting, a setting for tracking down really good vegetarian sandwiches, and one that located the nearest extremely horny homosexual man, a function upon which Hermes had applied for a patent. Sadly, he had decided it was too dangerous to allow the technology to fall into mortal hands, and had never manufactured the product. However, he had received a very interesting letter from one of the attorneys working at the US patent office. It read simply:

to: Hermes Trismegistus,
PO Box 333, James A. Farley Station,
New York NY 10001.

Dear Sir,
HAHAHAHAHAHAAHAHAHA
Pervert! I hope you burn in hell.

Yours Truly,
Eldon P. Forsyth, Esq.

Wince had framed the letter, and it now hung above the desk in his apartment at Eros's Palace on Olympos.

Mercury wiped the lens with the sleeve of his caftan. The deospectrometer kept fogging up. He was currently using the device merely to guide him toward his selected target. This was working nicely, because the energy reading from the target was unusually robust. Searching for an Immortal Incarnate usually offered a slight challenge, requiring that Hermes be within a quarter mile to read the signal. If his quarry were a god merely visiting the earth, the device tended to pick up a signal from up to ten miles away. In the case of Luke and Persephone, the two were broadcasting a wide-spectrum supernal signal that was detectable at fifty miles. Wince could not entirely account for this, but it was certainly making his job easier.

Wince had now zeroed in on the coordinates: a derelict vehicle, boxy and originally bright red, rusting away in the tall grass near a house that overlooked the Willamette River, just south of the city. Apparently, Luke and Persephone were inside.

Hermes paused, considering what to do next. He needed to talk to his sister, and would have preferred to do so alone, but obviously that wasn't possible.

He was starting to realize that should have brought Demeter and Zeus here immediately. Hades could discover the truth about Kore at any moment, and when he did, it would be too late to summon reinforcements.

***Eternity* – The Obsidian Palace, Hades**

The moment Hermes departed, the Lord of the Dead rose and approached the expansive, mirror-like wall of obsidian behind his gargantuan desk.

"Project Carnality," he uttered darkly. Instantly the outline of a file drawer appeared upon the featureless stone, and slid open. Hades pulled out a folder marked *zombie–data*. He opened it and perused the report within,

"Here's something new," he said thoughtfully. "Who is this Rosetta Stone? Hmm. The signal originated in Brooklyn, New York . . ."

Death moved to the adjoining wall, which was of even greater proportions, upon which tiny lights in amber, red and green twinkled in hundreds of long rows. He placed a fingertip over one of the green lights and pressed it. A narrow paper tape began to slide out of the wall from beneath it, and he scanned this tape, muttering under his breath. "Sykes. Swope. Svenska. Sudyka. Stone, Xavier. Stone, Samantha L. Stone, Reginald. Hmmm. No Rosetta Stone here." He scratched his beard. "Damnable device! Wait . . . what's this? Stone-Delgado, Penelope R., 198 17th Street."

The King of Hell tore out a piece of the tape, proceeded back to the file wall, and intoned, "Penelope Rosetta Stone." A drawer slid open, he riffled through the folders, and removed one.

"*Penelope Rosetta Stone, born 1960. Currently resides in Brooklyn, NY. One child. Husband, Aron Delgado. Occupation: visual and performing arts.* This must be the one." He leafed through to the notes. "*Category: Prismatic Love Node.* Ah, interesting. She'll broadcast a strong signal at transition, something that cursed adept will surely pick up. Excellent, excellent.

"Hmm. She has a guardian angel, I see. Molière! My, my, the great playwright has a debt to discharge, does he? Well, well, well. I'll have to deal with that comedian first, I suppose."

Hades picked up the receiver of the old-fashioned telephone on his desk, and pressed a button.

"Dispatching," a voice replied in an Eastern European accent.

"Give me the life status on mortal number–" he read from the tape, "57464679.243"

"Very good my lord." There was sound of papers riffling. "Status, living. Condition, illness, non-chronic; life-threat, mild to moderate, prognosis, favorable."

"That's very convenient. What is the sickness?"

"Streptococcal infection. Possible complications: liver damage, meningitis–"

"Meningitis, yes–We'll bump it up to that. Go to coma, take her right to the edge," Death muttered.

"What did you say, Lord Hades?"

"Nothing. I'd like to arrange a booking on her. Please prepare the volume."

"Very good, my lord. Shall I send an agent?"

"No, I'll take this one myself." Death put down the receiver with a smile curving his lips and a light in his manic eyes. He laughed softly. "I do believe the zombie will be mine."

He reached into the pocket of his oil-slick-colored pinstripe suit and pulled out a simple black cap of the Phrygian style. "Hermes, you faithless ape, I know your trickster heart. You'll not deceive me again." And he pulled the cap down over his stiff white locks, and vanished.

Jean-Baptiste lurked in the corner of the bedroom, feeling uneasy. He did not like the way that Rosetta's breathing rasped and labored. He did not like the slowing of her pulse, the depth of her slumber.

Guardian angels could only do so much. He could interfere via dreams, or at most in ways that were small and unnoticed, and then only with his own two hands. He had no tools to fight viruses or bacteria. He had no magical powers to heal the sick. He was merely a ghost, not a god.

He reproached himself. He ought to have stepped in more forcefully, long ago. Why had he permitted the man to wear down her spirit? Why had he not done something dramatic, as he had when she was fourteen?

In fact, he remembered now, he *had* stepped in. He had sent Rosetta pointed dreams more than once–she'd been particularly disturbed by the one in which Delgado was portrayed as a vampire.

She had not heeded the message. *It's only a dream,* she had insisted to herself.

Jean-Baptiste was incensed. When she failed to believe in her dreams, in her instincts, she stopped believing in herself.

And now here she was, desperately ill, and Jean-Baptiste understood why. Her energies were being thwarted, her desires frustrated, her visions dismissed, and she was turning her anger in upon herself.

This couldn't go on. He had to interrupt her downward spiral.

But what could he do? The most potent force to call her back to herself would have been the presence of her child. But the boy was far away.

Could he somehow bring Antoine to her? It seemed a thing beyond his powers.

Jean-Baptiste now became aware of a tiny spark of light hovering near the bed. It slowly grew into a luminous ball that floated above Rosetta's sleeping form. Jean-Baptiste approached with trepidation. Suddenly the sphere shot toward him, and lengthened, resolved into the form of a tall winged man in silvery robes, all aglow. His long white hair was swept up from his pale forehead in a widow's peak. Everything about him was pale. Only his eyes were as black as night.

"Why have you come?" asked Jean-Baptiste, with his heart in his mouth, moving to stand between the Angel of Death and the girl's sleeping form.

"I am come to take her. Stand aside, Molière."

"No, Monsieur Death. It is not her time!"

"She has lost the will to fight for her own life," the Angel of Death intoned.

"Then I'll fight for it!" The playwright hurled himself at the figure before him. Though considerably shorter, he was stocky and surprisingly strong, and succeeded in locking his arms around Hades' waist.

"Unhand me!" The apparition staggered back, then lunged forward, seizing his opponent's upper arms. Jean-Baptiste froze, locked eyes with Death, then kissed the end his nose.

"Don't be so coy darling," he simpered with a wink.

"Buffoon!" the Grim Reaper snarled, trying to throw the comedian to one side. But Jean-Baptiste clung to him, and Death only managed to swing him in a circle.

Molière landed like a cat, and using the momentum, twirled Hades around. Lifting one of Death's arms with a graceful flourish, the actor trilled like a ballet instructor.

"Et coupé-jeté–en tournant!"

"You dare to toy with me?" Hades hissed, snatching his hand away, and shoved Molière backward.

"Ah no, mademoiselle, I do not toy!" He seized Death's hand

again, falling to one knee. Hades snatched his bony fingers away and raised his arm threateningly. Jean-Baptiste flinched with an exaggerated motion.

"It's marriage I dream of, I swear it!" he declared, snatching melodramatically at the robes of the fell visitor, and dragging him down. With some difficulty Death tore himself away from the comedian's grip, and pointed a long finger at him.

Blue flame spurted from Hades's fingertip, and Molière threw himself backward. He struck a pair of French doors, and they burst open. A cold blast of air swept through the apartment.

Is kissing Death terribly bad luck? Rosetta's guardian angel wondered, just before he vanished.

April 7, 1994 – Portland, OR

How soon after the husband dies is it okay to ask a chick out?

Charity is so hot. And so famous. And so fucking rich, especially now! Would she even date me?

Well, why not? She married Luke Mandrake, and he was a psychopathic drug addict. Next to him, I'm gonna look pretty darn appealing.

Ah, this time it was Pete Portnoy, mover and shaker in the entertainment business. Handsome and suave and oh, so useful, with his fat Rolodex of luminaries. Damn him! Another so-called friend, scheming on his widow before Luke's side of the bed was even cold.

What a self-serving fake. People were so revolting. Luke was filled to overflowing with rancid disgust.

He lay curled up under an old blanket, occasionally feeling himself here and there for signs of muscle tone. This was inevitably a disappointing exercise. Since the memorial, he'd remained stuck at a stage of decomposition which, though less disfiguring than before, was far from zero. Luke was emphatically still a zombie, and the bones that jutted through the skin at his wrists, knees and ankles were there to prove it.

Luke had chosen to hide out in a broken-down van that stood on its rims in the back lot behind the next door neighbor's house. The spot allowed him to use telepathy to scan the vicinity while remaining unseen. Even Charity had no idea he was nearby, watching over her. In the bowels of the ancient Toyota Luke had secreted a length of heavy steel cannibalized from a department store mannequin stand, with which, considering that he himself was virtually un-killable, he was sure he could totally fuck up anyone, if necessary.

If a threat to his family arose, he would be ready.

So far the only serious threats he'd encountered were to his own ego.

Not an hour went by when Luke did not wallow in his own personal acid-bath of regrets. Masochistically, he had gone out and acquired a stack of newspapers and magazines with cover articles about his suicide, using some of the money that Charity had thoughtfully tucked into the pocket of the bathrobe. The sensations he experienced while reading news items about himself were as unpleasant as they had always been. The way he was depicted was so different from the way he saw himself, the things the articles focused on so far from what he thought was important, that he barely recognized himself.

For example, the fatuous accounts of his decline in Rolling Stone and Creem had made no more than a passing mention of his activism, if at all. It seemed as though his lifelong advocacy of causes like gay rights and feminism, although he'd talked about them at the slightest opportunity for years, was not even on their radar. There was however endless nostalgic coverage of Luke's rise to stardom–as if that were his primary achievement, rather than his great tragedy! The global influence of his musical style was extolled, and then his dirty laundry always got another airing. Yet all the hand-wringing tales of woe, the tsk-tsking over his marital troubles and his depressive, bi-polar tendencies, failed to resurrect him as a man in any meaningful way, much less capture the essence of his music.

Fercrissake! I was in pain, not insane. And yes, they really were out to get us. Of course they were. Nobody gets it!

But that was nothing compared to the newspaper and TV coverage. So-called journalists displayed nothing more than an obsession with the grisly details of his shocking suicide, nearly all of them fabricated. The sensational media blitz surrounding his demise ensured that Luke was, if anything, losing ground in the fight against zombification.

On the other hand, sales of their latest album *Open Womb* were way up. *Ha ha ha.*

The circumstances he found himself in were in short becoming thoroughly unbearable. If he'd had a useful task to focus on, it might have helped. But the Riverwood police had been vigilant lately in guarding their most luminous celebrity, so there had been no sign of attackers, no frightening nut jobs to terrorize, and even the paparazzi were but thinly distributed in the vicinity. Most importantly, Jules had not put in another appearance. It seemed that there were no bad guys around except for Luke himself, who was well on the way to becoming a stalker, waiting in the night to knock the stuffing out of Charity's next boyfriend.

And obviously he had nobody to blame but himself.

Luke slid inexorably back down into the acid bath. Misery, misery, that was what he was known for now. That was his future identity, his sole legacy. He was nothing more than a lesion on the consciousness of humanity. And he felt so sorry, for himself, for the friends *(well, except for those fucks lining up at Charity's door!)* who had meant hope and joy to him, for the legion of broken kids with whom he had once shared the healing power of music. *Forgive me,* he begged them all silently, *for being such an idiot, a weakling, an ass!*

In the depths of his despair, a voice rang out in Luke's mind.

You are forgiven! A profound and limitless grace surrounds you. Only believe!

For a few seconds, Luke felt it, a healing compassion, a warm glow of merciful love. For a few seconds, he almost did believe.

What the–? Where was that voice coming from? Who had spoken to him in that way?

Luke's mind cast out after the fleeting sensation, trying to follow it home. It seemed so far now, so faint.

Then he saw her before him: the large expressive mouth splashed over a delicate-boned, boyish face; the turned-up nose, the shock of punk-short hair with its gothic widow's peak, the penetrating gray-green eyes under devilish brows.

Jesus. Rosetta Stone? Androgynous yet maternal, painfully lovely, she stood in his memory, embodying everything he longed to be, could never hope to possess.

But now, unaccountably, she had contacted him telepathically, had prayed for him so powerfully that her thoughts had reached him from somewhere far away.

Did she know what he was going through now? Was she that clairvoyant?

"Luke," Buzz rasped, "Let's get outta here. I need to stretch my wings."

Luke stirred, checking the neighbor's house for signs of activity. It was misting a bit, but it seemed like it was safe to take a stroll. And Buzz was right, he needed to take a break from this obsessive vigilance. Listening to the greedy, self-congratulatory fantasies of a parade of persistent pals, arriving to "comfort" his bereaved wife, was turning Luke homicidal and suicidally depressed by turns.

He crept out from under the moldy blanket, and slid open the van door as quietly as he could manage. When he glanced around the yard and noticed a figure standing nearby, he almost yelled. If he'd known somebody was out there, he would at least have made sure his hooded robe concealed him. How had he not known? But the figure gave a friendly wave.

"Hello, Wince," croaked Buzz.

"Kore!" Wince greeted her. "Sorry to drop in on you unannounced, but it's urgent."

"Let's go down to the riverbank where we're less visible," she rasped.

"Very well," said the man, who was dressed in a broad-brimmed leather hat, a brown, bathrobe-like garment made of some rough woven stuff that he wore open to show off his smooth, well-muscled chest, and silky balloon pants. He was incredibly good-looking, Luke noticed, tall and dark, and with a jaunty, gravity-defying bounce to his step that was a little bit irritating. When they were climbing down the path to the river, he wasn't paying any attention to where he put his feet, and always seemed to be on the verge of falling, but he betrayed no anxiety about this. And his shoes were unlike anything Luke had ever seen, tall boots of soft leather with winglike projections on the sides.

Nobody spoke until they were down by the river in the shelter of a stand of cottonwoods that had taken root in the wash zone under the cliffs. Buzz broke the silence.

"Luke, this is my brother Hermes. Hermes, Luke Mandrake."

Luke put out his un-manacled left hand. Hermes seized it in his right, then gave Luke a one-arm hug. Buzz, perched on Luke's other shoulder, flapped her wings a little and preened.

"Nice robe," said Hermes.

"Thank you, uh, Hermes," said Luke, flicking the end of his boa flirtatiously.

"Call me Wince," Hermes insisted. "All my friends do. Look, Kore, I'm glad I was able to find you. Our Dad is searching high and low for you, and your Mom is going crazy trying to get in touch with you. They've gotten Hades to agree to remove the sentence, and let you go home."

"No shit?" said Buzz, looking over at Luke.

"Wow, that's so great!" Luke said, feeling an enormous rush of relief. "That's fantastic news, Buzz! You–"

"But I've got to tell you," Wince interrupted, "Death wants vengeance, and you, Luke, are in dire danger."

"So if we go with you now to Hades, Luke's a goner," Buzz croaked.

"Basically, yes," said Hermes.

"Well that's not going to work, is it?" she rasped. "I can't–"

"Kore, what are you saying? I mean–of course we have to go–" Luke said.

"–Can't do that to Luke after everything–" Buzz went on.

"Seriously, don't worry about me, I can handle Hades–"

"No, Luke!"

"He's going to incinerate you, body and soul, guy!" said Wince.

"But last time he–" Luke began.

"It's my decision, damn it!" screamed the condor, and the other two stopped talking and stared at her.

"Okay, thank you," she went on. "Wince, if I know you, you've got an alternate plan already cooked up. So let's hear it."

Luke felt a wave of nausea wash over him.

Hermes shrugged. "Me, I got nothin'. I think you'd both better go immediately to Demeter, and put yourself under her protection. And frankly, I'll come with you."

"Okay, well, let's talk about transportation," Buzz said. "Do you think you can carry both of us all the way to Greece? I can try to fly it, but that'd take days. I've a feeling we don't have that much time."

Don't have that much time . . .

Luke was feeling very strange. He was descending into a dark place, there in the deep shade under the trees, listening to the lapping of the water. There was a threatening shape taking form in his mind, an apparition of terrible sadness, a dreadful summons. Luke felt helpless and exposed. Tears rose in his eyes and he suddenly began to sob.

"Luke, get a hold of yourself!" Buzz snapped.

"I'm–I'm sorry!" he cried, "I don't know what . . . something's wrong!"

"What is it, Luke?" Hermes spoke gently. "Be more specific, please?"

"It's really bad. Somebody . . . somebody I know is . . ." Luke struggled for the words. "Rosetta! . . . She's dying!"

Luke began to lose consciousness as his astral body zoomed toward the scene of the woman's deathbed. He found himself high above a great cityscape. Then he felt a sickening lurch.

Spring 1994, The Caverns at Eleusis, Greece

Dearest Hera,

I hope this missive finds you well. I'm writing to ask your advice about a very serious matter, so please forgive me if I get right to the point.

Hades has gone too far! After all his despicable acts, he has done poor Persephone to death, and her spirit has fled into the mortal world, to be incarnated I know not how or where. I sit now beside her lifeless corpse, so lovely and so still, and weep until my eyes are likely to go rolling down my cheeks in a flood of tears.

And how did such an egregious act of violence come about? Because our brothers believe that they can get away with anything, and never be accountable. Even now, as I must suppose, Zeus sits on his throne chuckling, waves his cup and calls for another dance from his latest concubine, when he ought to be convening the Council to consider what punishment Pluton must suffer for his iniquity. I fear the beast will in the end be meted no worse a penance than the blow to the head that Jove has already delivered unto him in a moment of rage.

Meanwhile, my precious girl's life is held hostage to merciless chance. It seems to me that the monsters whose laws have condemned her, have no thought for anything but their own pleasure and dominion.

How long must we continue to bear this injustice? The Olympi-an gods have lorded it over us for thousands of years, behaving as if, having steadily smashed one another's skulls in since the Stone Age, this barbarity entitles them to deprive females of all serenity and gratifica-tion, forever.

Well, I've had quite enough of it, Hera. And I expect you have a grievance or two yourself, that requires redress. So, what do you think we ought to do about it?

I say the time has come to reignite our long-plotted Revolution, and to that end, I am calling a secret meeting of goddesses, to be convened here in Eleusis, in the deepest and most private chambers of my complex. Are you in?

And when do you think it would be best to schedule the convocation? We must choose wisely, for it is essential that the brutes know nothing of our plans.

Please advise me of your thoughts. My messenger will await your reply.

With love and devotion,
Your sister Demeter

The corn goddess signed the letter with a flourish, and placed it upon a stack of similar pages she had already penned that day. She inhaled deeply, stretching her torso, her hands on the small of her back.

"Auntie Demeter," said Hebe, the enchanting goddess of eternal youth, entering softly, "your single-mindedness is admirable, but perhaps you'll take a rest now?" She held up a silver dish piled high with fresh fruit. "From Hecate, with her compliments."

"Why thank you, Hebe." Ceres bit into a strawberry. "I've written letters for you to take to Hestia, Hera, Eirenne, Metis, Nike, Rhea, Selene, Eos, Themis, Baubo, Aphrodite, Hygieia, Iris, Phoebe, Leto and Tethys . . . But I'm hesitant to include Athena. She's such a tattle-tale. Do you suppose it's wrong to leave her out?"

"Well, I know for a fact that she's pissed off with Ares for supporting *Don't Ask, Don't Tell.* She's been trying to get him to permit women in combat roles for years, but he always puts his foot down."

"That's promising. But you know, she's such a daddy's girl."

"You mean was. She's been freezing Zeus out lately, too, because he still won't apologize for eating her Mom."

"Good for her. What a wicked thing that was to do, to deprive a girl of her mother, and then take credit for giving birth to her himself, into the bargain. All right, Athena goes on the list, but you must sound her out first."

"I know I can turn her," Hebe proclaimed.

The sound of raucous screams echoed through the cavern. "The peacocks," Demeter said. "Could you be a dear, and go see who it is?"

Hebe returned with an enormous and statuesque Titaness clothed very simply in shimmering gray robes of wool. Her sole ornament was a gold pendant fashioned as a functional set of scales.

"Ah, Themis," said Demeter, "your arrival fills me with delight!"

"Darling Ceres," the goddess of divine law said, and bending down, she held out her arms to her niece, and they embraced.

"You always know when you're needed, Great Aunt," said Hebe, giving her cheek a kiss.

"My dears, I have come in timely dedication to our cause. For as you know, the women of Olympos must soon unite for a single purpose," said the grave and formidable Themis.

"I knew it!" cried Demeter. "I've been writing letters for hours, calling upon all the goddesses to convene for a revolutionary council!"

"I am aware of your design," Themis said, "for I had foreseen it. But I have come, dear Demeter, to offer recommendations for action, and to warn you that our cause cannot proceed until we have a champion."

Hebe shivered. "A champion!"

"And whom do you propose? For I do not believe we can trust a single one of them, not even Hermes," said Demeter.

"You must know of whom I speak. For who was our warrior of old, our ancient advocate and defender?"

"Artemis!" Hebe breathed. "But she is long lost to us, and we have searched for her in vain."

"Not in vain," Themis intoned. "For I have seen the future, and I know what I know."

"If only you were permitted to tell us," Demeter complained.

"For long I have abided by the law of the Olympian Council, which proclaimed that only to Zeus may I transmit my knowledge of days to come. For centuries I have therefore kept my silence, revealing only those things to our king, that would result in the least harm done in service of his overreaching ambition. When pressed by him I would but moan, 'the future is dark before my eyes.' "

Demeter chuckled softly, and Hebe gave a tinkling laugh.

"But today I am on a pilgrimage to every one of my sisters, their daughters, and their daughters' daughters. I cannot reveal all that I know, but I will give counsel to each according to her role."

"Only tell me," cried Demeter, "will Persephone be saved?"

"Kore's life is in the balance, and much depends on what we now do," Themis replied.

"I agree," Demeter replied. "Tell on!"

"Of late under the stars of Pisces, I attended upon the Queen of the Dead, and gave her my counsel. Unto Kore I unveiled some small part of the Divine Plan, that series of events that must lead to the rebirth of Artemis, our champion.

" 'Through these Halls, where once I reigned as Supreme Judge, will come such a one as has the power to find Artemis, and restore her to her rightful place in the Heavens,' I told to her. 'And so be vigilant, and do not fail to greet each mortal that rises toward the firmament on the wings of ardor. For he will come to thee clothed in flame, garlanded with the laurels of renown, and carrying a burden of suffering beyond a mortal's portion. That none may know him, he will come armored with ignorance of his own nature, and a dark cloud of mystery will surround his origins. But he is that One before whom all the gods must bow, whether they will or no. And it is for him a divine destiny, to sow what cannot be sown, to reap what cannot be reaped, and to unearth that which has been buried for a long, long age in the hearts of men. When he comes to thee, help him, protect him, but do not betray his true nature, not even to himself. For should you do so, all the deep machinations of Isis, and indeed all the impassioned strivings of our sex, will come once more to naught, and another age must go by before balance is restored and humankind enters an era of blessedness.'

"Brave Kore swore to obey, as I had enjoined, the edicts of this Divine Destiny. And it is because of this that she now lives among mortals, in the shape of a hideous vulture."

Demeter let out a strangled bark of horror. "A vulture!" she whispered bleakly. "The monstrosity of it!"

"Such were the dangers that Proserpina faced when she under-took to vouchsafe the passage of the redeemer of Artemis into the Kingdom of the Blessed. But she has not failed us, for even now, the presaged Destiny unfolds. Yet Kore remains in peril, as we see, and swift action is required to mend the circumstance that Hades's hatred and savagery have engendered."

"But I don't understand. If the goal is to resurrect his divine twin, would not Apollo be our first resort?" suggested Hebe.

"Better to ask thy husband Herakles to set aside his passion for sport, and take up the spindle," Demeter retorted. "Know thee not that Apollo's claim upon Artemis is false? The sun god would rather that Diana remain buried in obscurity, than that, her divinity ascendant, she be revealed: a being far more ancient, and in days past more puissant than he." The goddesses had walked together to the bier where Persephone lay in state, and stood around her body, which was arrayed in living flowers, speaking in quiet, reverential tones.

"Of all the crimes committed by Zeus, that of deforming great Artemis to his purposes stands among the vilest," Demeter went on. "For she was once the defender of all the forest creatures, the champion of women and girls. But Jupiter proclaimed that she be shamed and defiled, not by rape but by the fear of it, and with his unremitting lust for conquest and control he reduced her glorious courage down until it was the twisted helpless rage of a slave. Not satisfied with this, through the lens of his cruelty he passed her, and made of her a huntress of animals and men, an ally to the dictates of male authority, and an enforcer of the double standard he had proclaimed as divine law."

"Indeed," Themis agreed, "for Artemis is the Queen of the Titans, firstborn of Gaia, having been birthed even before her twin brother, who is called the eldest of the gods. And it is he who is the redeemer foretold."

"But this is wondrous to me," spoke Hebe. "Why has the truth been kept a secret for so long?"

"Think you that only Artemis was beaten down by the relentless brutality of the warrior gods?" said Themis. "If she, the greatest of all, Mother of Amazons, was defeated, then so much further has been the descent of all other goddesses. Much was lost to memory in the fall, and much has been suppressed in fear, that would condemn the Olympians in their own eyes were it known today. It is for this reason that Zeus and Apollo, Ares and Hades have taken such pains to keep Artemis's whereabouts secret."

"Their crimes will be exposed ere long," Ceres muttered darkly.

Themis rose, and took Demeter's hand. "Send not thy letters, dear Demeter, for now, but await my signal. There is however one thing you must do."

"Only tell me," Ceres replied, "I am yours to command."

"Kore's companion in exile, an undead creature, is in peril of annihilation, for him would Hades unmake, if he could, or thwart if he cannot destroy. Know you that Zeus and his league would certainly support Pluton in this wish, if they knew the true identity of the zombie. Therefore must you preserve him from harm, for though he has like his twin been twisted and demeaned throughout the many centuries, until he has become a miniature, a shadow of his former glory, he too must be restored to his proper place in the Pantheon, for balance to be achieved."

"But who is this mysterious deity of old," Hebe begged, "this Titan from the primordial days?"

"I cannot reveal that," Themis replied, "and not merely because of my oath to the Council. Events that have already been set in motion must result from those yet to come, and to speak of it now may ruin all."

And with that she took her leave, and Demeter and Hebe were left to wonder, in awe and delight, at the miraculous providence of her coming.

April 7, 1994 – Brooklyn, NY

Luke floated above Rosetta, where she lay in bed beside a paper bag overflowing with tissues. He listened to her raspy, shallow breaths. She was sinking deeper and deeper. He felt her mind close up like the pupil of a cat's eye in the sun.

Buzz, Luke called out mentally, *help!* He turned to see that Persephone was already floating next to him. Of course. Their bond was unbroken.

Kore! he cried. *Can't we do something?*

What's wrong with her?

I don't know. She's slipping away!

If we follow her, we can try and send her home, the Queen of the Dead replied. Luke instantly understood what the danger was. On the other side, Hades was waiting.

He took Persephone's hand. In projecting their astral bodies, they had shed their imprisoning forms. It was almost worth it to be annihilated by the Lord of Terrors, seeing her this way again.

You are so beautiful, Kore.

So are you, Luke.

Shall we? he said, and beat his wings. Together they dove down the dark tunnel after Rosetta's retreating wisp of a soul.

It seemed at first that they had lost her. Rosetta had sped on ahead, and vanished where they could not follow.

She's gone, Luke mourned.

She could be nearby, lost, Kore said. *I believe she still lives.*

Then let's try searching from above, Luke suggested.

Soaring over New York City, they worked together to scan the neighborhoods Rosetta would have frequented in life. The city was dense with disembodied spirits, appearing in translucent mono-chrome, colored according to their spiritual state, some red, some green, some blue; some dark, some bright. At last they spotted her shade, glowing a silvery white, wandering the back streets of Alphabet City in a daze.

What now? Luke wondered.

We must first guide her to a place between the worlds, Kore answered, *where souls gather before their fate is decided.*

I don't want her to see me, Luke worried. *She probably knows I'm dead, and it might frighten her.*

"Here," Proserpina put her hands to his cheeks, and he shrank down to the size of a kitten. In her fingers, Kore now held a rag boy doll, still attached to the goddess's silver collar by a fine chain. Persephone shook herself and her splendor was covered with a pink sweater and dove gray jeans, white tennis shoes on her feet.

I will lead her to the mansion, she said, *where they wait, who may soon return.*

Kore swooped down, walked alongside the confused spirit.

"I have to find Aron," Rosetta said faintly, not looking at her.

Poor thing. "Talk to her!" Luke hissed.

"Ssh!" Kore whispered.

"What's that thing?" Rosetta asked, pointing to Luke.

"It's a doll."

"What's his name?"

"He has no name."

Rosetta looked at Kore suspiciously.

"Come to my loft," Kore urged. "We're having a party. Everyone will be there."

"Where is it?"

"I'll show you. It's an amazing artist's loft," said Persephone.

Rosetta followed the goddess as she whirled through the streets, up to 14th and over to 6th Ave, then uptown again.

"Where are we going?" Luke whispered.

"I know a place where there's a spirit door," Persephone

breathed.

This turned out to be a loft building on West 38th Street. The three of them entered the elevator, and Kore pressed the Penthouse button. When the lift reached the top floor, Kore seized Rosetta's hand. The elevator came to a halt, but she, Luke and Rosetta kept on going up, right through the ceiling.

They found themselves in a loft space crowded with spirits from all the nations of the world. These, it seemed, were mortals lingering between life and death. Most of the spirits spent a short time here, camped out in the main room. The cavernous space reminded Luke of a makeshift shelter set up in a community center during a flood.

"This place is gorgeous!" gushed Rosetta.

"Come, Rosetta," Kore said, "I'll take you on a tour."

Kore tucked the Luke doll face-out into the bosom of her tight V-neck sweater, and led the spirit of the dying woman into the kitchen. Luke was lodged firmly between Kore's fragrant breasts, and he could feel the beating of her divine heart. He also had a fine view of Rosetta as she floated about the loft. It was quite exhilarating and terrifying to be so tiny in the hands of these enormous women.

Now Rosetta was admiring the ornate glazed tiles in the kitchen ecstatically. He remembered that blazing smile, but she was even more lovely than he'd expected. She'd filled out in the past few years, he noticed, gaining inches at the bust and hips, an improvement that her form-fitting nightgown showed off effectively. Her hair was longer now and framed a face, softened yet refined in maturity, that had a classic beauty all its own. Like Sophia Loren, she just seemed to get more lovely with the passage of time.

What a tragedy it would be if she didn't live out this night.

Kore entered the area where the longterm residents were housed. It was less crowded, and there was a blue and white ape lounging excitedly on one of the couches. He immediately flapped toward them on bat wings and landed nearby. Rosetta lingered behind in the kitchen, looking enviously at the multiple sinks.

"Is he here?" Kore asked the monkey in a whisper.

Rosetta hurried up just then, calling. "Wow! How many bed-rooms does this place have?"

Instantly, an energy field formed a bubble around Luke, ex-panding out in all directions. Seconds later he found himself in a sort of ship's cabin sunk into the floor of the loft. Kore was beside him, but all the mortal spirits had been left on the decks above, including Rosetta.

The flying monkey straightened, flushed brown and resolved as a lovely big-eyed young Persian boy with a dancer's body. He wore a hat with little wings on it, and winged, boot-like sandals.

Hermes!

Luke looked up to the spot where they had just been moments before, and could see a tall man with white hair talking to Rosetta. The fellow turned his head and met Luke's eyes, and smiled trium-phantly. He took Rosetta's arm, and waved at Luke over the railing.

"Shit!" Luke interjected. "Who's that dude talking to her? He's creeping me out."

"It's Hades!" Kore said.

"Come on, let's go help her!" Luke cried. But his feet seemed to be rooted to the ground. "I–I can't fly!"

"I can't do anything now," said Proserpina. "The more I think about it, the heavier I feel."

"Kore, look!" Luke said, "she's following him! We can't just leave her in the hands of Death."

"There's no point in trying," Wince said. "Pluto has us locked in a Defeatist Zone."

"What's that?"

"It's a bubble where the only things you can do are things you don't care about," Persephone said. "The more you want something, the less you can make it happen, and the less you want something to happen, the more likely it becomes."

"Man, that's really evil!" said Luke.

"There's nothing we can do if we stay here," Kore remarked. "Might as well give up trying."

"Do you want to be a zombie again, Luke?" Hermes asked.

"That's the last thing I want to do right now," Luke retorted.

"How about you, Kore, do you fancy being a vulture again?"

"Not at all," she admitted.

They awoke by the Willamette River. Crickets chirped in the shrubbery, and water lapped noisily on the shore in the wake of a passing motorboat.

"Wow, that was horribly bizarre," Luke said.

"I hate it when Hades does that," Buzz agreed.

"Where's Wince?"

"Give him a minute," the condor croaked, preening her feathers. "He's gotta fly back here from wherever he is now."

"What if he's still trapped in the Defeatist Zone?"

"I think he's clever enough to get himself out of there," Buzz retorted.

"I guess we just have to wait then," Luke sighed. He reflexively reached out with his mind toward the house to check up on Charity and the kids. Everything seemed normal.

Twenty minutes later Hermes soared down through the drizzle, and landed beside them on the riverbank.

'Ugh," he said, "I'm never going to be able to un-see that!"

"What?" Buzz asked.

"German kids at fat camp. Interpretive dance class."

The look on Wince's face was so woebegone that Luke burst out laughing. "Sorry guy. I guess we owe you one, big time," he said.

"What now?" Buzz said. "It seems like my husband is on to us."

"Alas," Wince replied. "Hades knew of your connection to Rosetta. He used the sick woman to lure you both into a trap. But fear not, Kore, for your mother is on her way."

"Is Rosetta going to die?" Luke asked.

"I'm sorry to say that it's entirely possible. Death has taken Rosetta captive, in order to enforce his command for your destruction."

"But if I submit to him, she'll be spared?"

"Perhaps."

"Don't do it, Luke!" Buzz interrupted indignantly. "She still has a choice, and Death can't deprive her of life untimely, not against her will."

"True, but he may use both deception and seduction to secure her compliance," Mercury observed.

"Then—I guess I'd better—" Luke began.

"Luke," Hermes interrupted, "first things first. Let's restore Kore to her mother directly, and then we can count on Demeter to help us in whatever way she can."

"Is she coming here?" the vulture wondered.

"No, I've arranged to meet her someplace where we can do what we need to do."

"But Rosetta—" Luke objected.

"The best way to help her now is to gather allies among the gods," Wince insisted. "But time is short. I'll carry you to the appointed location."

The messenger god put an arm around Luke's waist, while Buzz held on tight to his shoulder. In a moment they were lifted from the ground and soaring up through the mist. In a rush of speed they burst through the cloud cover. The slanted rays of the sun picked out the undulating shapes of the strato-nimbus layer in gold.

"It's a bit chilly," Hermes apologized, "but this won't take long." They zoomed south, wind whistling in their ears. Tears streamed out past Luke's temples, and he was freezing. Buzz closed her eyes, her beak clacking. Wince didn't appear to be affected by the cold, but when he noticed that his passengers were shivering, he pulled off his cloak and drew it around them.

At last they began their descent. They had left the clouds behind, and landed at the summit of a cluster of stone pinnacles. The rocks glowed bright orange in the sunset.

Luke's legs were numb and he staggered when he was set down, and would have fallen, but Mercury's strong arm caught and steadied him.

The view from their position was spectacular. In every direction the natural rocky towers jutted, the formations marching in a harmonious rhythm randomized by gulches and stream beds. Dark green scruffy bushes clung here and there, their roots burrowing into crevices.

Before Luke could fully catch his breath, there came a blinding flash of light. When he could see again, there was a flying serpent a few feet in front of him. In fact there were three flying serpents, hitched to a chariot that looked like a two-person wheelchair, also with wings.

Seated in this was the most beautiful pregnant woman Luke had ever seen. Her skin was the color of mahogany and her ebony hair fell to her feet in slender jeweled braids. She wore a sheer white himation and over this a gossamer mantle of deep blue, sparkling with actual stars. Beside her in the chariot slumped Kore, or at least her lifeless form.

"Kore? Is that you?" the goddess called upon catching sight of the vulture. She leaped from her seat and ran toward them. "What has the monster done to you! My poor child!" she cried, tears welling up in her eyes, as she stroked the condor's glossy feathers.

"Hi, Mom," Buzz croaked.

It didn't take long for the loving mother to detect the existence of the chain.

"And what is this!?" she demanded, taking notice of Luke for the first time, and casting upon him the kind of look that so many insects must experience as their last impression in life.

"Mother, this is Luke. Luke, the great goddess Demeter."

"Howdy Ma'am," said Luke, doffing an invisible hat.

"What's the meaning of this?" the great goddess Demeter demanded. "Do you make a pet of the Queen of the Underworld?"

"Mother, Hades did this to me, not the boy," Buzz interposed.

Ceres stared intently at Luke, covering him with a searching gaze. Her stern look softened with a dash of amusement before she turned her attention back to her beloved child. "You've been made a fool of, haven't you my girl?" she chuckled.

Buzz stuck her beak up at this. "Luke has been a true friend," she rasped.

"Your Majesties," Mercury interrupted with a bow. "Time is short. Await me here, and I will endeavor to fetch from Hades the key that will undo the curse that links these two lovebirds."

He soared away, leaving them there in the rocky landscape, steep and barren except for juniper, scrub oak and gnarled, red-barked manzanita shrubs. Luke looked down at his zombie hands, and the chain that kept Kore bound to him. It wouldn't be long now before she was rid of him forever.

"Themis has been to see me," Demeter whispered to the condor. "She has told me much about your quest." And she cast a sidelong look at Luke that made him feel rather queer.

"Is she angry with me," Buzz wondered, "for making such a mess of things?"

"No indeed, she praised you courage," Ceres answered bracingly. "If she had but known what you've suffered . . . " she went on, looking again at Luke with a shudder.

Luke was feeling more and more uncomfortable.

"Excuse me, oh great goddess Demeter," he interposed, "but Hades has abducted a friend of mine, and may kill her if we don't stop him. Can you help us save her?"

"A mortal?" the goddess wondered.

"Yes, Ma'am."

"Well really, they all die in the end, don't they?" she said dismissively. "Does it matter so much whether it's now, or later?"

"Mother, please?" Buzz croaked. "It's only fair that we try to protect her."

"Kore dear, it's you I'm concerned about. How can I think about a mere mortal when your life is in peril? Now, tell me what you've been doing with yourself, down here among humans."

"Actually, starving is what I've been doing the most of. It's hard to hunt when you're chained to a zombie."

"Oh, my dear child! Why on earth have you not been feeding her?" she said accusingly to Luke.

"Hey, I fed her! I gave her a hamburger this morning," Luke protested.

"A hamburger!" Demeter was shocked. "Darling, I'll summon up a snack for you. How about your favorite, peach ice cream with pecans?"

"No thanks. I eat carrion, Mom." Demeter winced.

"Oh, yes, of course. What do you prefer, a horse? A goat?"

"It's all right, mother. I'll wait till I can eat real food again."

"Are you sure? Maybe just a piglet, to keep you together," Ceres urged.

"Really, I'm fine."

"Buzz, we have to do something about Rosetta," Luke said urgently. "There's no time to waste. Hades could be killing her right now!"

"What do you propose, Bozo?"

"We have to astral-project ourselves back into the spirit loft."

"Agreed," croaked the vulture. "We can at least try,"

"Okay then. One–two–three!"

"Darling, what are you doing–?" Demeter cried, just as the zombie dropped, senseless. The unconscious body of the scavenger bird landed beside him on the stony soil.

April 7, 1994 –Portland, OR

"And when was the last time you and Charity had a date?" Dennis Defoe asked. He was standing out in back of a burger and falafel joint called Sam's, talking to Louie, the prep cook, beside a dumpster that reeked of ripe garbage.

"I wouldn't call it a *date*. We're friends," the young man said, scratching his head. Tattooed on his shaved scalp, Mickey Mouse was being fellated by Donald Duck.

"Were you friends with Luke Mandrake?" Defoe pursued, his pen poised over his lined tablet.

"I knew him. Mostly through Charity." The youth had chipped black polish on his nails and there were inch-thick plug-rings in his earlobes. Tattoos crawled over his skin like maggots. Dennis stared at Louie's pale arm. Was he hallucinating? No. They were indeed actual tattoos of maggots, eating the lad's flesh.

"And how do you know Charity?"

"Look, I don't see what this has to do with anything. I've already told you everything I know, everything that has anything to do with when and how Luke died. So if you don't mind, my break is over and I have to get back to work."

"Uh huh," the detective said, sticking his tongue in his cheek. *Refuses to answer any further questions,* Defoe wrote in his notebook.

"What the hell are you writing?" Louie said. He grabbed the notebook out of Defoe's hands and looked at it.

Defoe reached inside his coat. Louie raised his hands, backing away, as Defoe pulled out a pint of bourbon and pointed it at the youth.

"Hahaha, you chump," Louie said. "You want your notebook? Dig for it." And he tossed it into the dumpster, and dashed back into the kitchen.

"Hey! Hey!!" Defoe shouted. But by the time he had replaced the flask in an inner pocket and pulled out his weapon, the door had closed on Louie's skinny behind. Much as Defoe wanted to charge into the kitchen and force Louie at gunpoint to retrieve the notebook, he was not quite drunk enough to embark on such a course.

On the other hand, there was no clear route to climbing up into the bin, no fence, no crate to step up on. And the eternally-winded detective was incapable of pulling his portly body up to where he could get a leg over into the receptacle.

Nor had he any desire to go dumpster-diving in a sea of stinky refuse.

Defoe looked around, and soon spied a homeless guy in baggy sweats wandering along SE Grand. "Hey there!" he called out. "My notebook accidentally got tossed out and it's in this dumpster here. I'll give you five bucks to get it out for me."

The man turned slowly and raked Defoe with a look full of wary hostility. "Watchoo say?" he whined, and spat between his several teeth.

"I said, I'll give you five bucks to climb in there and get my notebook out," Defoe repeated. "Police business," he added authoritatively.

The homeless man stood frozen, staring bug-eyed at the gun the detective still clutched in his hand. Defoe cleared his throat and replaced the weapon in its holster. "So, whaddaya say?"

"You wammee ta break my neck?" the tramp said plaintively.

"Ten bucks," he amended his offer.

The old codger pressed a finger to one nostril and blew a blob of snot onto the blacktop. "How, den?" he parried.

"How 'bout if you climb up on a chair, or a box or something?" Defoe pursued, sounding slightly desperate.

"Ain't see no chair. Ain't see no box."

"You know where I can find one?"

"Why ain't you ask 'em inside? Dey got chairs."

Defoe inhaled sharply and let out his breath in an irritated whuff. He was getting nowhere here. Maybe it would be easier to just reconstruct his notes from memory. He had a very good memory.

*   *   *

Charity Ball lounged in graceful mourning on the brocade settee in the formal living room of her Riverwood home. She was wearing a ballerina skirt of black taffeta over multiple layers of stiff tulle, from beneath which her long, shapely legs emerged, encased in fishnets. One leg was tucked beneath her and the other trailed, shoe-less, down to the Persian rug. A spider-woman corset in black satin and purple lace set off the perfection of the rock star's bosom and sculpted shoulders. Long black lace fingerless gloves completed the ensemble, and her flaming hair fell in loose curls, accented by an enormous purple silk bow.

"Mrs. Mandrake–" began Greg Fernley, reporter for the New Musical Express.

"Ball. *Ms.* Charity Ball."

"Pardon me, *Ms.* Ball. Thank you for kindly consenting to go ahead with this interview, so soon after your husband's tragic demise."

Charity cocked her head to one side and regarded him limpidly. "I'm a professional, Greg. Life must go on, and I have a responsibility to promote my new album, Dura Smell, which is coming out in two weeks," she said pointedly.

"Wonderful, wonderful Mrs.– ah, Ball. And I'd love to talk to you about Dura Smell, and about your band, Void. But first, what kind of life did you have, being married to Luke Mandrake? If you could describe him in three words only, what was he like, as a husband?"

Charity looked down at her hands, admiring the perfect laven-

182

der polish on her nails. Then she skewered Greg with a direct gaze from her luminous brown eyes.

"In three words?" she said, softly and gravely. "*Best. Fuck. Ever.*"

Just then the phone on the side table rang.

"I'm so sorry, Greg, but I may have to take this call, if it's my pediatrician. Haddy's had an ear infection all week." She picked up the cordless and frowned at the caller ID, then put the phone back on the table. She could call Louie back later.

"You were saying?" she said.

April 7, 1994 –Spirit Door #39655

Luke and Persephone materialized in the spot where they had last seen Rosetta. Naturally Hades and his victim were no longer in the loft.

"Where do you think he's taken her?" Luke whispered. He was eying Kore and hyperventilating a little. As always when she was so close to him wearing her voluptuously lovely form, he felt a powerful urge to taste her lips. Furthermore her outfit made him dizzy, the way her bare nips protruded above the shelf of the quilted and heavily jeweled bra-and-jacket combo, a Cretan confection that had to be the most brilliant invention of the ancient world, into which her sweet melons were nestled. Luke's anxiety about Rosetta's fate battled urgently with his lust, and won a grudging détente.

"There are only two ways out of the loft," the Queen of the Dead said. "The elevator, by which souls return to the world of the living, and the escalator."

"And that goes to Hades."

"To Hades, yes, and also to Olympos, although few are permitted to pass that way."

As she led him through the high-ceilinged room above 38th Street in Manhattan, with its long windows facing both East and West, Luke could see the lights below, a panorama of living jewels.

Now they stood before an opening in the brick wall. One could hardly call it a door, it was more like a part of the wall where there was nothing. No light, no dark, no substance, texture or color. Luke shivered.

"Are we going through that?"

"Take my hand," Kore said, and they stepped through the portal.

The two found themselves suspended above a shimmering,

sloping waterfall of light. There were no steps on this escalator, but there were black rubbery handrails, and these, Luke observed, moved in two directions. To their right, the seams in the band were moving upward, and to the left, they went down. A green neon sign suspended above their heads read *Please Hold Handrail.*

Persephone placed one hand on the skyward railing. They began to move slowly up.

After a time, they approached a layer of mist that obscured the top reaches of the escalator. As they rose into the cloud, Luke unfurled his wings nervously, but he did not attempt to blindly fly upward.

They passed through the fog, and gradually Luke began to hear a faint sound of tambourines and flutes filtering down from above. At last the mist cleared, and he saw that they were standing before a massive arched double door that appeared to be sculpted in solid gold, set in a marble facade that was fronted by a grand colonnade. The dozens of panels on the golden gateway depicted deities, with august Zeus at the apex, flanked by an eagle and a lion. The music could be heard distinctly now, along with voices issuing from within.

Kore turned to him with an anxious face. "We cannot allow ourselves to be seen here," she said softly. "We must only watch and listen, and not excite any comment. Therefore hold this in your mouth, but do not swallow it." She had opened the cover of a tiny basket that hung from her belt, and handed him a white lima bean, smooth and dry. She placed another under her own tongue, and instantly vanished from sight, as did Luke upon following her example. Silently she opened the gigantic doors just enough to admit them, and holding hands, they slipped into Olympos.

Just inside was an enormous reception hall with two large skylights, situated above a pair of circular cisterns. These pools contained matched fountains in the shape of many-headed snakes. However instead of water a liquid spurted from the mouths of the hydras which, judging by the thick scent in the air, could only have been wine. One of the fountains dispensed red wine, the other white. One also contained a fat naked man who sat in a wine-bath holding a wide shallow goblet to catch the stream issuing from the fanged mouth of a snake head. Near him wallowed a plump woman, equally nude, picking and eating grapes from a stem that she clutched between her toes.

Beyond the fountains, six openings issued upon a small amphitheater. The scene within was extraordinarily chaotic. Luke gazed around with interest at the celebration. The first thing that captured his notice was the crowd of musicians on the stage, prancing about playing an assortment of instruments that included a tortoise-shell lyre, a double flute, skin drums, a saxophone and a ukulele. The chorus sang woozily:

Then, come, put the jorum about,
And let us be merry and clever,
Our hearts and our liquors are stout,
Here's the Three Jolly Pigeons for ever !

They sang with the determination of revelers who have long ago performed all the company's favorites, and are scraping for any song at all. Few of them knew the words, but they sang along somehow. Those not actively performing were either asleep, sprawled here and there among the damp pillows and puddles of spilled wine, or necking, to put it euphemistically, on the upper tiers. A few revelers staggered about shouting incoherently. The atmosphere of boredom, satiety and banal decadence reminded Luke of an open mic that had sadly extended into the wee hours, long after anything interesting was likely to occur onstage.

"It's the 2500-year anniversary of the Dionysia," Kore whispered in his ear. "The Jubilee has been going on for weeks."

She led him down the steps toward the stage. The theater was lavishly appointed, with wide curved terraces of marble for seating. Near the stage, armchairs had been set out for the audience. Above these, the stepped seating areas were covered in cushions and bolsters, and dotted with low tables laden with carafes, cups, bowls of fruit, and platters containing the remains of bread, cheese and pastries. As they passed by three aged ladies sitting close together on folding stools, Luke tripped on a piece of clothing, or perhaps a tablecloth, that was heavily drenched with red wine. He fell against one of the women where she sat quietly staring up at the domed ceiling of the theater.

"Sorry," Luke said, before remembering that he was not supposed to talk to anyone.

"Who's that?" the crone creaked, turning the empty sockets of her eyes toward him. "Enyo, pass me the eye!"

"What do you need it for, Deino? It's still my turn."

"Somebody stepped on me," Deino complained. "I want to get a look at his face."

"It's my turn to watch the show," said the middle of the three ancient hags. "You've had the eye long enough, Enyo."

"There's nobody there, Deino," Enyo grumbled. "You senile old hag."

"I like that!" croaked Deino. "You're the eldest!"

Kore took Luke's arm and they continued rapidly down the steps while the Fates argued.

"Let's sit here," Persephone whispered, urging Luke toward a vacant place a few tiers up from the stage. To get there, they had to carefully step over a passed-out guy in an army uniform, spattered with vomit. It seemed like a place where they would be relatively safe from being sat upon by one of the guests.

The song had ended, and a member of the chorus cried out thickly, "Monks of the Screw!"

He began to sing in a loud and melodious voice:

When St. Patrick this order established,
He called us the "Monks of the Screw!"–

"It's Wince!" Luke whispered. "Is he drunk?" He certainly appeared to be as he bellowed out the drinking song, one arm around a huge red-bearded fellow. The giant grinned, swaying back and forth and swigging wine from an outsized goblet, and occasionally barked out a single word of the lyrics, "screw!"

What was Hermes up to? He was supposed to be getting the key to set Kore free of her chains. He was supposed to be helping them rescue Rosetta!

–Good rules he revealed to our abbot,
To guide us in what we should do.

But first he replenished our fountain
With liquor the best from on high . . .

As Mercury sang, a tall figure with white hair flogged a kettle-drum. "Look, it's Hades," Luke hissed to Kore.

"Play Cherniy Voron! Play the Black Raven!" a man shouted. He was sitting right in front of them, had pince nez and a beard, and wore a vintage suit, as did the man beside him, who was quite thin, and sported a bowler hat.

"Nobody here knows a thing about Russian culture," the man with the pince nez complained. "They are all idiots."

Luke and Kore were sitting close, touching. He could smell the musky fragrance of her skin, her sex. Unseen though they were, their astral forms were as real here, as their bodies had been back in the solid world. And he was her angelic boy again. In propinquity to her curvaceous features, he grew giddy with lust.

"Didn't they appreciate you new play, Anton?" the thin fellow wondered.

"Oh, they applauded, as they will to anything, like apes. But try and have an intelligent conversation with one of these lunatics, Franz! Ugh! It's more than I can bear."

Luke swallowed some wine that he had retrieved from a table nearby, then offered it to Kore. She accepted the mysteriously floating goblet and sipped it, while Luke carefully draped an invisible arm over Kore's invisible shoulder. The silver chain attached to his wrist tinkled, but nobody seemed to notice.

Luke glanced at a couple a few rows up, a satyr and a half-naked nymph. She was straddling the goat-legged fellow, moving her hips in a highly erotic gesture, while the satyr fondled her derrière suggestively.

"I don't bother," Franz replied. "But at least you have the comfort of writing, and seeing your work produced."

"Ha!" Anton retorted. "What I wouldn't give at this moment for a bottle of vodka, and a machine gun."

"But tell me of the play you entered into the Festival, for I was at work, and unable to watch. More wine, my friend?" Franz asked.

"No, thank you," Anton Chekhov replied.

Ninety-six bottles of beer on the wall, Ares bellowed.

Luke was losing focus. All he could manage to do was speculate about how Kore would react, if he seized her right now and sat her on his lap. He knew what he would do to her if he got the chance. Hell, they were doing it right and left in here. And the two of them were invisible anyhow. What was to stop them?

Franz Kafka drained his glass and poured himself another.

"The play? A sad little comedy, is all, a frivolous tale called *Rasputin's Mistress*. Rasputin played himself. He's actually got quite a gift for acting, you know," Chekhov said.

"How extraordinary. And did it win any honors?"

"It was well received, but the prize went to Aristophanes, as always. They really only invite me to be polite, which is to say, to have someone the Greeks can be compared to favorably.—But tell me Franz, are you working on anything?"

Eighty-one bottles of beeeeeer . . .

Luke's left hand had succeeded in creeping under Persephone's skirt and now began insinuating itself between her thighs. Several verses ago the right hand had quite impetuously captured a nipple, and his fingers refused to release the prisoner, a hostage to the tender assault occurring below.

Kafka drained his cup again. "I'm rotten to ripeness with despair, and nothing comes out except vile recriminations and complaints," he sighed. "My inspiration is all eaten away from within like a worm-ridden apple. It's this job, and why I am set to it day after day is a mystery. I believe Pluto thinks it a grand joke to have me as his dispatcher, and treats me as if I were an animal, trained to do tricks for the amusement of the guests." Kafka dropped his head into his hands. "And the worst of it is, that he knows it torments me, and he takes pleasure in knowing."

Luke's left hand wriggled like a fish swimming upstream. Persephone did not seem to want to escape, as she shivered in his arms, making delicious little sounds that only he could hear. Instead, she stroked his invisible cheek with a loving hand, and covered him with kisses.

"What is it that troubles you most, the boredom and dreariness of it? Or the senseless cruelty of fate?" Anton wondered.

Luke had gradually maneuvered the goddess's callipygian extremities into the preferred position. His tensed sex was knocking on heaven's door. Kore moaned, wriggled against him. Luke enclosed her in his arms, kissing the back of her neck, and whispered huskily, "My Queen . . . I am at your command . . . !"

"Honestly," Kafka complained, "it's being asked to do things that are entirely against the spirit of the rules, by a fellow who's otherwise fanatical about regulations when it comes to every detail. For example, today Hades set out to endanger the life of a young woman whose body was perfectly capable of conquering her illness."

I'd better listen to this . . . Luke checked the grinding motion of his pelvis.

"How so?" Chekhov wondered.

"He was determined to take her to the very brink of death, which could only be done by compromising the immune system. He did so by causing the room to become unsalubriously cold."

"And did the girl survive?"

"She lies now in a coma, and Hades uses her fate as a bargaining chip in some game he's playing with his wife."

Kore squirmed deliciously as he took possession of the other nipple. His hand burrowed into her cave like an eel. "Unng! But– Luke! We have to pay attention!" she whispered.

"Relax," he breathed, trying not to let the bean slip out. "I'm totally . . . paying . . . oh! . . . ye-e-es . . ."

"I pity you, dear Kafka. I know that if you were to fail or refuse to follow his orders to the letter, Hades would exact a diabolical penance."

"It's always the same: if he supposes I've made a mistake he transforms me into a gigantic cockroach. How I wish I'd never written that infernal story!"

Luke clasped the goddess to him in a profane embrace, his hand burrowed relentlessly, while his manhood stood at attention before the entrance. Kore had not ceased to writhe and wiggle in his lap, drawing him ever further into her ecstatic secrets. Now she began to shudder and buck, and Luke groaned, responded with sudden ardor so that she gasped, and cried out!

Chekhov and Kafka turned and looked behind them. But they saw nothing.

"The unspeakable irony of it, Franz! If this were fiction, it would be comical."

"So far he has relented and restored me to my own form only because I've repeatedly proved my usefulness to him. But if I were to openly defy him, I'd soon be lurking in the shadows of hell, striving to avoid being eaten by bats."

"And there would be no forgiveness, I presume."

"His cruelty is surpassed only by his affection for oblivion. My primary duty lies in securing pharmaceuticals for his insatiable appetites."

"There must be some compensating entertainment to be found in that?"

Luke could not hold back any longer. Clutching the delicious goddess, he lurched to his feet, turned her to face him, lifted her. She wrapped her legs around him and clung to his neck, impaling herself wildly on his excitation.

Ahh, Kore! Luke had to bite his lips to keep from making a sound as dizzying bolts of ecstasy hummed through his body. If he hadn't been using his wings to keep his balance, he would probably have fallen over. *Ah, yes, my Queen–I am yours!*

"Now and again," Kafka admitted. "For a time he had a craze for tree-frog venom, and securing the drug was an adventure, for I had to journey to a remote jungle in the Southern Americas, and bargain with the shamans of lost tribes. But Pluto inevitably imbibed too much of the substance, which caused him to become demented, and he began to accuse me of fabricating excuses when I was unable to obtain it in sufficient quantities. I spent a good long while as a bug, a victim of his arbitrary vengefulness. Whether because of the lack of resourcefulness of my successor, or because the population of tree-frogs dwindled, the poison eventually became impossible to obtain at any price. When Hades had returned to saner mind, he remembered me and restored me to human form."

"Ah, Kafka, if you don't write down some of these stories immediately, I shall have to start stealing them. Tell me more about the trouble between Hades and his wife. I must hear every morsel of gossip!"

Luke had draped Kore over a pile of cushions, and the two now engaged in delightful shenanigans that might have attracted quite a bit of attention, even in this temple of iniquity, had they not both been cloaked in invisibility. The freedom to absolutely fuck the wench senseless, right in the middle of a crowd, had completely gone to Luke's head, and not the one he used for thinking. The main thing was to keep those beans in their mouths, otherwise he did as he pleased, and she submitted to his creativity with the usual melting surrender. Christ, she was intoxicating!

Kafka glanced warily over his shoulder, then looked over to the stage. Pluton was still banging away at the drum, singing in a deep booming voice:

Nothing in nature's sober found,
But an eternal health goes round.
Fill up the bowl, then, fill it high,
Fill all the glasses there; for why
Should every creature drink but I?

"All right, but you must drink with me, Chekhov. It won't do to sober up. This is a tale that requires hilarity." Franz refilled his own cup, and Anton's.

Luke was conscious that he was having his way with Kore, and she with him, right there in front of her beast of a husband–and

Death didn't know! The knowledge filled him with a dangerous sense of infallibility. He indulged in the crazy conviction that he could keep fucking her like this pretty much indefinitely, staving off the explosive conclusion for all eternity. Maybe it was because he was still listening with one ear to the conversation between the two authors. The distraction was good for his endurance, at least.

Kafka leaned in close to Chekhov, lowering his voice. "Persephone has been transformed into a vulture by her Lord, for infidelity," Kafka began, and proceeded to briefly outline the main points of the tale, up to the moment at which Kore's body was taken away by her parents.

"So I got a call earlier today from Hades," Kafka said, "as I mentioned before, asking me for details about the woman, Rosetta Stone, to whom the zombie had apparently formed an attachment during his life. The Lord of the Dead planned to handle the case himself, using the girl as bait to lure the undead creature and Kore into his power. Some time later Pluto contacted me again to arrange a booking." Franz lit a cigarette and inhaled smoke before continuing.

"When I say booking I am speaking of a particular way of concealing a spirit in a dimensional fold from which it cannot escape, nor can it be found, unless the searcher is aware of the nature of the trap. Are you familiar with this practice?"

"No, Franz, I don't think I am."

Luke had remained poised mid-thrust since he heard Rosetta's name mentioned, and he was trying very hard now to listen attentively. It wasn't easy with Kore filling his arms, soft as a fuckable custard tart, but he prided himself on his control. Anyway he had no choice, as he doubted she was paying any attention whatsoever to what the two authors were saying. If she were, he'd feel a bit insulted, honestly. He'd been doing his best to drive her completely out of her mind, a thing for which, as a telepath, he had always had a certain gift. As he listened unmoving to the conversation, he fondled and pinched Kore with his fingertips in the most exquisite way, squeezing and milking the soft fuzzy hood of her twat, that was already so stoutly impaled, in a way that pressed the whole clitoral mound gently and firmly against his pelvic bone. He thus urged her on into continuous seismic, orgasmic shudders. The only thing that was keeping Luke from losing it entirely, was that he was forcing himself to stay focused on the business at hand.

"Well for heaven's sake don't breathe a word of it, for my fate would be sealed if Death discovered I'd revealed the secret. But it's called *booking* because the soul is literally hidden inside a book."

"But this is fantastic!" Chekhov breathed. "Can any book be used?"

"No indeed, that is the reason Hades required my assistance. The book must be the story of the person's own life. And Death contacted me to write this book."

Suddenly Kore was wriggling away, and Luke reached for her as she rose, and kissed his mouth hungrily, pushing him down into the cushions. When she mounted him ravenously, he did not resist. *Your wish is my command, my Queen!*

"How long did it take you?" asked Chekhov.

"Not long. It was primarily a matter of assembling and augmenting the materials in Stone's existing dossier. She's a prismatic love node, an operative of Eros, and so a fairly comprehensive file has been kept on her as a way of monitoring the love god's activities."

Pay attention, pay attention. –Don't come! Pay attention . . . ! Luke told himself. Rosetta, working for Eros? The mental image these words summoned up wasn't helping him in his efforts to delay ejaculation.

"This is because of the ongoing conflict, I suppose," Anton observed.

"Naturally. In order to create the book, I merely had to scrape together some information about her most recent activities, to bring the story up-to-date. And then, and here's the crucial point, the book has to continually be added to, so long as the spirit is imprisoned, updating the narrative to reflect current circumstances."

"So . . . as long as the book describes the soul as residing in its prison, the spirit must remain there, is that what you're telling me?"

Luke sat up quickly, seized Kore and held her still. "Holy shit!" he whispered in her ear. Realizing something was happening, Kore froze.

"Exactly," Franz replied. "There are only two ways for the ghost to escape: one is for changes to be added to the book by its original author, describing such an event, and the other is for the spirit herself to gain access to the book, enabling her to write an ending that changes the narrative."

This was precisely the information they'd been hoping to overhear. The lovers clung to each other, breathless with ecstasy, and listened.

"But I don't understand. You said that the soul was trapped inside the book, did you not? Where is she located, precisely?"

"That's where it gets interesting. The book creates a dimensional fold, in that by repeating a single unique action by the mortal being, it captures her spirit in an eddy outside of time, within a single moment re-occurring, in theory, infinitely. Therefore she is now located precisely nowhere, unless and until the storyline advances."

"How fascinating," Anton said. "I would enjoy very much to see such a book."

"I'm afraid that's impossible," Kafka averred, "the risk is too great. There are caveats, I should add. The first is that the motion of the repeated action does eventually decay due to the laws of physics. When that happens, free will kicks in and the story can advance in unpredictable ways. The second is that this method won't work as well with those who have living relatives or are well-known, as the thoughts and dreams and ideas of the living speed up the process of decay by creating pressure on the existing narrative. Therefore a constant attention is required to keep the event stable. The more famous the individual is, the more quickly the stasis breaks down, so it's impractical to use on real celebrities."

"Well that is a boon, for those of us at least who enjoy a little renown," Chekhov opined.

"But all this puts me in mind of the fact that I must go now and add a line or two to the volume, as is my painful duty, before the event expires." Kafka rose to his feet.

Luke scooped Kore up in his arms as he stood upright. He felt like a god just now, as he reveled in his strong, sinewy angelic body, his powerful wings and not to mention, his completely functional, non-zombified, certifiably monstrous cock.

"A pleasure, Franz," Chekhov said, kissing him on both cheeks.

"For me also. I'm grateful that the nature of the assignment has permitted me to escape my own cell and attend the festival for a short while, and to speak with you."

Luke launched aloft with Persephone, as the two men embraced.

The tender goddess swooned with pleasure in his arms. Luke took a deep breath. He needed to keep his head, or they would both plunge to the ground. Anyhow, he had to somehow manage to retain his senses, if he were going to trail Kafka to the location of the fatal tome.

However, Luke's erection was still a dowsing rod of lust pointed relentlessly, feverishly at the sweet, engorged pussy of the goddess of Spring. And so when Kore entwined him again in her ravishing legs, he surrendered in midair to a satisfying conclusion long delayed.

April 7, 1994 –New York, NY

"–You'll receive one volume per month for four months, plus your free, suitable-for-framing reproduction of the Magna Carta with the first shipment," Phil said in his most cultured tones. "Absolutely, Ma'am. I urge you to–oh, cripes." He blinked his large, heavy-lidded eyes, then set the phone receiver down, and peered around the wall of pitted pressboard that separated his tiny cubicle from Aron's.

"I sympathize, sir, but you won't be billed for sixty days, so–" Aron switched the receiver to his other ear. "Absolutely you can use a credit card. Yes, we will hold your invoice for sixty days. Thank you, sir, we pride ourselves on our excellent customer service. I'm sure you'll find this to be an invaluable reference. May I confirm the shipping address? Yes, we can ship to your office . . ."

Phil waited until Aron had finished completing the sale and then whispered, "Did you hear about Marky?"

"No, what happened? Is he all right?" Aron answered. He'd heard that Marky had collapsed suddenly during the morning shift, and been taken away by ambulance.

Phil looked around to make sure the shift supervisor wasn't watching before he answered. "No, he's not. Mina called me a few minutes ago from the hospital. He's dead!"

"What!!?" Aron responded. "Dead? How–why?"

"They said it was pneumonia. Apparently he didn't know he had it."

"Christ!" whispered Aron. "Was he shooting up?"

"Of course. That's why he had no idea how sick he was. By the time he got the antibiotics, it was too late."

"Fucking hell. That's horrible," Aron replied. He was deeply shaken, and it felt like a fist was clenching his chest.

Anxiety reared up in him to the point of panic. Rosetta had

been down with something all week, and for the first time, he worried about her. What if it was something serious? Hadn't she told him she was going to the clinic this morning?

He dialed their home number and listened to it ring. When it finally picked up, it was the outgoing recording.

"Hello, you've reached Aron and Rosetta, and the world headquarters of the Windup Teeth," his own voice said. Aron hung up. He would try back later, he decided.

A frown clouded Charity's brow as she dialed Dennis Defoe's number. *That moron never returns my calls.* Of course, it went to a recording.

"Hello, Detective Defoe? We have a problem. I just got a call from an old friend of mine, Louie Carmichael. He was very upset. What on earth did you say to him?

"Frankly, Detective, I'm flabbergasted at the ham-fisted way you've gone about your job. I hired you to find my husband, and you've taken it upon yourself to harass and intimidate our friends. This has got to stop.

"I'm calling to let you know that I'm terminating our contract, effective immediately. Please submit your final bill, and it had better be reasonable, considering that you've failed to deliver results on every single one of the objectives we outlined in our original conversation.

"And Detective Defoe, since you haven't bothered returning my calls up until now, please don't bother returning this one. I have nothing further to say to you. Good day, Detective."

Charity clicked the phone off, and leaned back on the settee. It had been an exhausting afternoon. The journalist from NME had needed to be browbeaten into talking about her new album for more than ten seconds. Meanwhile, she was already starting to receive letters from Shambala fans, letters she couldn't bear to open, much less read. Maybe some of them were sympathy cards, but many were definitely angry rants. One of them was addressed to "Charity Ball, Diseased Cow." Another had a cartoon of a round, lit bomb on the back.

And now this Defoe guy was creating havoc everywhere he went, causing bitter complaints. No doubt Luke's friends were eager to judge, and to malign her behind her back for siccing the heat on them. Nobody ever gave her the benefit of the doubt, she'd noticed.

Could she get away with taking another Valium? Maybe two? She badly needed to calm her nerves. Meditation was all very well, but the stress of the day's challenges was starting to stimulate the incoherent cloud of rage that sometimes threatened to engulf her.

Why were there so many assholes in the world? And why did they always seem to target her with their stupid, sexist bullshit?

She took a deep breath, and tried to calm down. The phone purred, and she let the machine take it. A nurse left a message.

"I'm calling from Doctor Gosling's office with the results of Galahad's tests. He has an ear infection, but everything else looks normal . . ."

Thank goodness it was nothing worse. Charity hoped Kaylen would be able to fill the prescription. She could not face venturing out into the world right now.

April 7, 1994 – Pinnacle Rocks National Park, CA

Demeter had been watching over the unconscious forms of the zombie and the condor, and the lifeless body of her daughter, since sunset. Now the first stars were glittering in a darkening firmament, and the nail paring of the waning moon was following the sun to bed.

The great goddess of agriculture was not amused by the delay. She had too much work to do, to waste her time with this sort of nonsense.

Why had Hermes brought her here, only to abandon her? Where was Hades? He had agreed to restore Kore to life. It was time for him to get on with it.

She would have left an hour ago if she hadn't been responsible for all these bodies. And two of the three were her own child, for goodness sake. What could she do but wait?

Then an idea occurred to her. All she needed to do was protect Proserpina from harm, and she would be free to go and discover for herself what was causing the hold-up.

Maybe she should drum up some reinforcements first. Her brothers could be very stubborn.

She lifted a whistle that hung from a cord around her graceful neck, and blew three trilling notes. It was only moments before a bird arrived in answer to her summons, and then another. Soon there were hundreds of them, varying in plumage and size, whirling around her under the starry sky.

Demeter blew two short toots on the whistle, and the birds crowded around the body of Proserpina where she lay in the chariot. In seconds she was completely concealed by the dark fluttering wings. The rustling shape rose up into the air, then descended close beside the prone figures of Luke and the raptor. As quickly as it had formed, the avian cloud dispersed. Now Kore lay on the stony soil beside the sleeping bodies of Luke and Buzz.

Ceres removed her starry mantle, shook it out into the breeze, and shook it again. Each time it grew longer and wider until it was large enough to cover the recumbent forms. She allowed the translucent fabric to settle gently over them all, and when she was done, they had vanished from sight.

"Let no viper pass here, nor any poisonous thing, nor any creature however large or tiny, that might do harm to my beloved child," she said softly. "Let her remain hidden until my return." For a moment the stars on the mantle glistened, then faded back into invisibility. Only the inaccessible outcrop and the fragrant shrubs that grew there could be seen.

Satisfied, the goddess stepped into her chariot, and cracked the whip above the winged snakes. With a clap of thunder and a flash, the vehicle disappeared.

Dionysia Year 2500 –Mount Olympos

"My Lord Pluton, I fear you'll topple me! It's pointless to try and best you at this game," Hermes moaned ruefully.

Hades laughed, *har har har,* and snarfed up a thick ribbon of white powder. "You are as much a coward as you are a thief, Mercury," he bloviated. "Go on, take the other."

"Shut up, both of you!" grunted Zeus from the massive couch opposite the one where Hermes and Hades were seated. They were backstage in the green room at the Dionysian Theater. The king of the gods was fondling two diminutive, nude girls, one of them draped over each thick leg, while a third knelt before him in a worshipful attitude, attending energetically to business. "I'm trying to concentrate."

"If my lord insists," Wince replied to Hades, pointedly ignoring Zeus, "but I'll not vouch for my ability to speak after such a feat." And he bent and began to inhale the matching line, not all at once as Hades had done, but in hesitant little whiffs.

"Suck it up! Or are you a girl?" Death taunted.

Zeus meanwhile looked on impatiently as the doll-sized blonde nymph stimulated him ineffectually with her tiny tongue. *This will never do.*

"Give me time, my Lord! I have not your hardy constitution," Hermes complained.

"You are fresh out of time," Hades retorted.

"Come my dear, and take a ride on the kingly dong," Jove said cheerfully. He lifted the yellow-haired poppet onto his lap and began to stroke and pet her vigorously, and with avid purpose. The concubine wriggled in his iron grip, but that merely added spice to the gigantic god's enjoyment.

Ahhh, yes. It was good to be king.

The three nymphs were miniatures in comparison to his bulk,

but they were simply ordinary-sized humans. These sweets, it happened, had only recently been freed from imprisonment on the Island
of the Damned, where they were held in thrall to a sadistic rape-mon-
ster native to that demonic realm. It was the titans Crius and Iapetus
who had retrieved them, on Hades's orders, and brought them to the
Bacchanal for Zeus's delectation. The treats had arrived still strapped
to carousel horses, interestingly enough, and wearing fetish gear that
was quite fascinating to behold. They longed to become Jove's group-
ies, Hades had informed him with a wink, and would be so grateful to
be freed of their contortionistic predicament, that they would surely
be honored to tend to the King's every wish.

Jupiter was only too happy to welcome the little dumplings to
Olympos in true royal fashion. Zeus liked his pets plump and in an
assortment of colors, and these were eminently suitable.

He'd found that it took three poppets at the minimum to keep
him properly amused, during those odd moments between more
monumental conquests. Lately his stock of sex pets had reached an
alarmingly low number–for some reason the creatures always managed to run off–so he was well satisfied with this peace offering from
his lordly brother. Twelve delicious captives from the land of the
dead, trained well, he was told, in the art of receptivity. They would
be attentive, he was assured, or at the very least submissive. Zeus had
drooled in anticipation, expecting that these concubines, with their
unique indoctrination, would endure even his most strenuous demands without complaint.

He had thus ordered them to be cut from their fetters and made
presentable. The three choicest maidens were to be brought to him at
the after-party, clad only in richly decorated golden collars, and taste-
fully bound together, like trinkets, on a single sliding chain.

He had been enjoying the blonde for some minutes now, but she
seemed already to have gone rather limp. Perhaps he had been too
abrupt in his attentions. She hadn't been properly tenderized, that was

it. Jove didn't think of himself as a cruel master, but he was conscious of the beneficial effect of spanking slave girls often and well. He ought to have had all three of them paddled before they were brought in. But unless it was done properly . . . slowly, firmly, with just the right amount of force, and for a good long time, that was his recipe.

But it was so difficult to find decent help.

Well, next time. Let her be, for now.

He put the blonde poppet over his knee, then reached with an enormous hand toward one of the captives straddling his broad thighs. He'd been bouncing them well, galloping them like bareback riders on his pony-sized thews, and he expected a delicious increase in tenderness as a result. He chose the redhead, with her creamy skin and fetching red twat, and seized her around the waist.

The dainty creature was reluctant to quit her perch. She had twined her slender legs around his thigh, and was gripping it with all her might.

How adorable. She is frightened, mayhap, of the Divine Phallus– as well she might be, oh ho! No matter, for massive impalement awaits each and every one of our little dumplings, willing or no. He had been grooming and jiggling this one most particularly in preparation for the honor, and she would not now be spared. He gently plucked her up, like a naughty kitten, and sacrificed her, squirming, to his mammoth godhead.

Zeus heaved a cheerful sigh, and then looked down at the third nymph appraisingly. This black-haired plaything was yet to be tried, and he relished her long fat titties, sinewy hips and bulbous behind. That delightful curvaceous bottom must receive his most energetic ministrations, ohh, yes indeed.

But what was all that noise? Jupiter scowled.

Below, the redhead squealed loudly in his monstrous grip. It seemed that she had no self-control, a sad failing. In private Jove could thoroughly appreciate the screams and sobs of his pets. In public however, the giant deity preferred that they be seen and not heard. Any sound louder than the faintest gasps and if necessary, whimpers which could not be suppressed, he found irritating.

But Jove was feeling indulgent, and merely pressed his thumb firmly over the girl's little mouth. *We can't have a scene, miss thing, every time we bless thee with a few more inches of our engorged divinity.*

Having taken care of this matter, he took the black-haired nymph in hand, mashing her softness against his bulging thigh. But before long he was forced to turn his attention again to the redhead, who was biting his thumb. *Ow! Oho, thou rebellious jade. Now wilt thou truly be punished!*

He usually tried to be careful with the little treasures, but this one had annoyed him with her noise, and now it seemed, she was a biter. Sometimes they simply needed to be taught a lesson. All Zeus had to do to accomplish this, in this instance, was take his pleasure with a bit more firmness and dispatch. After all, he didn't *have* to be nice. He was nothing if not a strict disciplinarian, and in this case duty and pleasure were joyously intermixed.

Yet for all the implacable zeal he brought to the task at hand, Zeus did not experience satisfaction. These pretty little poppets were deliciously snug, it was true, but he could only apply so much force, and even then they could not fully encompass his magnificence.

Still, one more poppet might just do the trick.

Stung by Pluto's taunts meanwhile, Hermes had snorted the last portion of the coca dose, which alone should have been enough to stun a rhinoceros, in one long drag.

Salivating with anticipation, Jove disciplined the third captive's rare haunches, spanking judiciously until the juice ran down his leg. She was quiet, keeping her hand over her mouth. *A fast learner.*

While Jupiter was thus occupied, he had kept a firm, even punitive, grip on the tiny redhead. Zeus glanced down now at the nippy ginger, who had fainted quite away. With an impatient grunt he deposited her back onto his massive thigh, where she collapsed, a more chastened pet, Zeus trusted. He lifted the next slave girl into place with a mighty arm. He was hopeful he would achieve satisfaction in the embrace of those small sweet buttocks.

But then–"Augh! My sinuses are bathed in freezing flames!" Wince squealed, clapping his hands over his nose.

Zeus was sorely distracted by this, and that made him plunk the poppet down roughly. She gave a yelp, and he sighed.

"Har har har!" The Lord of the Dead laughed. "That will teach you to play tricks on me, monkey-man!"

Jove was nearly frantic to relieve the pressure that had been building up during his frolics. *Thor's Balls! Fuck it!* he thought, and seizing his reluctant plaything by the teats, he sanctified her most emphatically and repeatedly with his majesty. She began to wail but he thrust a huge finger into her mouth, silencing her, and bore down.

"Why do I let you outsmart me?" Hermes mourned, tears running down his cheeks.

Jupiter was getting so close. But it was impossible to concentrate. "Damn you two! How can I enjoy my pleasures with your bickering hurting my ears!?" he thundered.

But the gods gave no heed to his complaints. "Wait until we get back to Hades," Pluto taunted Mercury. "I have something special lined up for you, a real zinger of an assignment, har har!"

Zeus was on the verge of really losing his temper. Despite all his care, the dark-haired poppet was not submitting gracefully to the urgent reaming administered by her lord, not at all. She was struggling ever more wildly, the little wretch. That always made him feel unappreciated. She was biting his finger too, damn her. Such ingratitude made him angry. When he got angry, the fragile little bauble he was wearing sometimes broke, and stopped being any fun at all.

This wasn't going to work.

Jupiter growled with frustration, and shoved the wild kitten away. He was going to have to start over. Let's see, the blonde was first in line before, so he would have a go again with her. He pulled her limp form closer, shook her and smacked her, but she barely responded. Incensed, he drew all three pets across his knee and spanked away vigorously at their reddened buttocks with a massive hand.

"Silence thy howls!" he ordered, "or I'll spank thee raw!"

These undersized nymphs are simply useless. Jove needed a proper fuck, damn it, and a proper drink. What he really needed was a friendly goddess, but these were in desperately short supply. It seemed as though magical twats were becoming as rare as unicorns in Olympos. *Fiend seize them all!*

"I'll do whatever you command, my Lord, only I beg of you, please don't make me breathe in any more of your demonic cocaine," Wince gasped. "It's turning me into an icicle!"

"Simone!" shouted Zeus. "Bring us a bottle of ouzo!" The collared trinkets still lay across his leg, weeping. They disgusted him. "You three, get up!" He dragged at the chain and made them straddled his thigh once more. "Sit there and be quiet!" he snarled.

"Ouzo!" Jove cried again, louder. Looking rather frightened, Simone, a magnificent female centaur, hastened up with the bottle, along with a tray full of cups and a bucket of ice.

"That's right, that's right, serve up these fine gods with the best of the vine. Dionysos!" Jupiter thundered. "Get over here and be toasted!"

The wine god was happily rolling on the floor with a pair of lion cubs. "Arrr! Rrowrr! Good grief, I've been toasted for a month, Jove!"

"Well, come and be toasted again," Zeus commanded.

Dionysos, he of the red cheeks, button nose and brown curls, clad in a green tunic, sandals and a wine-red cloak, approached with a wide grin and a cub squirming under each arm. He attempted to present the baby beasts to the despondent maidens decorating Zeus's thigh, but the cats were over-excited by their play and proved more than the ladies could manage. One scratched the redheaded nymph on the arm and she shrieked.

"Get those damn lions away from here," Zeus growled. Dionysos hastened to oblige.

"You're bleeding, Bacchus," Hermes pointed out.

"All in a day's romp," Dionysos said cheerfully, and having handed the lion cubs over to a nearby Titan, he accepted the cup of milky liquor that Simone offered him.

"Stop your obsessive fiddling with that razor blade, Pluto, and pay attention," the thunder god rumbled. "I'd like to make a toast to our host, Dionysos, whose Festival has surpassed all others this millennium." Zeus immediately tossed back the cup of raki in one gulp, holding it out for more. Simone refilled it obediently.

"Hear, hear," the other gods said politely, and drank. Simone took the bottle of liquor round again, clop clop, her large bare breasts nodding.

"And to my lovely daughter, Persephone," Jupiter went on, "whom my dear brother Hades has sworn to restore to life this very night, that is, if he wants to keep his jawbone attached to his ugly head!" He again swallowed the contents of his tumbler, then glared around intemperately. "Come here, Simone," he beckoned. She trotted up and refilled his cup, then started away.

"Simone, get over here," Jove said thickly, as he took her shoulder. "Where have you been hiding all night? Ha ha ha! I have a nice long drink for you, you lazy brood-mare, and then a special treat." He pinched her nipples, and smacked her chestnut rump.

Simone bridled, whereupon Jupiter seized her by the hair. "Drink, damn you!" he commanded impatiently, forcing her head down. "Relax and enjoy the party."

"Why must you be such a brute, Zeus?" Pluton complained with evident distaste as he watched the inflamed monarch compel the centaur-girl to her knees before him, while pouring liquor down his own throat. "That's bestiality, if you ask me."

"I?" shouted Jove in sudden rage. He hurled his tumbler at the onyx coffee table, where Hades had begun to array another phalanx of coke lines. The cup smashed into shards, scattering ice everywhere, and causing the others to jump back and shield their faces. "I, a brute? It is thou who'rt a brutal beast, Pluton!"

Hades jumped up, livid with rage, and Zeus leaped to his feet as well, letting the trio of concubines tumble to the floor. As the gods squared off, the bruised nymphs scrambled out of the way, then crawled behind the ottoman and crouched there, arms about one another's shoulders.

"Now, now," Dionysos said cheerfully, "I understand that we've all had quite a lot to drink, quite a lot, but–"

"No, you don't understand," Zeus said menacingly. "You see, this old goat here has killed my girl, and it's up to him to bring her back, and now he thinks he can just sit around and stuff his nose with candy, doing nothing about it, and keeping me waiting. But he knows I don't like that. Don't you, Pluton?" Zeus strode over to Hades and pushed his red face right up close to his brother's pale one. "Time's up!" he snarled.

By now Simone had helped the chained concubines to climb up onto her back. She trotted hastily from the room without being observed by Jupiter.

"You think you can force me to bring her back?" Hades retorted coldly. "Well think again, Zeus. I was going to, but suppose I've changed my mind. Go ahead and beat me to a pulp, brother, you always were a bully. But maybe my honor is more valuable to me than the doubtful benefits of obedience to your dictums. Have you thought of that?"

There came a sound of applause from close by. Demeter stood there, clapping her hands together. "Very, very good, brother Hades. Excellent work, brother Zeus. I salute you both," she said quietly.

Eternity – **Hades**

Kafka took the escalator, Luke and Proserpina invisibly following. They descended down, down past the exit to the spirit loft, and into the bowels of the city.

A story could be read in the walls, which seemed to carry them backward in time. They first passed a level of pipes and tiles, and then a layer of rubbish and worms, and then a course of wet and leaky masonry, which gave way to solid granite, and beneath that a matrix containing large and mysterious bones. Below this was a layer of ash, atop fragments of worked stone displaying elaborately carved architectural ornamentation in a style Luke had never seen. Underneath, a thick level of sediment contained the remains of extinct sea creatures.

Luke held Kore's hand tenderly in his, still giddy from the delicious sexual union they'd just enjoyed. He was becoming a much stronger flier, and that opened up interesting possibilities, which distracted him with their promised delights. More importantly, he understood now that their ability to astral project into this realm, abandoning the miserable bodies they inhabited in the solid world, was the magical switch he'd been looking for, to get him back to his angelic form, and to restore to him the goddess he adored.

At last a crust of incomprehensibly ancient metamorphic crystals gave way to open space, and they entered the caverns of Hades.

Kafka exited the escalator in great haste, and the pair of spies followed as quietly as they could, Luke beating his wings softly and bearing Persephone aloft with him so that their footsteps would not echo through the chamber. Their guide dashed up a long spiral stairway lit by guttering torches, and then stopped at a landing where a heavy door was set in an opening carved into a wall of living basalt. Franz removed an iron key ring from his pocket. The massive keys clanked as he opened the door.

Luke and Kore were barely able to squeeze through before Kafka shut the portal behind him. The rustling of Luke's wings must have caught the author's ear, for as soon as the door was closed he called out, "Who's there?"

Luke had fluttered up above Kafka's head and caught hold of a wrought iron balustrade, from which he hung, holding his breath and trying not to move a muscle, while Kore clung to him. After staring about for a few beats, perspiration starting on his forehead, Kafka opened the door again and stuck his head out, listening. At last he closed and locked the door from the inside, then trotted to a ladder leaning against the wall, and began to climb.

They were within a spacious circular room. Looking up, Luke saw that though the chamber was ten meters wide, it extended upward hundreds of meters, with no ceiling in sight. Every five meters or so, a rickety-looking catwalk circled the room, and each had its own ladder that could be rolled along the bookcases to give access to the books that crowded the shelves. The same ladder could also be used to reach the catwalk above.

Luke cautiously pursued Kafka, fluttering upward with Persephone in his arms, always pausing before he got close enough to alarm the writer with the gusts of air raised by his wings. As he waited a couple of levels below for Kafka to climb further, he glanced at the titles on the shelves. None of them were books Luke had read. He noticed one called *Paul Verlaine, by Arthur Rimbaud*. It appeared that the books were all biographies alphabetized by subject, presumably with the A's at the top. All of the titles he could see, aside from the Verlaine, were names he did not recognize.

Kafka appeared to have found what he was looking for. Luke fluttered up and landed on the catwalk. He looked around at the books: their subjects bore surnames beginning with *S*.

Franz had already pulled a volume from the shelves. Now he climbed again, five more levels up, and retrieved a second volume.

Luke flew upward, hovered, landed as quietly as he could. As Luke and Kore crept toward him, Kafka sat down on the catwalk, laid one of the books open before him, removed a pen from his inner coat pocket, and began to consider what to write next.

Luke scanned the page. The text read simply:

Rosetta sat on a bench in Dutch Kills Green, enjoying the flowering trees.

"You distract him, and I'll grab the pen," Luke whispered into Kore's ear.

Kafka looked up at the sound. "Who's there?" he cried again, a terrified expression on his face. At that moment, Persephone lifted the writer's bowler hat and then dropped it back down onto his head. As Kafka put one hand up to steady the hat, Luke seized the other hand, taking hold of the pen, and wrote firmly,

Just then, Luke and Kore arrived with Rosetta's biography.

Moments later, they were standing in a city square. It appeared to be a place outside of time, with its modern cement benches and planters, surrounded by faded Victorian homes and a fragile-looking church.

Rosetta was sitting quietly on a bench, her hands in her lap. Luke and Kore still had the beans of invisibility in their mouths.

"I think it's best if we don't reveal ourselves," Persephone whispered. "This may only work if she figures it out for herself."

Luke placed the book on Rosetta's knees, with the pen tucked inside. Slowly the woman bent her head down to look at the object. She took it in her hands.

It was not bound like a conventional library book, but in orihon fashion, that is, the pages comprised one long sheet, which was folded accordion-style. The blank end-paper had been wrapped around to the front, enclosing all but the final page, which was the only one that could be read, as the edge of the end-paper was sealed to the inner margin of the last page of text with glue.

They watched as Rosetta lifted the wedge of paper in her hand, turned it over. She then looked at the binding, a cardboard solander covered in green fabric, that encased the folded pages. On the front and spine it read: *Rosetta Stone - by Franz Kafka.*

Rosetta raised her arched brows. She examined the orihon book again with greater interest. It was clear that there were pages inside the sealed packet that she couldn't open. She carefully detached the end-paper and unwrapped it, turning the book over to reveal the first page. With a puzzled half-smile, she began to read.

Dionysia Year 2500 –Mount Olympos

"I applaud you, my Lords, but," Demeter said, pacing smoothly toward the group of gods, "I've waited long enough for that which is my right, and so has Persephone." She turned her head and gestured to the luminous group of feminine deities standing behind her. Like Demeter, they all smiled as they stepped forward: red-haired Hecate, with a raven on her shoulder; girlish Hebe bearing a cup of amber wine; tall Themis, grave and stately; beauteous Hera, with her golden spindle; fair Leto, with skin like alabaster; golden-haired Aphrodite clothed in clouds and rainbows; and last of all gray-eyed Athena, wearing the gorgon on her breast, her helm and spear glinting in the candlelight.

"I've brought seven goddesses with me to witness this glorious moment of achievement," Ceres purred. "Because this is a moment that will go down in History, the moment when you, Pluto, graciously hand the key to Kore's chains over to me, her loving mother."

"Ow–ow–out of the question!" Hades stuttered.

"And not only will you surrender the keys, but I firmly believe you will gladly swear never, ever to harm poor Kore again in any way. Isn't that wonderful, Ladies?"

"So just," said Themis.

"Hades is a pillar of manliness," Athena agreed.

"Such a dear, sweet fellow," said Aphrodite, floating toward him slightly on a cloud of butterflies.

"And so handsome!" sweet Hebe added, batting her eyelashes at Hades. He began to cough.

"And I feel sure that in the interests of peace, dear Zeus, you will be glad to apologize to Hades for any offense you may have caused, with the passionate way you communicated your wishes."

Zeus only looked at her darkly, shifting uncomfortably from

one foot to the other.

"You have nothing to say?" Demeter said sadly. "Then you leave me no choice but to call for assistance from one who will not ignore my pleas." She lifted both hands palm upwards, and cried, "Isis, mighty and benevolent,"

"Isis, mighty and benevolent," intoned the other goddesses with their hands likewise raised.

"Thou who rulest both land and sea," Demeter went on, and the other goddesses repeated her words as she continued her prayer. "Thou who conquerest death and wieldest the life-giving magic . . ." Zeus, Hermes and Dionysos all looked at each other nervously, and then at Hades, beseechingly. "Thou who art the Queen of Serpents, and the Milk of all the world! I call upon thee to–"

"Stop!" Death barked. "Do not–please! Do not summon Isis! I . . . I will give you the key."

"How kind!" Leto said, smiling at him beatifically.

"How prudent," added Hecate approvingly.

"And will you swear not to harm her again, for any reason?" Demeter went on.

Hades opened his mouth angrily, and sputtered, "You ask too much!"

At this Ceres gasped, her eyes wide with horror. She then gazed sorrowfully round at the other goddesses. As one they all raised their hands once more, palms pointed to the heavens, and began to intone beseechingly, "I call upon thee to–"

"Hades!" Zeus cried desperately. "I do apologize! I–I ought to have asked politely. I beg you, don't let them bring Her here!"

"Come on, Pluto!" Dionysos put in. "You know how angry She gets. She'll turn Mount Olympos into a volcano before She's through."

"Damn it, all right!" Hades snarled. "I swear! I-I won't lay a hand on Kore, or . . . anything else! Not unless she wants me to."

"Go on," Demeter said.

"What else do you want me to say? I'll treat Proserpina like the Queen she is, with respect and forbearance, forever more. Is that good enough for you?"

"Almost. Just one more thing. Themis?"

The ancient deity of Divine Law stepped forward. "It is the opinion of the Council of Goddesses that the obligation of Persephone to return to Hades for half the year is forfeit by this act of murder. As she has died, and is to be resurrected in a new life, all such contracts are to be declared null and void. Do you agree, Lord Zeus?"

"I agree," Zeus growled.

"Lord Hades?" Themis went on.

Death gazed at the Titaness balefully. "Fine," he said. "Let her be free to choose. She'll come back," he smiled, "as she always does."

"The key, Lord Hades," Demeter said softly, holding out her hand. Reluctantly, Hades produced the key, and dropped it into her palm. Demeter bowed her head graciously.

"Thank you, great Lords, for your generosity and foresight. Esteemed ladies, I call upon you to witness the glorious achievement of these exalted gods!"

"Amen!" intoned the goddesses. Then the seven beauteous deities turned and together exited, accompanied by the tinkling of their jewels and the soft rustle of their garments.

"Phew, that was a close one!" breathed Hermes.

"Well done, Pluton!" Dionysos cried heartily, clapping his uncle on the shoulder.

"Those infernal, meddling females," muttered Zeus. He blamed Hera especially for his current distress. The biddable little sylphs had slipped away, as they always did when his wife appeared. Would Hera comfort him in his moment of need? *Not likely. Not she!*

"I must depart on urgent business," Death said abruptly, and vanished.

Hades wasted no time in descending the escalator to his domain, and as he did he thought about Luke, and about how he was going to pulverize him and scatter the atoms across the Milky Way.

He also thought about Rosetta Stone, his hostage. She might still be useful. If Demeter had taken the zombie kid under her protection, he would need a plan.

The god of the dead hastened to the round library, where he searched in vain for the book entitled Rosetta Stone. He stormed back to the Obsidian Palace, and dialed dispatching. Kafka did not pick up the phone.

The Lord of the Dead was becoming increasingly perturbed.

Hades summoned five rats to his study, and with a wave of his hand, caused them to become paralyzed. Then one by one he stomped on their heads with a grunt, crushing them into the black wool carpet with his heel.

This did not make him happy, but it did help clear his head a bit.

It was apparent that he was going to have to take matters into his own hands. He needed to travel to the time eddy where Rosetta was trapped, and make sure that she was secure. Without the original book, he was going to have to resort to a manual override. He opened a file drawer and removed the folder with Rosetta's name on it. It disturbed him that Kafka, always punctilious in his duties, was not at his post, but fortunately he had returned the dossier promptly after composing the book.

Hades opened his desk drawer and extracted some cello tape, a piece of paper and a pen. First he taped the folder closed, then he taped the blank piece of paper to the folder. On this sheet he wrote:

Rosetta Stone,
by Pluto, Lord of Hades
(Override Code HD-AO3)
Trapped in a time eddy, Rosetta was surprised to discover that a

That stranger's name was Death.

Moments later, Hades found himself standing in a city square. Flowering trees surrounded him. Seated on a cement bench, Rosetta was reading the very book that had disappeared from his library of booked souls. Death walked over to her.

"That looks like an interesting book," he said pleasantly. "What's it about?"

The woman looked up. "It's the story of my life," she said, "and it says here that–" she gazed down at the page with a puzzled frown, then back up at Pluto, taking his measure. She opened her mouth as if to go on, then closed it, and shut the book and clasped it tight, holding the pages against her heart.

"Aren't you going to finish it?" Hades wondered.

"Not right now. I think I'd rather wait to see how it turns out," she replied.

Damn it, she was cleverer than he had supposed. Who had brought her the book? Whoever it was, he or she was probably still trapped here. He sensed a presence, but could not see who or where it was.

Hades berated himself for leaving the dossier behind on his desk. As long as Rosetta had that book, she could still re-write her own story, and if he took it from her by force, it would only break the spell. He had to use cunning. A burst of excitement filled him. This was getting interesting. Perhaps he could get her to reveal the position of her helper.

"There's a hidden treasure here somewhere. Can you draw me a map, so we can find it?" he suggested.

"I have no idea where the treasure is," she pointed out, "so how can I do that?"

"Why not try? You may know more than you realize," Pluto

urged.

"If you want, I can help you look for it," she added politely.

"Yes, that would be very kind. Where should we begin looking?"

"Umm, well, treasure is usually buried underground. Maybe it's in that empty lot over there."

"Good thinking." Pluton held up his two hands and a spade materialized in each. He handed one to Rosetta and she began to dig energetically. Unfortunately, whenever he got close enough to see what she was doing, she moved to another location.

She seems to find me suspicious, Death thought. Surreptitiously, he pulled a white hood out of his pocket, and drew it over his head. It was the Mask of Familiarity. Wearing it, he would appear before her as someone she knew and loved.

Rosetta looked up from her work and spotted him. "Oh, hello Amber," she said cheerfully. "We're digging for treasure, would you like to help?" Inside his hood, Death smiled.

Immediately Rosetta spotted something. "It's a foot!" she said. The "treasure" was emerging from the earth, and just as he had hoped, it was the zombie kid, Luke.

No doubt he was the one who had brought the book to her. So far, his plan was working nicely. All Hades needed to do now was find a way to destroy him.

"We'd better get him inside," said Hades, still in the guise of Amber, whoever she might be. "You take the head, and I'll take the feet." Together they hauled the body into the parlor of the Victorian mansion that stood next to the empty lot.

"Do you know who this is?" Hades asked, indicating Luke's corpse.

"It's the avatar of a god," she replied without hesitation, "and a messenger." Pluto was taken aback by this revelation. Could it be true?

"Do you know who I am?" he asked curiously.

She looked at him with those penetrating gray-green eyes. "You're Death," she said.

This woman Rosetta was disturbingly perceptive. The Lord of the Underworld hadn't had such a stimulating exchange with a mortal in some time. He was beginning to feel distinctly attracted to her, with her adroit mind and arresting beauty. This kind of cat-and-mouse game was–well it was refreshing, actually, to be enjoying his work again.

"So . . . it would seem that both he and I have divine messages for you," Death pursued.

"You're a god, not a messenger, I think," she said firmly. "You have nothing to say to me."

That damnable woman! I must possess her! I shall take her back to Hades with me right now, Death thought urgently. *What's to stop me?*

"You can't do that," she retorted, divining his thoughts. "It's not my time. And you won't break your own rules." Had she read that in her book?

"For Death," she declared, giving him a heart-stopping look from under those devilish eyebrows, "is a gentleman."

That was when she vanished, and the zombie's muddy corpse along with her.

April 7, 1994 – Pinnacle Rocks National Park, CA

Luke woke up wondering what was going wrong with his vision. When he opened his eyes, everything was blurry, splotchy. He sat up, groggy and confused, and realized that there was a light piece of fabric covering him.

Buzz was struggling to escape from the same web. Luke pulled the covering away. It was Demeter's star-spangled cloak.

"Buzz? I can't see you."

"Ack! Ack!" The vulture suddenly appeared, as the white bean came shooting out of her throat.

"What happened? Where's Rosetta?" he said.

"Last thing I saw was her winking out. I think she disappeared at the same time we did. So presumably, she's waking up now, too."

"I hope she's okay. And that Hades isn't too hard on poor Kafka."

Buzz hopped up onto Proserpina, walked along the thigh and up to the abdomen, eying her own body curiously. "Yeah, I felt bad about doing that to him, but oh, well."

"I hope you're not hungry enough to commit auto-cannibalism," Luke replied.

"I'm not gonna eat me," Buzz insisted, waddling toward the head of the corpse. She stared at the face with interest.

"Maybe it's best to remove the temptation." Luke rose to his feet and lifted the condor in his arms.

Just then a maelstrom of lightning scorched the pinnacles of rock nearby, as a series of thunderclaps caused the formation to shudder. Several boulders broke off and plummeted down into the canyon with a rumble and a far-off crash.

Five winged chariots hovered above them, each containing the resplendent figures of one or two goddesses. The vehicle of Ceres landed gently nearby and the goddess sprang out, while the other four chariots slowly circled the outcrop, their beauteous occupants one and all gazing at Luke curiously.

Demeter approached, and held up a small iron key. This she fitted into the lock that held Buzz's collar in place. She turned the key and the collar sprang open. Instantly the condor rose upon powerful strokes of her wings, paused to look down at Persephone for just a moment, then with a rasping cry, flapped away.

Kore stirred, sat up.

"Persephone!" cried the corn goddess, falling to her knees and casting her arms about her daughter with a sob of relief.

"Mother," Kore murmured weakly.

"Oh my darling girl," Demeter wept, caressing her child. Persephone turned her head toward Luke, looking a bit groggy.

"Mother, please? I need to say something to him. Then you'll have me all to yourself." Kore struggled to rise, and failed.

Ceres appeared as though she were about to object. Then she kissed her daughter, saying, "Be easy, my child. I will await thee." She rose to her feet and turned to Luke.

He stood watching the magnificent bird sail up toward the crags, trying not to cry.

"Take this key, my boy, and loose your bonds," she said gently.

"Thank you." The tiny key felt strangely heavy in his palm.

"Will you assist her to the car?" the goddess said.

"Yes, Ma'am," Luke replied. Demeter walked back toward her chariot.

Luke was not sure where the keyhole could be, but it seemed that the key knew its business, snapping into place at an opening that appeared on the manacle quite spontaneously. Luke removed the fetter and cast it away.

Still a zombie. It figures.

He knelt down beside the lovely goddess of Spring, and took

Kore's hand. He knew what was coming.

"So . . . this really is goodbye, isn't it?" Luke said, cursing himself for the break in his voice.

"It looks like it," she answered gravely. The color was returning in her cheeks and she rose to her feet without permitting Luke to assist her.

"I'm glad you're free," he said simply, biting his lips now, as his nose and eyes stung.

She smiled tenderly. "I love you, Luke, you know," she said.

"Funny kind of love." Luke regretted it the moment he said it.

Why doesn't she want me? The answer to that was too obvious to even mention, but he asked himself the question all the same.

"Let me help you walk to the chariot," he begged.

"That's okay, Luke, I'm fine."

So this is how it ends. She's a lovely, divine being, and I'm a living, rotting corpse.

He wanted to say something charming, or funny, or debonair, but he couldn't think of a single thing. She raised one hand as she turned away, gazing back at him with pitying eyes, and wiggled the fingers slightly.

"Kore-!" he blurted.

"I'm not–" she had tears on her cheeks too– "I'm not the one, Luke. I'm not . . . your destiny. I'm just a helper along the way."

"How do you know that?" Luke said, a little too wildly. Almost he seized her in his arms, but he mastered himself. "Maybe my destiny is something *I* should have some say in!" he blurted.

"Luke, we are all playing a part in something bigger: you, me, Hermes, even that condor, whose life was miraculously given back to her just now. And your part is more important than you know."

Then why not give me a little more information, Kore? he wondered savagely. But what he said was, "Why make me do this–this whatever it is–blind, tormented and alone?!"

"I do have something to tell you." She was clearly anxious to conclude the conversation and get away, Luke thought.

"I'm listening."

Kore leaned in close to him, and whispered, "The cowrie shell–guard it with your life!" Then she kissed him on the wrinkled green cheek, pulled back, gripping his upper arms gently for a moment with her small, strong hands. She lowered her eyebrows and raised them meaningfully.

"*And thank you!*" she whispered. She smiled, brushing away her tears, turned and walked away.

Kore. Come back. Don't leave me here. Luke wanted to shout these things, but instead he lunged for her skirt and seized it. She half-turned back toward him with an inquiring look.

"Don't go back to him, Kore!" he begged. "Please? Just–just don't go back to Hades. That's all I ask."

Persephone responded with a sad smile. "And if I return not to the Land of the Dead, will I ever see thee again?" she wondered.

Luke released her dress. "This isn't about me," he said gruffly. "I just need to know . . . that you're gonna be okay."

"Luke, I promise. I'm going to be okay." She nodded as she spoke. "And–and so are you, Luke. You really are going to be okay."

He watched her as she walked away, in the windy night under the glittering stars. She stepped up and seated herself beside her divine parent. She waved to him again, and he waved back. Then the five chariots rose majestically up into the clouds, and vanished.

"So what have we here?" boomed a loud voice. Luke turned.

There stood Hermes, and beside him, a gigantic man with a huge red beard and muscles like pumpkins.

Oh boy. It's Daddy.

Zeus strode over to Luke, and when he got near to the boy his arm shot out and he seized Luke by the shoulder. Luke could feel the fragile bones disintegrating into fragments inside the god's iron grip.

It hurt real bad, but Luke held his breath so that Zeus wouldn't hear him whimper. He'd had plenty of experience with bullies like this guy.

"You fucked her, didn't you, boy?" Zeus said softly. Luke kept silent. "I'd end you right now, if it weren't for your usefulness to me." And he took both of Luke's arms and spread them out like he was examining a slave at the market, and laughed deeply and cruelly at Luke's emaciated body. "But the thought of you existing to be a thorn in Hades's side is much more lastingly delightful than the brief pleasure of crushing you to a powder."

"My Lord Zeus," Hermes bowed, "Hades . . . has sentenced this one for destruction."

"Fuck him!" Zeus bellowed. "I like the little monster alive, you hear me?"

"Remember, my Lord Zeus, the undead are an abomination on the earth. Perhaps the zombie should be returned to Famebeau, from whence he came."

"But won't he be at my brother's mercy there?" Zeus rumbled. "He won't last an hour!"

"My Lord Zeus, if you will but relieve me of my duty to serve the Lord of Death, as I have so often begged you to do, and set me instead to protect this one . . . "

"What? You fancy this boy? What's your name, lad?"

"Luke, sire."

"I do fancy him," Hermes smiled, "and what's more, the Queen of the Spring herself doth call him friend," he added persuasively, "and Her would I serve with all my heart, were you to command me or no."

"Well then, I free thee to follow thy heart, good Hermes. For thou hast served her well, at thy peril, and for that I owe thee much, and more. What boon thou mayst have in thy heart to ask of me, ask it now."

Luke watched and listened, feeling that he was being treated more like a pet than a person by these drunken, illustrious beings. It made him nervous, and unwilling to call attention to himself.

"Father, you know my wish," Hermes murmured, bowing low.

"You wish to serve above all others, the one you love, am I right?" Jupiter roared. "Eros, eh? It was ever so with you, always Eros this, Eros that." The kingly god seemed perplexed by this, more than angered. "Well, be it so. Thou'rt commissioned to't. Serve him, and be damned with the both of ye pudding-heads."

Zeus turned away, chuckling, and pulled a glistening lightning-bolt-shaped object from out of his ass, or so it seemed to Luke, who truth be told wasn't actually watching very closely. He was occupied with looking into the gentle, loving eyes of the messenger god, and with speculating about what fate awaited him, with this beautiful youth as his protector.

Meanwhile Zeus hurled a thunderbolt into the air, and it soared up, leaving a trail of sparks, along which path the thunder god zoomed heavenwards, with a final wave to Mercury and a booming laugh.

April 7, 1994 –New York, NY

Aron had phoned the house several times, but no-one had answered. He'd already left two worried messages for Rosetta, but she hadn't called back.

At 6:00 when everyone at the office called it quits, Phil stood up and wrapped a brown-and-tan scarf around his neck.

"Poor Marky," he said gently, shrugging on his denim coat. His Little Richard hairdo had somehow become flattened into a misshapen wedge, and his expressive features were exceedingly morose. "We should all go and get a beer in his honor. Right, Aron?"

"Sorry, but I'll have to pass," Aron said. "Rosetta's really sick, and she's not picking up. I need to go check on her."

"She's probably just sleeping," Phil urged. "Let her rest."

"Umm . . ."

"Just one beer?"

". . . No, really, I'm worried it might be something serious. I'd better go home." He embraced his friend, noticed that Phil had tears in his eyes. "Steady on," he said in his best British accent, and patted Phil's shoulders bracingly. He gave him another bear hug, waved goodbye to the others.

"Sorry, gotta go!" he called out. "Have one for me!" And then he hurried out of the building.

On the subway, Aron retraced in his mind the events of the past week. Was there some clue that he was overlooking? Rosetta had seemed awfully sick. Why hadn't she called him when she got back from the clinic? She was usually so good about that sort of thing. Was she in the hospital? Wouldn't somebody have contacted him, if that were the case?

He couldn't get it out of his head, that something was terribly wrong.

When he arrived at the stoop of their building, he took the steps two at a time. He fumbled with the key and cursed, trying to unlock the front door. When he stepped inside, the apartment seemed strangely chilly. He raced into the bedroom. The window was wide open, and it was freezing. He shut it.

There was Rosetta, lying in bed under the covers, quiet. She was just sleeping. Wasn't she?

Aron kicked off his shoes and crawled under the covers, fully dressed. He pressed his body against his wife's. She felt so cold! He wrapped his arms around her, felt her deep rhythmic breathing. He felt his scalp prickle as relief flooded through him.

It had been silly of him to worry. She was only asleep. He stayed with his arms around her, holding her to him, warming her.

God, how he loved her. She would never know how much. He could never tell her. Every time he tried to say it, his throat closed up, and panic seized him. He had no idea why it scared him so much to say it. Why he felt like he had to keep her guessing, keep her at a distance, or . . . or he would fall, lose his footing completely. He would be utterly lost.

But if something happened to her . . . !

She hadn't stirred, and he was reluctant to wake her, but he had to know that she was okay. "Rosetta?" he murmured in her ear.

She inhaled, made a small sound, a wordless "hmm?" before turning in his arms, nuzzling his chest. Then she slept on.

Aron breathed in deeply, shivering, let it out. He was being foolish, overly emotional. She was fine, of course she was. Rosetta wasn't a junkie who was recklessly driving herself into an early grave. She was a healthy woman, in the full flower of life. She'd been to the doctor today, probably gotten some medicine or whatever. Everything would be okay.

Aron closed his eyes and for a little while, he drifted off to sleep. Then he got up, heated himself a bowl of soup, and had a beer.

Franz Kafka sat at the desk in Pluto's study. He was considering what to write next. The surface he was gazing upon was a piece of paper taped to a folder. On this paper the following had already been written in a florid, firm script:

Rosetta Stone,
by Pluto, Lord of Hades
(Override Code HD-AO3)
Trapped in a time eddy, Rosetta was surprised to discover that a stranger had arrived. That stranger's name was Death.

Next to Pluto's moniker, in a loose, spidery hand, Kafka had added the words, *and Franz Kafka.*

Beneath the lines Hades had written, Kafka had also written some of his own.

Rosetta found what she was looking for, and woke up. Luke and Persephone returned from the Time Eddy safely. The Lord of Death, to his great surprise, remained trapped outside of Time, where he took a long, restful vacation

Kafka inhaled sharply, and began to write:

. . . and pondered the following joke:
Once a man told a joke, and he wasn't joking. And that's the joke. Get it?

Franz sat at the desk, rereading what he'd written. Then he added:

Ha ha, just joking. There was no joke!

Kafka sighed. How long could he afford to wait between additions? Death was, after all, pretty famous. To keep him imprisoned in this sidebar of Rosetta's story was going to be a task that required Kafka's unswerving attention. And a good deal more paper!

Kafka frowned, reached into his pocket and removed a book. He'd been carrying this around with him, since his last visit to the Library. He had forgotten about it until now.

The solander was stamped in gold:

Jean-Baptiste Poquelin de Molière, by Franz Kafka.

Kafka removed the book from its case. The glue that bound the pages into a circular narrative had come unsealed. On the final page, he saw what he himself had written:

Before Death could incinerate him with a fatal blast, Molière vanished. He found himself in a vast, circular library, filled with biographical tracts. He began to search for a book about himself, written by Franz Kafka. At last he found the book.

Below this someone had written:

Fortunately, Molière had a pen and paper with him. He quickly sat down and wrote a biography of Franz Kafka. This book described the book that Kafka was writing about Hades.

Kafka would continue writing this biography for a long time. Perhaps it will never be finished . . .

But in his spare time, Franz Kafka also wrote a book about Molière.

These are the last lines Kafka wrote in Molière's biography:

After that, there was nothing more. Kafka peered inside the solander, and shook it. A note fluttered out and landed on the desk. Franz picked it up and read it:

Dear Kafka.
I congratulate you, my friend.
Finally, you've managed to finish a book!
–Molière
P.S. Tell Death he forgot his teeth on my bedside table. But not to worry. He's sure to be much more fun in bed, without them!

Kafka knew what he had to do. He drew Molière's biography toward him, took up his pen and wrote:

Jean-Baptiste returned to Brooklyn, where he found Rosetta alive and well.
He remained with her for the rest of her long life.
But Molière continued to work on the biography of Franz Kafka for a long time. Perhaps it will never be finished . . .

April 8, 1994 –Brooklyn, NY

Rosetta opened her eyes. She felt so . . . so very ill. She started to drift off again.

But the phone was ringing. The answering machine beeped in another room. Somebody was leaving a message.

Aron had already left for work. She had a fuzzy memory of him bringing her some orange juice and toast, of drinking the juice and falling back to sleep. The toast was still sitting there, on a plate on the floor next to the bed.

What time was it?

She pulled on a sweater, and made her way to the blinking machine on the kitchen windowsill. She punched the listen button.

Hello, this is Methodist Hospital, calling with a message for Penelope Stone-Delgado. We've got your lab results. Please call us back at (718) 780-3000.

Rosetta dialed the number, rubbing one bare foot on top of the other to keep them warm.

"Hi, this is Penelope Stone-Delgado," she croaked. "You called just now about my lab results?"

"One moment please while I look up your records." There was a rustle and the nurse cleared her throat. "You tested positive for strep. We have your prescription here for antibiotics."

"Okay . . . How do I . . . where do I go to fill it?"

"It's up to you. You can come back to the hospital, or you can go to the clinic."

"Umm . . . I guess I'll come to the hospital, thanks."

"It'll be waiting here for you."

Rosetta dragged on some clothes. Dragged herself once again, on foot, to the hospital a mile and a half away. Dragged herself up to the counter at the Emergency Room, and explained about the antibiotics.

"You have to be admitted before you can see a doctor," the clerk said.

"But . . . it's just to pick up a prescription."

"You still have to be admitted," the woman said coldly. "Do you have health insurance?"

"No."

"That will be eighty dollars. Will you pay now, or would you prefer to receive a bill?"

"Please bill me."

Rosetta sat down in the waiting room. *Eighty more dollars!*

She filled out the forms as best she could, dizzy and exhausted. Added up, what ought to have been a simple visit to the doctor had cost the equivalent of her family's food budget for a month. It was infuriating!

She waited to be called. And waited, wrapped in a cloud of rage and misery. After sitting there and worrying for a while, she decided to jot down the dream she'd had the night before, while it was still fresh in her memory. She usually carried a small sketchbook with her everywhere, and she pulled this out of her purse along with a pencil, opened the book to a blank page, and began to write.

I'm riding on a subway train, on my way to meet Aron at a show. I'm late, feeling anxious. The train stops at an unfamiliar station, the conductor announces that it has gone out of service. I get off. On the bench in the station a book is sitting open, face down, left behind by some rushed commuter. Printed on the spine in gilt letters, Love in the Time of Cholera.

I wait for the next train, picking hairs off my coat. I am amazed at the variety of hairs I've been carrying around with me: short and long, red, black, yellow, brown and white, straight and curly, seeming to derive from every species of creature. The hairs float in the air in a beam of light coming through a hole in the ceiling. Suddenly they are blown upward as wind comes whooshing through the tunnel.

A train pulls into the station, puffing diesel smoke. It's a work train; more like a garbage scow than a subway car. A man with a mop, riding on the open bed of the single yellow car, waves me on and I climb aboard, ripping my stockings on one of the hooks attached along the side to hold long-handled brooms and rakes in place. The work train heaves out of the station and I balance like a surfer, trying not to fall off.

The train is slow, bumping and squeaking along, first on an elevated track, then between dark warehouse walls of corrugated tin. The man with the mop hooks his thumbs under the braces of his overalls and grins at me, spitting liquid out in a thin stream from between his front teeth. I move forward in hopes of staying out of range of the spit, but this is made difficult by the buckets of rubble and bags of trash that take up most of the space on the surface of the narrow car. I crawl along between heavy-duty black garbage bags and construction sacks.

The train has begun to shrink, I realize, and before long it's only two feet wide. Then I'm riding on the engine like it's a small pony. Next thing I know, I'm walking along the tracks, wondering where I am.

I realize I'll never get to the show on time. I plod on, determined to find Aron. Even the train tracks have petered out now, and I tread on patches of grass and gravel, walking past the back fences of houses. I've ended up somewhere in the suburbs.

Then the scene changes, and I'm strolling down a sidewalk in a cityscape, alongside a chain link fence that has plush animals stuffed between the wires, rotting and sagging like bodies hung from gibbets. Within there's a garden, its paths overgrown, rank and weedy. I walk on over broken pavement, down lonely streets where even gypsy cabs rarely venture.

"Oh dear, what's this thing called?" says an anxious voice close by.

I turn to look at the speaker. Beside me walks a woman, petite and plump, with dark hair and Native American features. She's clutching a rag boy doll, stained and pale, with holes in the fabric where the button eyes have been torn off.

"It's a doll," I say.

"But what's his name?" *the woman wonders. There's an edge of hysteria to her voice. I don't know the doll's name, so I don't answer. Instead I wrack my brains for any excuse to escape from this woman. She seems unhinged.*

"I live in an artists loft. Would you like to see it?" The woman asks.

"Yes," I say politely, although I am not so sure that I do. I follow her through urban canyons, to another part of town, Hell's Kitchen maybe: commercial office buildings, skyscrapers, industrial buildings. We enter one, go up the elevator. When the lift emerges through a hole in the floor at the top level, I step out immediately, which is fortunate. The roof and sides of the elevator-box have already retracted, and the floor of the box slides into the floor of the loft, disappearing like the steps on an escalator, leaving an empty void in the middle of the room.

I say to myself, "She should have warned me, I might have fallen in."

The loft is clean and luxurious, and the prewar details, the white painted pillars and moldings, are in pristine condition. The floor is pol- ished wood, and the space is vast and alive with activity. Although there are people everywhere, the ceiling is celestially high, and it does not feel crowded.

The occupants are of every nationality and color, and apparent- ly they all live here and sleep in this main room. At first I suppose my guide to be one of these, but soon I surmise from her manner that she is either the owner or the leaseholder. Perhaps she comes from a wealthy family and is making the space available to others as a charity. Perhaps she is charging all these people rent to stay here, in which case she must be making a fortune, or so I imagine. I do not question her, but merely speculate.

She takes me on a tour of the rooms. There is a long, narrow kitchen with yards of tiled counter space, and a multitude of huge spoons and cook-pots and frying pans hanging from wooden pegs along the walls. Beyond this we pass into another room. I assume that it is going to be my host's bedroom, but it turns out to be another large living room that resembles a hotel lobby, dotted with modern black leather couches and armchairs, and chrome occasional tables. There are several groupings of blinding white sofas surrounding massive mirrored coffee tables. Bowls of pomegranates and grapes, and ferns in square ceramic pots, add color to the space, which is otherwise a composition in black, white and brown.

Near the entrance are two wooden trestle tables flanked by long benches. A number of individuals, who have the appearance of immigrants, are being served a meal there.

At the back of this enormous room are doors that open onto smaller bedrooms, five all told: two opening off the main room, along with a huge bathroom, and three more accessible via a short hallway to the left. A man emerges from one of the bedrooms. His ponytail is white, and he has a small yellowed goatee under his lip.

"How much is the rent on this whole place?" I ask him.

"Oh, around $1200, I'd say," he replies.

"Oh, surely it's more than that!" I exclaim. Even if it were two or three thousand, it would be an amazing deal, it seems to me.

To the right I see that part of the room is separated from the rest by a low curving wall, covered all along the top in metallic shiny silver. Upon further examination I can see that it encloses a sunken study, divided from the main area by a glass partition. Several people are relaxing in this space. One of them is a slight young man, blond. He looks familiar, but I can't place him. There is a large ornate fireplace of carved black marble. It appears that the sunken room can be reached only through some hidden door, perhaps in the kitchen.

Suddenly I am out-of-doors, sitting in a public square. It's a beautiful day, and I'm reading. The loft isn't in midtown Manhattan, as I had supposed, but in Long Island City. It's really a huge old Vic-torian house, one of several on the block. It seems to me that my new acquaintance must have purchased the house, or perhaps her husband purchased it for her back when she was married, years ago when the neighborhood was run-down and dangerous. Now it's become a ritzy area. The square is paved in red sandstone, and there are deep stone planters, containing a thick tangle of daffodils and honeysuckle, from which blooming tulip trees rise, their trunks curved like graceful maid-ens. Along one side of the square, a cathedral reaches toward the sky.

I'm relaxing on a bench in this peaceful place, reading my book, when a man walks up to me. He is dressed in a dark pinstripe suit, and has a thin mustache and a cultured air.

"You seem fascinated by that book." This is the gist of his remark, although his exact words aren't clear.

I start to tell him the story of the book, but I don't get very far be-cause I realize immediately that it's actually the story that is happening to us at that very moment. I mustn't get ahead of the plot.

Apparently there's a missing treasure map. We must search for the treasure in a muddy plot of land near the house. Because nobody can find the map, I start digging around randomly. The man with the thin mustache is helping me. I find a large cowrie shell and think, "this is important." Instead of showing it to the man, I put it in my pocket.

We are about to give up and go look for the map when I notice a foot sticking out of the mud. Then I see an arm, and then the face of the dead person. I am struck by the realization that we are not supposed to find the corpse yet, it's too early on in the story. I consider not saying anything about it, but the thing is done, so I just go with it. The dead man has stringy hair and is gaunt and pallid, but he isn't very large. My sister Amber comes and takes hold of the feet, and I have to carry the other end of the mud-caked body, which makes me shudder. Somehow we get the body into the house. At first I worry about tracking mud into the fancy rooms. But there is something about the unearthed corpse that strikes me as otherworldly.

*"He is going to be for us the means of communication with a god,"
I tell Amber. As I say this I realize I am talking to the man with the thin
mustache. He looks exactly like me, except that he's male.*

*"And you're Death," I point to him, but I don't speak aloud. He
hears my thoughts, and I hear his, for words aren't necessary between
us.*

*"So we are both vessels of communication for a god," Death replies
in the telepathic way we have of communicating.*

*"No," I correct him, indicating the corpse, "he is a vessel. You are a
god."*

*Death responds playfully. "Then I must have the power to make
you (taste/smell) the (spicy/dangerous sensation) any time I want?" I
know very well what the spicy, dangerous sensation is. "What's to stop
me from doing that to you right now?"*

*"Death is a gentleman," I reply boldly. "You are a god, not the
Devil. Remember, Death is not evil."*

*I awaken understanding that I am part of a larger cycle of Nature,
one that is inevitable, that must be respected, one that operates by laws
all creatures must obey.*

April 7, 1994 – Pinnacle Rocks National Park, CA

"How's your shoulder?" asked Hermes.

"Well, I can't move my left arm," said Luke. "But it's already starting to feel a bit better. It's amazing how fast I heal."

"That's good," the messenger god nodded. "Zeus is a brute, but you handled him well." He no longer appeared drunk. Had it all been an act?

"But–what about Rosetta? Will she live?"

"If she wishes to, yes. Don't worry about Rosetta, Luke. She seems to be very well able to take care of herself. But now I must return you to Famebeau, for your destiny lies on this plane no longer."

Hermes put an arm around Luke's waist and lifted him into the air. His shoulder still ached horribly, and being carried this way wasn't helping. *Will I ever return to my real form?* he wondered.

There was a tremendous whooshing sound, and pressure that went on for much longer than Luke would have liked, with wisps of cloud whizzing past. At last they emerged above the stratosphere, surrounded by a starlit sky. And they kept on rocketing up, up toward a shadow that was growing above them, blotting out the stars. Closer and closer they came to the shadow until it filled the sky. And then at last they arrived at a small iron platform, at the end of a ladder that extended downward from the black shape above. It was hard to make out in the dark, but Luke got the impression of huge boulders and layer-cake slabs of stone. It was as if a mountain had been ripped out by its roots and set to orbit the earth.

"Isn't Famebeau in Hades?" Luke wondered aloud.

"Well, yes and no. It's ruled by Hades, yes."

"Won't he pulverize me as soon as he gets the chance?"

"Not if I have anything to do with it," Mercury laughed. He had by now lighted on the platform, and he reached up and touched the rock into which the ladder was anchored by enormous bolts. Instantly the stone slid open, revealing a vertical passageway up which the ladder ascended.

"Go on," said Hermes.

"I thought . . . I thought Hades was deep underground," Luke stammered.

"So it is. But Famebeau is in the heavens."

And so Luke climbed up into the dark tunnel, the messenger god close behind, and they soon emerged into a chamber, vast and echoing, and filled with marching pillars that rose into the light-filled atmosphere.

"The hall of Persephone!" Luke gasped. "Is she here?"

"The Hall of Ten Thousand Pillars belongs to every god, and every demon. What a man meets here, is his destiny."

Perhaps Kore really is my destiny.–Although that's not what she told me. Luke thought this, but kept his silence.

"Come on," Hermes said. "There's somebody I want you to meet." He led Luke through the pillars, toward a wide opening between the columns. Bright sunshine flooded down from above. There was a long flowerbed much like the poppy path that Luke had encountered on his previous visit to the Hall. Little stone paths wandered across between the bushes, and as he walked with Wince beside them, Luke could smell the spicy scent of the yellow blossoms.

Before long they saw the throne toward which their path was leading them. Drawing closer, Luke made out a very large woman seated there, with amber skin and long eyes. She rose from her seat and held aloft a pair of scales. Her black hair flowed down across her shoulders in a smooth sheet, all the way to the floor. Her gown was simple, a silver robe with long wide sleeves. Upon her head was a crown of olive leaves.

"Themis!" called Hermes. "Goddess of Divine Law! I bring you Luke Mandrake, the champion of Proserpina."

"I'm no champion," Luke objected.

"Come closer, child of humankind." The deep musical voice of the goddess thrummed and thrilled through Luke's body in a marvelous, relaxing way. He stepped forward, looking up into the face of the giantess, which was long and a little bit sharp in the chin, with a long thin nose. Her dark eyes were narrow and seemed to see far into the future, and deep into his soul.

"And what did you find on your journey, Luke Mandrake?" she intoned.

Luke felt at his throat for the cowrie shell, the one that he'd kept on a silver chain around his neck ever since Kore had given it to him. The one she'd told him to protect with his life.

He found only the chain. He pulled the chain forward, searched with both hands all the way around to the back. The cowrie shell was gone.

"Nothing . . . " he said, closing his eyes in shame. "Nothing I haven't already lost." A sense of hopeless abandonment rose up in his heart, and closed over him like deep water, cold and smothering. Tears pricked his eyelids. *No! I won't cry!* He squeezed his eyes shut, fists clenched.

Then Themis spoke in a gentle, vibrating tone. "Do not grieve, Luke. What you long for is not lost, any more than a seed is lost when it is planted in the winter earth."

Luke looked up into her eyes, pleadingly. "Can you just tell me when? When will I finally be–be . . . ."

"Loved?" Themis murmured. "Thou art loved, and beloved, dear child, more than thou knowest."

Luke sighed. Why couldn't he feel it? If only he could believe himself worthy of that love, then he might change his opinion on the matter.

"I have a gift for thee," Themis whispered. Luke saw that her enormous palm was extended toward him. In it, small as a grain of rice would be in his own hand, rested a tiny Tinkerbell figurine of yellow metal. She was poised in flight with golden wings outstretched, and her feet rested upon an openwork ball, filled with tiny iridescent crystals. From the back of the gem protruded a circle meant for stringing.

Mia. She knows about Mia.

Luke took the fairy pendant and attached her to the chain. "Thank you," he said hoarsely.

"Whenever you are in need of help, hold the pendant to your lips, and aid will surely come," said the goddess.

"Thank you, my Lady," Luke said again. "Your kindness is . . . very much appreciated."

"Luke, we must continue on upward," said Hermes.

"Fare well, beloved child. Do not forget who you are," Themis called out, as Hermes once again took Luke around the waist and carried him up, and up. They passed uncomfortably close to what appeared to be a blazing miniature sun that hung suspended in the air above the throne of Themis, and then rose further still, into the mists that gathered in the heights. As they soared heavenward the fog grew ever thicker and condensation wet their skin.

"Take a deep breath," Hermes instructed him, and Luke did.

Seconds later the air had turned to water, and they were rising to the surface of a vast, unending lake. It was dotted as far as the eye could see with round stones, which emerged from the surface in a regular pattern.

They rested together on one of these stones: two youths, one lissome and strong, the other frail and ghastly.

"You're home, Luke," said Wince. "Where do you want me to take you?"

Luke stared curiously at Hermes. Why was this god so interested in assisting him?

"I really don't know much about the lay of the land around here."

"Well, is there somebody you want to meet?" Wince wondered.

But Luke had been puzzled over the round stones. "Of course!" he cried. "They're the tops of the pillars, aren't they?"

"Yes indeed. But where to now?" Hermes prompted again. "I can introduce you to anyone: Voltaire, Socrates, Cleopatra . . . you just give me the name."

"How about Billy Taylor?"

"Never heard of him."

"It's–it's just somebody I know. He came looking for me, and . . . and I wasn't very welcoming. If he's still around, I want to apologize."

"Well if he's here, we'll find him," Hermes said cheerfully.

April 10, 1994 –Portland, OR

When Dennis Defoe entered the office of the Medical Examiner at Legacy Emanuel, Dr. Lupercan hastily closed a filing cabinet drawer. He appeared to be wiping his mouth surreptitiously.

Defoe instantly recognized a kindred spirit, at least in his affinity for spirits.

"Doctor, thank you for meeting with me. I hope you can clear up a few questions I have about the death of Luke Mandrake."

Lupercan stiffened. "Wa-wa-what do you want to know?" he stammered.

"Well, Doctor, I've read the autopsy report, of course, but I was wondering . . . what was the overall condition of the body when you examined it?"

"He . . . he was dead, Detective."

Oh boy. This guy is a real maroon. And I thought he was going to be a tough coconut to crack.

Defoe was no longer employed by Mrs. Luke Mandrake. But that hadn't stopped him from continuing his investigation. In fact, being fired had made it much easier to proceed with his investigation in the manner he desired. He no longer had to worry about having to be accountable to Mrs. Luke Mandrake, for asking leading questions about the possible nefarious activities of Mrs. Luke Mandrake. And this, to put it bluntly, was the line of inquiry that interested him, and the potential investors he was courting, the most.

"Were there any bruises on the body, perhaps faded bruises? Any signs of previous abuse or physical neglect?"

"No, Detective. There were not. Detective, are you associated with the Portland Police Department? Because if so, my full, annotated report is on file at your office."

"Let me clarify myself, Dr. Lupercan. I am engaged in an independent investigation, on behalf of clients whose identity I am not, ah, at liberty to disclose. However, this is a case in the public interest. And there are those in the public who suspect that Charity Ball has something to hide."

"Let me assure you that Charity Ball is a fine woman, an up-standing member of the Portland community, and someone I count as a personal friend."

"Doctor, a beloved icon, a man whose fame has reached around the globe, has died under mysterious circumstances. And all his worldly assets, wealth which he gained by his own talents and efforts, are about to pass into the hands of his widow, a woman he has known for a handful of years. This is a case that requires vigilance, objectivity and determination. I will learn the truth, Doctor, and if I need to get a court order to gain access to the truth, I will get a court order."

"All of the documents are on the public record, Detective, ah?"

"Defoe, Doctor."

"Defoe. So please, if you have no more questions . . . "

"Too busy to care about the pursuit of justice, Doctor?" Defoe challenged. Lupercan only gazed at him woodenly. "Listen, Doctor, I am not here to create trouble for you, or your department. I'm simply trying to do my job. What do you say we go out for a drink after you get off work, and have a discussion . . . off the record, shall we say?"

Dr. Lupercan stood up, his face shiny with sweat, and began to speak more rapidly. "Detective Defoe, I do not know, nor do I care who sent you here. But I resent your suggestion that there is some hidden 'truth' beyond that which is to be found in my reports. Your assumptions are in error. Good day, sir."

As Defoe stood and gathered up his trench coat and briefcase, he stared at Dr. Lupercan with a secretive, gloating smile. With this case, Defoe had hit upon the mother-lode of pop culture gossip, specula-tion and innuendo. Who knew how long he could milk it? Book deals, documentaries, docudramas. He was high on the endless possibilities.

This cat knows something he's not telling, I can smell it. And that sheen of nervous sweat on his brow is all I need, baby, to start me off on a wild ride to fame and fortune.

Dennis Defoe was on the hunt.

April 10, 1994 –Pinnacle Rocks National Park, CA

The condor had returned to the rocky outcrop hundreds of times since she abandoned her empty nest. Oddly, the scavenger had not taken any interest in picking at the flesh of the recumbent cadaver.

She had flown far in search of her mate and chick, but to no avail. Perhaps the male condor had met with a fate similar to her own. The newborn chick, unprotected, would soon have perished. Perhaps they had been captured by scientists. Either way, they had vanished. And so the female condor's urge to nest had been transferred back to this lonely spot, and to the human corpse that was the sole object of her maternal devotion. Each time she returned she had brought with her a stone, or piece of wood, or a spray of foliage clipped from a nearby shrub, and laid it carefully on the bony form that huddled there in its purple velour robe.

At the start, a terror of humanity had kept the ravens and other scavengers from approaching the still figure. Upon her return, the condor had taken to roosting in a cleft twenty yards from the cairn, from which she could both see and hear, should any creature attempt to feed upon the corpse. These she would drive away jealously.

Day by day, the barrow had grown. Condors are not by nature builders, but she was obsessive. Sometimes she walked about, moving bits of stone from here to there, striving to keep the cairn intact. She left a whitewash of droppings, which helped somewhat to glue the stones and twigs together. Now the mound of materials almost completely covered the body.

And still the condor watched over the barrow, added to it, departing only in search of food. Her transmitter destroyed, she was tracked by none. She alone, and the rising and setting sun, kept a vigilant wake over the remains of Luke Mandrake.

"Here she comes!" Rosetta whispered to the others.

Jessie walked into the little cafe near Tompkins Square Park, spotted her friend, and made her way to the table with her daughters in tow. She was surprised to see Virgie, Chandra, Violet and Fester. Even Peter was there.

"Happy Birthday!" yelled everyone.

Jessie cried, "Ohh! A surprise party! Oh Rosetta! I can't believe it!"

Rosetta grinned. "Happy Birthday," she said again. The two women embraced.

"Happy birthday to you, too, Rosetta!" Jessie said.

"It's your party," Rosetta insisted. "You deserve it."

"But it's your birthday, too," Jessie objected. "Ohhh Rosetta!" Jessie cried again when she saw the gifts stacked next to the home-made cake. "You didn't have to do that."

"They're just silly things," Rosetta said. "For fun."

It had been a hard week for her friend, Rosetta knew. Two days ago, Jessie had gone to the welfare office to apply for emergency food assistance. The upstairs neighbor had agreed to watch the kids. Unfortunately the woman had allowed the girls to play in Jessie's apartment unsupervised.

The youngsters had gotten a bright idea when the noticed tiny beads of Styrofoam escaping from the seams of a gigantic stuffed Barney doll: they would make it "snow" inside the house! The supply of foam pellets had been nearly limitless, and when Jessie got home, they covered every surface. The lightweight bits of statically-charged fluff were inside the drawers, all over the clothing. They clung to everything they touched and were nearly impossible to get rid of. Jessie had phoned Rosetta in near-hysterics.

Knowing all this, Rosetta had lured Jessie to the Life Cafe, where the Windup Teeth were to perform that night, for a mutual birthday toast. She had organized attendees for the last-minute surprise, and in honor of the occasion she and Antoine had created a small pile of gag gifts, using cheap items from the drugstore as fodder, and giggling the entire time. The biggest hit was a can of air freshener re-branded with a picture of Barney, drawn on construction paper and taped over the canister. The label read, "Barney B-Gone: Just One Spray Keeps Barney At Bay."

When she saw the can, Jessie laughed her long, loud, uproarious laugh. Rosetta beamed with sisterly affection. Even Alice and Kimberly could share in the joke, and the gay atmosphere was a welcome respite from the distress at home. Watching Antoine and the girls as they romped around on the empty stage squirting silly string at each other, Rosetta felt a deep satisfaction.

By the time the Windup Teeth were setting up to perform, Peter was getting the kids ready to be ferried back to Brooklyn in Jessie's old Dasher. At Rosetta's behest, he was taking all the children to her and Aron's place, having arranged to baby-sit as a birthday treat.

Now Peter's girlfriend joined the party. Jessie greeted her with remarkable friendliness. *She's a saint,* Rosetta thought.

While Jessie was outside getting her coat from the car, Aron approached Rosetta and offered her a small wrapped box.

"Happy Birthday," he said.

Rosetta tore off the paper and took out a silver pendant on a chain. It was a Cretan goddess, her bosom bare, wearing a tiered skirt. In each hand she gripped a writhing snake.

"I love it!" Rosetta said, and offered Aron a kiss. He kissed her back, a real kiss on the lips, the kind that they used to get razzed for at parties because it went on for way too long. And then, he kissed her again.

"What are you two lovebirds up to?" Jessie cooed.

"Look!" Rosetta said, displaying her prize. She gazed at Aron adoringly.

"I guess Rosetta's feeling better, eh, Aron?" Jessie winked.

"Completely recovered," Aron proclaimed, as Rosetta flashed her 500-watt smile.

"Showtime in ten minutes," Aron called out. "Calling all Wind-up Teeth!"

That night when they got home, and Jessie had departed with her sleeping children, Rosetta and Aron frolicked with tipsy abandon. It was such a relief to have her husband back, her delicious man, diving onto her, kissing and laughing. Driving into her, impassioned, urgent, the way he used to, back before they got married, before the pregnancy that had changed everything. Afterward, Rosetta quietly wept tears of happiness, curled up against Aron in the dark.

April 15, 1994 –Brooklyn, NY

Dreamed I was chosen to be the Queen of May after someone named Kore opted out. It was an ancient dance to songs remembered from days long ago–the line of the moon, old words in an "English" no longer spoken, performed by men on a green field in a soft Spring landscape.

Two giant witches were trying to stop us from holding the festival. I was running late, and had to change clothes. To get to the festival I would have to travel through a secret tunnel. Oddly, it widened at the far end and was lined with shops.

It was while I was getting ready that they called to tell me that I would be Queen. I was surprised, but pleased.

A gentle, handsome young man was watching me. He was dark, sexy, with a mischievous smile, and I believe he was a doctor, or perhaps a doctor's son. He had long, curly hair, was short and muscular, and was wearing a tailored coat with wide, buttoned cuffs. He had a friend with him, who had light, shoulder-length hair and a little beard. The friend was also short, but much slimmer.

The two youths gave us a van to get to the dance.

We arrived at the appointed place but had to abandon the van. The witches were after us. To them, we were like tiny worms or insects. We hoped to distract them from noticing our flight by rolling seeds toward the miniature abandoned van.

The two witches were male, they were giants. One was dominant, and he thought of himself as the brains of the pair, constantly complaining of the other's lack of sensitivity and insight. The other was hugely muscular and frightening, and had the head of a bull.

The truth was that neither was smarter than the other, one was just more pushy.

*   *   *

Jean-Baptiste reread the sentence he had just written, as he stretched out his right arm, and flexed the fingers on his cramped hand.

Searching Pluto's study, Franz found several long sheets of paper, ready-folded, in a drawer in the sideboard.

How long can we keep this up? he wondered. It was madness, really, trying to trap Hades in a time eddy indefinitely. As far as the comedian knew, nobody had ever attempted anything like it before.

The idea had come to Molière in the round library, when he realized that Kafka had brought him there, intentionally, to find his own biography. The way the books were used to stop time, to rewrite the plot of a person's existence, had of course fascinated the play-wright. If Franz could use this method to snatch Jean-Baptiste from the clutches of Death, then perhaps he would be able to employ it further, to keep the maniac busy for a while.

That's when Molière had conceived the notion of writing a book about Kafka, in which he did exactly that. And astoundingly, it had worked very well. Between the two of them, they had managed to stay ahead of Hades–so far. While Kafka spun the tale, Molière sealed up the cracks in time, making sure nothing unexpected could happen to stop him.

He bent to write another sentence.

Trapped as he was outside of time, Hades could not know who it was who was writing his biography from moment to moment.

Of course, eventually something would go wrong, that was inevitable. It was the nature of eternity. Jean-Baptiste fervently hoped

254

Kafka would succeed in making Death forget all about them both, by the time the Dark Lord exited his prison.

At least things were going well for Rosetta at the moment. Aron seemed to have snapped out of his childish discontent. But had he truly outgrown it? One could but hope.

Molière spared a moment to check in on his charge.

What's this?

An image arose in his mind, of Rosetta looking at him trustingly, gratefully. *It's a dream she's having . . . we're offering her a vehicle of some sort.* Himself and some other man together were providing her with assistance.

Rosetta was dreaming about him? That hadn't happened in decades. His heart filled with a warm, gratifying sensation. He thought she had forgotten him long ago.

But who was that other fellow? The blond youth she had associated with him in her dream was nobody he knew.

Ah yes, he remembered now. The dead musician–she had recently grieved for him, had prayed for his soul.

As a rule Jean-Baptiste did not focus overmuch on Rosetta's dreams. She had a rich inner life, and it would have been a massive effort to track all of that material. It was far more important, in his thinking, to focus on the very real threats that could emerge within her daily existence.

But now Molière began to take an interest in the cornucopia of visions, that arose within her subconscious. When he peeked delicately into the archives of the woman's mind, he immediately understood that he had overlooked something important.

This ghostly youth had haunted Rosetta's dreams during the days leading up to her illness. Apparently he was an encroaching spirit, who had played a central role in certain recent events–events that had nearly caused her death!

Jean-Baptiste compressed his lips, his eyes narrowed and his eyebrows lowered. From now on, he would be on the alert for this ghost boy, Luke, who had toyed so destructively with Rosetta's fate. When the lad returned, as he surely would, Molière would deal with him.

Jean-Baptiste smiled. He chuckled softly, recalling that until quite recently he had been bored, to the point of despondence. Now, his hands were more than filled with tasks, but this did not distress him.

Come on back, Luke Mandrake, he thought, *it will be my great pleasure to meet you. Do you even know who Molière is?*

If not, you will soon learn that Rosetta Stone is not unprotected. Oh, yes. You will learn.

April 16, 1994 – Portland, OR

The phone rang in the Riverwood house. Again.

It had been ringing every three minutes, for half an hour. Whoever it was, they would always hang up without leaving a message. Charity had already turned off the sounds on the downstairs phones.

But not up in the bedroom. *Brrrinnng. Brrrriiiinnng.*

Stupid paparazzi, she thought with irritation.

She switched the ringer off, yawned, and started to undress for bed. She could just hear the answering machine's outgoing message filtering up from the floor below. Somebody was actually leaving a message this time. Whatever it was, it could wait until the morning.

Charity crawled under the covers and switched off the lamp. That was when she noticed something weird: there was a beam of light playing on her window curtain.

Somebody was out there, shining a flashlight up at her window.

Damn it. She should call the cops. She reached for the phone, then froze.

Shit. What if it's Luke?

The light was still zipping and bobbing over her curtain. Charity pulled on a dressing gown and crept to the window facing the back yard. She peered cautiously out of the crack in the curtains, but whoever was directing the flashlight beam at her bedroom was shrouded in darkness. She opened the curtains a little wider, and the light hit her face, blinding her for a few seconds.

When she could see again, the light had been redirected to a handmade sign that the figure brandishing the torch was holding. The sign read:

PAY UP–OR YOU'RE NEXT!

Charity couldn't see who was standing out there, but the hairs on her neck prickled. She hastily closed the curtains and stepped away from the window. She stood there in the dark, breathing loudly. *Fuck, fuck.* What the hell was going on?

She jerked open the door of her room and ran downstairs on bare feet, halting before the flashing answering machine in the front hall. She stabbed at the play button.

"Charity, it's Enoch." The Void guitarist's voice was hoarse. *"Fuck, I'm so sorry–"* he broke down and wept for several seconds before continuing. *"I'm so sorry to have to tell you this. Kaylen,"* he gasped out finally, *"Kaylen is dead!"*

Charity made a wrenching sound, and put a hand to her heart. She felt like she'd been stabbed. *What the fuck, what the fuck? Kaylen, dead?*

Kaylen!

"I–I just found her, I called 9-1-1, they're on their way. But it's too late," he sobbed. *"She's gone."*

Gone. Overdosed. What else could it be?

"I don't get it. She hasn't used in over a year!" Enoch broke down again. *"And–and she was always so careful. It had to be a hot shot, that's all I can think of. Where the hell did she get it, though? She wasn't even using. Who could have given her that?"*

Charity put her hand over her mouth to smother the sounds that were coming out, the dry rasping shrieks she didn't want the kids to hear. Tears dripped onto her nightgown.

"I'd better go. Charity, be careful, okay? Be careful," Enoch said in a strained voice. *"Love you kiddo!"* And then the message ended.

Luke found Billy not far from where he'd seen him last, there in the barren hills of the desert, near the entrances to the mines. While he'd been gone, Billy had been hard at work, building walls and laying floors, using the slate and marble and limestone that he had quarried from inside the mesas, and clay that he had dug from the beds of dry streams. Now there were the beginnings of a house on the ridge, and several rooms had been roofed with tiles. There was a well that gave fresh water.

When Luke and Wince found him, Billy was whitewashing the adobe walls surrounding a little garden that he'd planted next to a cabana. They landed on the patio nearby, watching him work, *slap-splotch, skush,* dipping the brush into the bucket. *Slap, skush.* He stepped back to examine his handiwork.

"Billy?" Luke said, and the young man turned.

"Luke!" he cried and, dropping the brush into the bucket, he ran toward them and threw his arms around the zombie boy.

"Billy! You look fantastic!" Luke said, not without a touch of envy. Billy had appeared almost as zombie-like as he had himself when they'd met on the first day he arrived. Now, the trans-man was flushed with his efforts, smooth-skinned and handsome as he'd ever been in life.

"Luke, I'm so glad you're here. I want to show you around the place."

"What a lot of work you've done. How did you accomplish so much?" Luke marveled. "When I left here not so long ago, all this was empty, barren desert!" he said to Wince.

"Very impressive," Hermes agreed politely.

"It's–it's all for you, Luke," Billy said shyly. "I wanted to show you how sorry I am . . . for what happened."

"Sorry? You?" Luke was shocked. "I'm the one who's sorry, Billy. I–I shouldn't have been so angry with you. That was just not cool. Honestly, I thought–" Luke stopped. Now why had he thought that?

"You thought I'd killed myself?" Billy said quietly.

"Yeah. I didn't even ask you what really happened."

"It's okay, Luke," Billy said.

"But I want to know. Please tell me what happened, and how you died," Luke said. "It's really been bothering me, not knowing."

"Okay. But come on, get out of the sun, and relax," said Billy, and Luke and Wince followed him, and sat down under the shade of the cabana in some Adirondack chairs.

"I haven't got much to drink, just water," Billy said.

"If you like, I can help out with beverages," Wince offered. The others applauded the notion, and Wince, pulling what looked like a seed packet out of the pocket of his caftan, removed some green grains and sprinkled them on the ground near the corner of the patio. Within a few minutes, a palm tree had grown up on the spot, and when a short while later it reached the height of a person, shiny round fruits began growing on the tree.

Meanwhile Luke and Billy filled him in on the events leading up to the fatal day.

"When I jumped ship at rehab," Luke began, "I'd decided that from now on, I was going to live as a hobo, like Frances Farmer–"

"Who is that?" Wince wondered.

"She was a rising starlet in the early days of cinema," Luke explained. "But she wasn't cut out for fame. She suffered from depression, drank too much and ended up running off and becoming a tramp. Later on, when they caught her, her mother had her committed to an institution, where they gave her a lobotomy," he shuddered.

"Ah. It's all clear now," Wince said. "Please proceed."

"So I tried to disguise myself. I fluffed out my beard, wore a cowboy hat, and talked in a fake southern accent. I started to hitchhike north. But I never would have been able to pull it off, if it weren't for Billy. We met at the first truck stop."

"I figured out right away who he was," Billy said. "But he asked me to help him travel incognito, and I told anybody who remarked about it that he was my cousin, who had a spooky resemblance to Luke Mandrake."

"I walked with a limp, too," Luke pointed out.

"Yeah, but you still just looked like Luke Mandrake, pretending to limp," Billy laughed.

"I can't believe we pulled it off at all. Remember that lady truck driver who kept staring at me?"

"She was totally on to you," Billy said. "She couldn't stop looking over at you, even though she was driving ninety miles an hour."

"I thought she was going to hit a tree!" Luke snorted. "Anyway when we got to Portland, I mailed the letter to Ded Leper, telling them I was backing out of my contract. I knew I had to get out of the business, and get off dope, or I was gonna lose my family, if not my life. But I had a plan. A really stupid plan, as it turned out," Luke admitted.

"It could've worked, if you'd been able to get the money," Billy said loyally.

"The idea was, I'd set myself up as a drug kingpin. Just on a temporary basis, of course, to deal with my most pressing financial obligations. I'd rent a hotel room, get a big pile of cash, buy a hundred pounds of smack, sell it all off in a few weeks, and make enough money to pay off my mortgage in one shot."

"Brilliant," Wince remarked. "What could go wrong?"

"It was way too much dope for me to use it all up, even if I tried," Luke protested. "Of course I couldn't tell Charity about the plan, she'd have freaked. But I was able to talk Liam into managing the celebrity sales, and I had Billy to help me set up the street deals. Billy, if you haven't noticed, is very resourceful and a real charmer."

Billy glowed. "Maybe too much of a charmer," he said.

"The problem was, I couldn't get the cash. I didn't want to set off alarms with the wife by withdrawing such a large sum, so I decided to cash advance ten thousand of it. But when I tried it, the bank refused the transaction. Apparently she'd put an alert on my accounts."

"Smart lady," Wince observed.

"In retrospect I understand why, but of course I was upset. I mean, it was my money," Luke said indignantly. "Anyway, when there was a delay getting the funds, we had to come up with another plan. I sent Billy, charming Billy to negotiate for me."

"I managed to persuade them to front us the goods for three days," Billy said. "We figured that we could probably move a lot of it real fast, and if Luke talked to Charity, he could get her to make up the difference."

"I also needed to purchase a couple of guns," Luke added. "After the scare in Paris, Charity had broken the lock on my gun safe by smashing it with a hammer. I think she was worried I was gonna do something rash."

"Why was she worried about that?" Wince wondered.

"I'd noticed that she was thinking about cheating on me," Luke admitted.

"You mean, she was acting distant? Or you actually found a letter, something like that?" Hermes pursued.

"I mean that I literally read her thoughts, and accused her of fantasizing about another man, I won't say who. Which she was totally doing, while we were in bed together!"

"It's not a crime," Wince pointed out.

"The whole thing must have weirded her out. Anyway I flipped, and I guess I made some stupid threats."

The messenger god raised his eyebrows.

"Nothing violent, at least, not towards her," Luke added hastily. "I was just . . . well, it was pretty immature. I did–I did threaten to kill myself if she divorced me," he said guiltily. "And after that I took way, way too many Valiums, and washed them down with a bottle of champagne, and almost kicked it right then and there." Painful as it was to make a clean breast of it all, it felt right, after everything that had happened, to share these dark secrets with Wince, who seemed already like an old friend. And Luke had come to cherish Billy with genuine affection.

Wince picked one of the bottles of fine cognac, which were now ripe, off the tree. "I apologize for the lack of snifters," he said, pouring the golden liquid into shot glasses that he produced from his sleeve.

Luke swallowed some of the brandy, marveling at the way he could savor each molecule while tracing its effects on his brain with infinite consciousness. He closed his eyes, and became aware that he was thinking longingly of heroin. Strangely, it was the first time since he died that he had gotten a serious jones. He wondered what it would be like to skin the sun in the afterlife.

"You were saying," urged Wince.

Luke shook himself. "Yeah. Anyway, right away things started to get real ugly in the drug-lord biz," he said. "Nobody was buying on the street. The distributor had dealt us a sting. And the high-end clientele we were depending on was taking too long to cultivate."

"I tried to find buyers," Billy said in an anguished voice. "But everybody was too scared to do business with us. It seemed obvious that Jules had intimidated them, threatened god-knows-what if they got caught buying from the new guy."

"It turned into a turf war," Luke said grimly. "I guess I should have expected it. I was just so naïve," he shook his head, amazed now at his own stupidity. "I called Charity, finally, but the conversation did not go well. She was a total hard-ass, and accused me of setting out on a suicidal rampage. She couldn't see what I needed so much money for, and of course I didn't tell her."

Luke sipped cognac, heaved a sigh. "What was I supposed to

do? If I contacted the bank directly, I'd have to contradict my own wife, which would have been a real shit-storm. Anyway I was in hiding. The last thing I wanted was for the guys at Ded Leper to track me down. Talk about ruthless fucks, they'll stop at nothing, with that kind of money on the line. When I couldn't convince Charity to wire me any cash, I knew it was over." Luke looked over at Billy.

"So we decided to try and give the stuff back," Billy said. "We didn't have enough money to pay for what had already been consumed, but we would promise them an extra two thousand next week, just to sweeten the deal." Billy swigged his brandy.

"We went to talk to Jules, but he sent somebody else," Billy went on, "and it turned out it was somebody I knew, though not well, from the old days in Santa Cruz. Even though he was awful friendly, I had a bad feeling about the guy, since I'd heard things about him from before, that he'd stiffed somebody in a deal. It turned out to be a big mistake, trusting Chester. Anyway, he accepted the return with a big belly laugh, and handed me a packet with a wink. 'This is something special for Luke, from Jules, just to show there's no hard feelings,' he said."

"That guy knew it was hot?" Luke put in.

"I dunno. But I'm pretty sure the shipment never made it back to Jules, because later that night he called me, asking where the stuff was, and he was screaming and cursing at me, like, *where's my money, where's my dope.*"

"Shit, that was exactly what I was afraid of," Luke said.

"Yep. I didn't know where to turn. I tried to wake you, but you were already gone." Billy began to weep. "Chester hadn't warned me, and it was such a small packet I didn't even think about it, but it turned out to be pure uncut smack," he sobbed. "I should have known. I shouldn't have let you take such a big hit, without testing it first," he said to Luke. "I'm the one who gave you that hot shot, Luke, and you right out of rehab. I'll never forgive myself."

"It wasn't your fault, Billy," Luke said. "I made that decision. The truth is, I was being totally reckless–with my own life, and worse, with yours. I suspected that one of those guys were gonna pull something, that they might come after me. I spent my final hours just sitting there at the window with my shotgun, looking out over the lawn like a paranoid hillbilly, thinking about death."

"God, it was so fucked up," Billy said. "I'd been sailing along, la-la-la, like it was all a game, and how exciting! And then there you were, fucking dead. After the call from Jules, I was so terrified, I didn't know what to do next."

"What did you do?" Luke wanted to know.

"I fucking ran. I grabbed a gun, whatever cash was in your wallet and the credit card, thinking that if they caught me, I might be able to buy my way out of trouble with it. I hit the trail like a scared rabbit."

"Shit. I'm so sorry, buddy." Luke shook his head slowly and then downed a large swallow of the fiery elixir. "I guess they caught you."

"It was down on the trolley tracks by the marina. Three, maybe four guys came out of the shadows and surrounded me. I shot one of them in the leg." Luke barked a laugh at that. "They grabbed me and dragged me into the woods. The last thing I remember was them pushing me down on my knees."

"Fuck. Fuck," Luke said. Wince poured him another shot. "I'm so, so sorry, man."

"Hey," said Billy, "I took the risk, eyes wide open, same as you. Nobody forced me to do it." Billy looked down at the jacket that Luke had given him, a precious hand-made artifact from the early days of a legendary band, and put one hand on the Shambala insignia stenciled on the breast pocket. "You know Luke, all my life I felt like I was living a lie. When I was a girl, it was a lie because inside I knew I was supposed to be a boy. When I was living as a boy, it was a lie because I knew that, physically anyway, I was still a girl. But Luke," Billy said, water starting in his eyes once more, "you took me for who I am, you treated me like I was a real person, like a man, and not some kind of freak. And you aren't just anyone, either–you're Luke fucking Mandrake. That's–that's huge!"

"Stop it. I'm just like anybody," Luke said, choked up. "Only more idiotic than most."

"No you're not. You're something else," Billy said. "You're the best friend anybody could have. I love you, man." Billy stood up, and embraced Luke tearfully.

"I love you too, man," Luke snuffled as he held him close for several deep breaths. When he released the boy from his arms, Billy vanished.

"Fuck!" said Luke. "What–where did he go? What just happened?"

"I guess Billy got what he needed, Luke. He's moved on," Wince said quietly.

Luke was silent, tears running down his cheeks.

"This is unbearable," he finally said. "Is this what I have to look forward to, for the rest of eternity?"

"Welcome to Famebeau," said Wince.

Who Killed Cock Robin?

Who killed Cock Robin?
"I," said the Sun.
"I loaded his gun.
I killed Cock Robin."

Who saw him die?
"I," said the fly
On the wall. "With my eye.
I saw him die."

Who caught his blood?
"I," said the Press.
"I snapped up the mess.
I caught his blood."

Who'll make his shroud?
"I," said his Mom.
"I've been spinning so long.
I've made his shroud."

Who'll carry the torch?
"I," said the drummer.
"I'll bear it till Summer.
I'll carry the torch."

Who'll be the Clerk?
"I," said the Detective
"I've got perspective.
I'll be the jerk, I mean Clerk."

Who'll dig his grave?
"I," said his Friend.
"I was true till the end.
I'll dig his grave."

Who'll be the Parson?
"I," said Money-Man,
A gold record in hand.
"I'll be the Parson."

Who'll be chief mourner?
"I," said his Wife.
"I got out with my life.
I'll be chief mourner."

Who'll sing his songs?
"We," said the Crowd.
"We'll sing long and loud.
We'll sing his songs."

Who'll carry his coffin?
"I," said his daughter.
"I'll bring it by water.
I'll carry his coffin."

Who'll toll the bell?
"I!" cried Mike Flash.
"I'll announce it for cash!
I'll toll the bell!"

All the freaks and teenagers
Fell to sighing and sobbing
When they heard on the air
Of the death of Cock Robin.

Then the Corporate Machine
Moved in for the plunder.
Who killed Cock Robin?
Well may you wonder.

RM, 1998